sudden moves

Also by CHARLOTTE VALE ALLEN

FRESH AIR
GRACE NOTES
PARTING GIFTS
MOOD INDIGO
CLAUDIA'S SHADOW
SOMEBODY'S BABY
DREAMING IN COLOR
LEFTOVER DREAMS
PAINTED LIVES
NIGHT MAGIC
DREAM TRAIN
ILLUSIONS
TIME/STEPS
MATTERS OF THE HEART
PIECES OF DREAMS
INTIMATE FRIENDS
PERFECT FOOLS
THE MARMALADE MAN
DADDY'S GIRL (autobiography)
PROMISES
TIMES OF TRIUMPH
MOMENTS OF MEANING
ACTS OF KINDNESS
GIFTS OF LOVE
BELIEVING IN GIANTS (reissued as MEMORIES)
BECOMING
JULIA'S SISTER
MEET ME IN TIME
RUNNING AWAY
MIXED EMOTIONS
ANOTHER KIND OF MAGIC
GENTLE STRANGER
SWEETER MUSIC
HIDDEN MEANINGS
LOVE LIFE

Writing as Katharine Marlowe

HEART'S DESIRES
SECRETS
NIGHTFALL

CHARLOTTE VALE ALLEN

sudden moves

ISBN 0-7783-2036-7

SUDDEN MOVES

Visit us at www.mirabooks.com

Printed in U.S.A.

First Printing: April 2004
10 9 8 7 6 5 4 3 2 1

For Maribeth Sullivan, whose friendship is an
ongoing gift, and for the Rhyming Couplet:
my daughter, Kim, and her husband, Tim,
whose happiness makes me happy.

Prologue
1997

Prologue

On her way to bed, Lucinda stopped in the living room doorway to look at the black-and-white pinspot-lit photographs of her mother and father on the far wall. Lily's was the famous 1957 Hurrell portrait, with his signature exquisite lighting and airbrush work. Simply made up (Lily had refused the usual false eyelashes, heavy penciled-in brows and overdrawn mouth), her deep-set, clear blue eyes looked directly into the lens as if offering a somewhat amused challenge. Her normally limp, naturally blonde hair gleamed in an elaborate upsweep that accentuated the length and vulnerability of her exposed throat, and her famous cleavage was on display courtesy of a tastefully low-cut, long-sleeved black moiré silk dress. No one would have known, from that photograph, how thin and tiny a woman she actually was, and how very unprepossessing in real life.

Beside it, in a matching frame, was the blown-up late-40s

studio photograph of her father, Adam Bentley Franklin. In his pristine white dress uniform, rows of ribbons on his chest, spine perfectly straight, he looked impossibly young. His slight smile was sufficient to show the appealing dimple in his left cheek—a man of evident good humor, despite the formality of the pose. He had the same hazel eyes as Lucinda's, the same mouth and cheekbones, the same high forehead and slightly squared jaw. But unlike her hair which was dark blonde, his was black, with the standard military short-back-and-sides cut. And unlike her complexion, which was pale like Lily's, her father's was dusky.

The first time she'd come to visit after Lucinda had hung the photographs, her grandmother, Elise, stopped in the doorway, her hand lifting to her heart, and said a little breathlessly, "Oh, but this is wonderful! How lovely they were, eh, *chérie*?"

Lucinda was perpetually awed at her parents being side by side, together for anyone to see—something they'd done in reality only a few times during their lives. Public or studio knowledge of her having a husband of color would have put an end to Lily's film career, and neither she nor Adam had been willing to risk that. Nor had they wished to risk stigmatizing Lucinda's life. So they'd gone to great lengths to ensure that their child wouldn't know the true facts of her parentage. Lily always said, "I've got no idea who your father was. Okay? It could've been a couple of different guys. What's it matter anyway? I did right by you, didn't I?" True. She'd done better than all right. She'd been a wonderful mother—easygoing and proud of her daughter's slightest accomplishment. It was just that she'd had a big secret she'd gone to extraordinary lengths to keep. There had been no other men. Only the one. And his identity had died with her, leaving Lucinda to search every avenue, using every conceivable resource, until all the possibilities had been exhausted.

It wouldn't have mattered, Lily, she silently told her mother's portrait, as she often did.

She'd have been happier knowing her family, spending time with them, instead of losing years, decades, to a paralyzing uncertainty that had, like a bizarre life-support system, kept her breathing but not truly alive.

June 1999

Chapter One

Lucinda stood enjoying the fragrant breeze and the early summer sun piercing the heavy foliage to lay splashes of warmth on her arms. Everything was in bloom and the colors were, she thought, like the primaries of a beginner's set of Crayolas. She loved spring. But full summer, when the air stood motionless and heavy, too thick almost to breathe, was unbearable. Despite having spent the first part of her life in California—the land of perpetual summer with the periodic peculiar effects of the Santa Anas that often drove otherwise rational people to do irrational things—she'd never tolerated the heat well. Lily hadn't either, and used to say she'd passed her native New England genes to Lucinda. Which was why Lily's first major expenditure on the Connecticut house had been the central heating/air-conditioning system. Her second and last expenditure of any significance was the installation of the swimming pool for Lucinda (Lily herself didn't swim). And that was that. Lily's taste in furnishings had been terrible. Lucinda had grown up with a woman who, while meticulous in most other areas, had been content to live with furniture the Salvation Army would've rejected.

Nearly thirty years before, when Lily's estate finally cleared probate, Lucinda had become the owner of a property that included the old farmhouse and barn on two acres of land (which had the local real estate agents salivating and phoning endlessly, begging her to sell), more money than she could possibly spend (given her limited needs and desires), and a number of cartons of highly collectible memorabilia from her mother's film career. By then, though, Lucinda was in a state perilously close to agoraphobia. With a desperate need to humanize the space that had come to contain her as tightly as a vacuum-sealed, see-through package, she had had the house renovated. But the barn had remained untouched, a repository for rusted-out farm implements, dead lawn mowers and crumbling wicker furniture; the home of nesting birds and small burrowing animals.

At last, in the grip of long-accumulated inspiration, she'd hired an architect—a then-recent graduate whose tidy features flushed with ambitious pleasure at the sight of the massive hand-hewn beams and weathered wood walls. And the previous May the renovation of the barn had finally been completed after thirteen months of noisy saws, migraine-inducing hammering, and workmen moving about to the accompaniment of bad music blaring from the paint-bespattered boombox that seemed to be a vital part of their equipment.

Sometimes now, Lucinda would be drawn down the driveway to let herself into the barn and wander around for half an hour or so, admiring the heavy beams, the wide plank flooring, the loft and steeply pitched roof—that were integral to the original structure. The rough plastering on the walls had been painted eggshell white, in appealing contrast to the age-darkened exposed studs and beams. A kitchen had been created at the far end of the living room, separated from the main area by a long countertop that served both as a work area and a dining table. Three utilitarian bedrooms had been created in the loft, accessible by an open, thick-planked stairway, and were faithful to the overall simplicity of the place. The bathrooms, too, were plain, with white fixtures and ceramic tiles.

Dropping by mid-construction, looking at the uncapped pipes and spools of wiring feeding in from all directions, Lucinda's oldest friend Gin had said, "I don't know how the hell you stand it—the horrible noise, and all the nasty butt-cracks on view. I think construction guys—plumbers especially—love flashing their ugly bums 'cause they're so sure no woman's ever going to say, 'Kindly *cover* yourself, sir. The view is *not* pretty.'" Lucinda had stared at her for a long moment. Then they'd burst into mad laughter that had bounced back at them from the ribbed roof high above.

The barn was now where Katanya and her mother, Loranne, and grandmother, Jeneva, stayed when they came up from Manhattan on weekends. In the past year, the three had taken to leaving personal items in their rooms so that they traveled on the train carrying only small overnight cases or, in Jeneva's case, a Bloomingdale's bag filled with containers of delectable food she'd prepared the night before.

Katanya's room had a bulletin board where she'd push-pinned pen-and-ink drawings she'd done, programs from school productions and the Broadway musical in which she'd appeared, and a ju-ju bag she'd bought in an African shop in Harlem that contained, she said, "... my good luck shark's teeth that probably came from a dog, what's supposed to be antelope hair but I think is rat fur, and for-real chicken bones." Several worse-for-wear stuffed animals sat tiredly on the bed, and her dresser top held clustered bottles of nail polish and perfume, hair ornaments and tangles of costume jewelry. There was a poster of Albert Einstein on the wall over the bed and, next to it, one of Savion Glover. It was definitely a young girl's room—but, clearly, no ordinary girl.

Jeneva and Loranne were more discreet, less proprietary, leaving nightgowns and a few changes of clothing; scented soaps and hair-care products in the bathrooms. Their different fragrances lingered in the rooms and Lucinda would pause in each doorway to breathe in the scents of the women who'd become so close, so important to her in the three years since Katanya had traveled outside of Manhattan for the first time, courtesy of the Fresh Air Fund. Those two weeks had changed everyone's lives—putting a welcome, albeit unnerving, end to Lucinda's twenty-seven years of self-imposed isolation and bringing Renee (of the nearby host family) and her little boy Jason to Lucinda's door.

Despite years of effort by private detectives, it had been impossible for her to track down her father. Defeated, feeling ever more fraudulent, her life had been put on hold. Lucinda had learned in the immediate aftermath of her mother's death that she wasn't a white woman after all, but a person of mixed blood, and she'd no longer known how to be what she'd been before or what she was now. How did you become a person of color? Were there codes of behavior, beliefs and values she had to know? If she continued to go out into the world as a white person, would she be denying her heritage? Would her travels be viewed as trespass? She was not naive; she knew the abuses, large and small, the prejudice suffered by those of color. But she had always believed that what lay beneath the skin mattered, not the surface. Was she supposed to come out, declare herself and, in the process, possibly tarnish Lily's memory? She didn't know. Nothing existed to inform her of a transformation process from white to black. She actually did lengthy internet searches, following links from one site to the next until it seemed she'd gone thousands of miles through cyberspace only to end up empty-handed. She was able to accept her status as one-eighth black. That wasn't difficult. But knowing how to behave, who to be, was a question that went unanswered. Years got used up; they dissolved, began and ended, over and over while she become rooted in place, almost stone, like the trees Lily had taken her to see in the Petrified Forest long ago, when on a location shoot in Arizona.

Then, at Katanya's urging, Lucinda had made up a flyer and sent it to predominantly black churches in the area, asking if anyone knew the man whose photograph gazed out from the page. Recognizing his late uncle, Lucinda's cousin, Paul Junior, had telephoned his grandmother to say excitedly, "I am on my way with something you must see. Lucinda is looking for us, finally."

And so, because Katanya had been directly instrumental in bringing Lucinda to the family, Katanya and Loranne and Jeneva together had served as the emollient agent to ease Lucinda's integration, and were welcomed whole-heartedly by the Franklins—as if they, too, had been long-lost relatives.

Lucinda's love for the trio was, like the love for her found family, a self-renewing revelation that seemed almost dangerous at times. Like someone who'd been rescued from a desert sandstorm, she wanted to drink too much, too deeply; she couldn't get enough and felt a low-level yet abiding shame at her unquenchable thirst for more time with her family, particularly with her grandmother. She had to keep pushing it down—a jack-in-the-box appetite that popped up repeatedly—in order to savor the pleasure of any given moment. And it might have been manageable had there not been the ongoing problem of her aunt Anne's active competition with Lucinda over Elise's time and affection.

After being out of touch with her mother for months at a time throughout her adult life, as soon as Lucinda appeared Anne contrived ways to pre-empt Elise's free time or actually to be there when Lucinda arrived for a scheduled visit. Her inability to like her aunt added to Lucinda's shame but, try as she might, she couldn't overcome it. The precedent had been established on the August evening three years before when every member of the extended family turned out to meet Lucinda and she'd encountered Anne for the first time. Elise had warned her that her eldest daughter was difficult. "She is the one, I think, you will find not so agreeable. She has a mistrusting nature, I am sorry to say." In retrospect Lucinda could only think that, as her mother, Elise had been overly generous in her description of her oldest child.

Anne was pretty in a pinched, malnourished fashion that sank her eyes deep into their sockets and made her cheeks concave. Her prominently corded neck semi-concealed by an expensive enameled choker of singular ugliness, her platinum hair gelled and sprayed into a stiff helmet, she'd been wearing a hot pink Ungaro suit with thick red cord piping. Lucinda could imagine Lily saying, "Done up like a whorehouse sofa," and was fighting down a laugh as Anne eyed her suspiciously. The woman offered a handshake so slight and fleeting—a silken, fleshless package of small bones stroking across her palm—that Lucinda shrank inwardly as the woman's glacial blue eyes swept over her in instant appraisal—as if Lucinda were for sale and Anne was deciding whether or not she was overpriced. Anne was as brittle as old cellophane and, Lucinda decided, just as likely to crumble on direct contact. This was someone who got her way because people were afraid she'd fall to pieces if they challenged her. Lucinda had seen lots of women like her when she was growing up in Hollywood—usually the wives of the studio executives who liked to wield their husbands' power as if it were their own.

"You're tall!" Anne had accused in a razor-edged tone.

"Not really. I—"

"Adam was tall," she stated, as if the fact of her older brother's height might possibly be a proving measure of Lucinda's parentage.

"I—"

Anne barreled on, saying, "Lily, as I recall, was a very small woman with unfortunately large breasts." She'd looked pointedly at Lucinda's chest, as if its flatness erased the point Lucinda had gained for her height.

"Actually, she was—"

Again, the woman interrupted. "I couldn't think what Adam saw in her, but they seemed devoted." This remark was delivered grudgingly—as if the couple's devotion was unimpeachable. There was an unpleasant subtext at work that Lucinda couldn't quite grasp. She tuned out for a moment, speechless in the face of the woman's harsh, accusatory manner, and looked down at her aunt's shoes—red patent Saint Laurent pumps with heels at least four inches high. Why, she wondered, would a woman of seventy-three wear shoes that emphasized the extreme thinness of her legs; shoes that could send the fragile woman on a spill that would, without question, result in a shattered hip. One misstep and she'd spend the rest of her life wearing Hush Puppies and pushing a walker. Unexpectedly, Lucinda felt a small surge of pity for her aunt. Only someone consumed by fear would be so unconcerned with other people's feelings and so bold about her footwear.

"What is it you hope for here?" Anne was asking in her grating voice when Lucinda tuned back in.

"I beg your pardon?"

"All these years later, turning up this way. You're after something," Anne declared, keeping her voice sufficiently low so that no one else would hear.

"I'm not—"

"There's absolutely no proof whatsoever that you are who you claim to be."

"No, because—"

"And I suppose it wouldn't bother you to have Negro blood, if it suits your purpose."

Anger beginning to eat at her innards like acid, Lucinda said quietly, "What bothers me is that you'd think I have ulterior motives—"

"*My mother* is a *very* wealthy woman," Anne cut her off yet again. "Suddenly, you turn up out of the blue, the long-lost grandchild. I find it questionable. Any reasonable person would."

That this woman considered herself reasonable astounded Lucinda. She could feel a migraine, like a homing device, targeting her skull. Struggling to keep her anger under control, Lucinda forced a smile and said in an equally low voice, "I'm wearing J. Crew, not Chanel or Dior, so you think you know the sum of me." Seeing by Anne's slight flinch that she had hit the bull's-eye, Lucinda had taken a quick up-and-down look at the woman and said, "Ungaro with Fogal hose, Saint Laurent shoes and a knock-off Bulgari choker." Shocked, Anne's hand had risen involuntarily to her throat. "A long time ago," Lucinda continued in that pleasant, conversational tone, "I used to get that sort of instant-take reaction from underpaid salesgirls in overpriced stores in L.A. They'd do a quick once-over, see the inexpensive clothes but fail to notice the telling details like the wristwatch and the handbag and the shoes. So they'd dismiss me as just a browser, not a genuine shopper. For the hell of it, I'd buy a three-hundred-dollar blouse or a pair of five-hundred-dollar shoes just to see them fall all over themselves." Thrown completely now and unable to help herself, her mouth quivering slightly, Anne glanced down, belatedly taking note of Lily's gold Tiffany watch on Lucinda's wrist. Keeping the smile glued to her mouth, Lucinda said, "*I* am a very wealthy woman, and my *only* motive in being here is to get to know my family. As for being bothered about having 'Negro' blood, my understanding is that—"

"Mother, shame on you! You're monopolizing Lucinda!"

Lucinda had looked over to see a handsome green-eyed brunette her own age smiling apologetically at her. Gently but firmly taking hold of her mother's upper arm, she'd maneuvered Anne away, saying, "I think Aunt Adele is looking for you."

With a last raking look at Lucinda—as if to say, *I'm not*

through with you yet—Anne allowed herself to be shifted. "*Such* an unbecoming color for you, Madeline," she told her daughter, flapping a bony hand in an up-and-down motion to indicate Madeline's actually very flattering mint-green Thai silk dress.

"Isn't it *hideous*!" Madeline had said happily. "I just *had* to have it."

With a disapproving sniff, Anne tottered off in search of her sister as Madeline turned back to take hold of Lucinda's hand in both her own and said, "Forgive her. She doesn't know how to stop herself. Try to think of her as a wrinkled eight-year-old who's jealous of anyone who takes attention away from her. I'm sure she was saying horrible things. I could see you were uncomfortable. Please don't take anything she says seriously. My twin brother and I can barely manage to be civil to her, and we've never understood how someone as gracious and open-hearted as our father could've lived with her. But"—she shrugged—"she's our mother and we're stuck with her. So." She smiled again and squeezed Lucinda's hand. "I'm your cousin Maddy and I'm delighted to meet you at last. We've all been so excited about tonight. And how pretty you are!" Her warm approval was like ointment on a burn. "Such beautiful eyes, like grandmother's."

Lucinda had to smile. "Thank you. That was very ..."

"Oh, I'm sure it was," Madeline finished for her, her eyes sympathetic, her smile gentle. "You heard her about my dress. It gives her some sort of perverse pleasure to imagine she's being honest when, in fact, she's just horribly unkind. Try to forget it because, if you let her, Mother can be the equivalent of an earwig. She'll crawl into your brain and eat her way right through it. Michael and I learned early on to ignore her, otherwise we'd both be basket cases now. Or maybe we are and just don't know it. I never wanted children and Michael's a confirmed bachelor, which should give you an idea of Mother's capacity to do damage." She laughed softly. "Oh, and don't be thrown when my brother introduces himself as Michael Eye-Vee. He's the fourth and thinks that Eye-Vee business is hilarious. It's forgivable because in every other way he's so much like our father, who was a divine man with the patience of a saint. Which, as you can imagine, he needed. Now, come let me introduce you to the others. We've all had to wait because Mother insists on a pecking order. As the older sister, she gets to go first, regardless of the situation. She lives in an alternative reality where asinine rules like that actually exist. And poor grandmother has given up trying to change her." Then, taking her hand again—as if they were children who'd vowed upon meeting to be best friends forever—Madeline led Lucinda over to meet the rest of the cousins.

The next day, when Lucinda had telephoned to thank her grandmother for what turned out to be—despite Anne's efforts to control everything from the topics of conversation to how the food was served—a lovely evening, Elise had said, "You must disregard my daughter, *chérie*. To Anne, to be one-quarter black, it is as cancer. We have all felt the sharp edge of her tongue. I am her mother and I have love for her, but no liking. But her children, Maddie and Michael, they are charming, are they not?"

Chapter Two

Two years before, Lucinda had agreed to baby-sit Jason while his mother went back to graduate school. Renee insisted on paying her, and Lucinda had reluctantly agreed to accept a hundred dollars for the hours she spent each week with Jason. In truth, she'd have gladly paid Renee for the privilege of spending time with the boy—despite the fact that she had never been completely comfortable with his mother, primarily because of her mercurial mood-swings but also because there was something not quite right about the young woman that Lucinda couldn't pin down. Jason, however, touched her deeply—perhaps because she recognized aspects of her childhood self in him. Not that she'd ever been as rowdy or as undisciplined as he was at the outset, and still could be on occasion. But his soaring imagination, his intellectual precocity and the play of emotions on his mobile features had a compelling appeal. As well, his trust in her was so total that it was like having a pace-maker in her chest. He was her touchstone, her internal regulator. Collecting him weekday afternoons to bring him to her house was, as well, the ideal motivation to get her out, past the driveway. She could scarcely leave a small child waiting while she dredged up the courage to start the car moving. So it had become her daily act of love and courage to drive a mile and a half to the school and wait, parked in a long row of cars, each occupied by a young mother or nanny.

The schoolbell rang, grounding her attention, and children began flying from the building like a flock of varicolored birds. Lucinda continued to lean against the passenger door of the Bentley, scanning the flock for Jason, wishing she could be content simply to be with him—as she'd been at the outset—without tallying the number of hours spent with him and not with her grandmother; and wishing, too, she could rid herself of her uncharitably negative feelings for her aunt Anne. The ongoing contest with Anne for her mother's attention gave Lucinda a permanent-seeming tension knot in her stomach.

Then, spotting Jason, she experienced a thrill of recognition and affection, wondering every time if this was how the young mothers felt as their kids came into view. She wondered, too, if the young mothers and nannies thought she was—this tall, too-thin woman with the dark sunglasses and broad-brimmed straw hat, in long, somehow melancholy L.L. Bean dresses—an eccentric but doting grandmother who, for any possible number of reasons, appeared daily in her mothership of a vehicle (a stately black standout in the row of predominantly silver late-model SUVs and high-end station wagons) to collect one of the children. Lucinda loved the idea of being mistaken for a grandmother.

"Hey, Soupboy!" she said with a smile as he came bounding over. How could she begrudge him even a minute of their time together? She adored this boy. And yet … Damned Anne! Why couldn't the woman just back off even a bit?

"Hey, Luce!"

His thick gold-brown hair was center-parted today, lending him a distinctly Dickensian look that was at odds with his low-slung baggy pants and yellow T-shirt, the plaid shirt tied around his waist, sneakers that looked impossibly large for a rather undersized boy of almost six and the bright red backpack he carried in his left hand. He crashed into her, grabbed a handful of her skirt and pressed himself hard against her—his show of affection—and for a long wordless moment this was their greeting. Then she opened the rear door of the sedan, he clambered inside, she fastened his seat belt, and then moved to get behind the wheel.

"Wait'll I tell you what happened, Luce," he began the instant she put the car into Drive. "We're all outside this mornin'. And Tristan—he's the one I told you 'bout, the one with the fire hair who's always pounding on everyone at recess? 'Member?"

"I do."

"Okay. So, he goes to push Emma—she's the one with the black hair and prepple eyes (he was unable to get his mouth around the word purple). 'Member I told you 'bout her?"

Indeed, Lucinda had been daily studying the faces of the children, hoping (but failing) to catch sight of one who sounded like the Elizabeth Taylor of *Lassie Come Home* and *National Velvet*.

"So," he went on, "Emma sees him comin' and *just* like a Jackie *Chan* movie she does this cool move, and, *fa-sham*, he goes *flyin'*! It was amazin', Luce! Then Tristan gets up and he's all mad, makin' this squinched-up, slitty-eyed face like he's gonna to kill her. But before he can do *anything*, Emma does this little spin and kicks him right in his *willy*! His face goes red red red and he puts his hands 'tween his legs and falls down. *Ka-plop*! All of us were cheerin' and clappin' and yellin', 'Yay, Em!' and she just smiled and went back to skippin' rope with Tiffany Kornfeld.

"You know what, Luce? I like Em better than anyone in the whole stupid school, 'cept for my teacher Mrs. Turner. Mrs. Turner's *nice*, and she talks v-e-r-y softly. Not like the others who're like mad all the time. Emma's the smartest of all the kids, not just the girls. She's not a show-off like that Tiffany, or a gorpo like Brittany Cronin, or a zomboid like Brandy Alexander."

"*Brandy Alexander*? That's the *name* of one of the girls?" Lucinda couldn't help but laugh.

"Yeah. Why's that funny?"

"It's the name of a cocktail, Jase, a drink people order when they go to bars."

"She's got the name of a *drink*?" Jason was astounded.

"I think," Lucinda said charitably, "her parents are probably very young and didn't know. They just thought it was a nice name."

"She'll still a zomboid, and it's a *stupid* name."

"Maybe Emma could come play with you one day after school," Lucinda suggested, changing the subject with a glance at him in the rear-view mirror as she appreciatively considered the description "fire hair."

He shook his head. "She's got this Filipino nanny who's pretty, but looks kinda mean." He paused, thinking, then said, "But maybe she's the one who showed Emma how to do the Jackie Chan stuff. I'm gonna ask her if that's who teached her. If she did, maybe the nanny will teach *me* how. I'd like to kick a whole *bunch* of those guys in the willy."

"You could hurt someone badly doing that, honey."

"*Yeah*!" he said gleefully. Then, seriously, he said, "'Course I'd only do it to rotten guys, like Tristan, who's always makin' the girls cry and beatin' up on the small boys. And he *never* gets caught. Everyone else gets in trouble, cuz he lies with his face all wide open, and says it wasn't him; he didn't do anything. Go ask his friends Rory and Aidan. Then the teachers say to the kids that told, 'Why did you say Tristan hurt you?' And the kids get scared, cuz Tristan's making signs behind the teacher's back that he's gonna *kill* 'em next time he catches 'em. So the kids don't say anything, and then they're in trouble. How come the teachers believe him and not us, Luce?"

Us. Jason was one of the small boys getting beaten up. It made her feel ill, made her wish she could personally throttle those bullies. Why didn't Renee know? And if she did know, why hadn't she complained to the school? Too often, Lucinda had the feeling that Jason didn't have his mother's complete attention. Renee's periodic air of distraction invariably gave Lucinda pause.

For now, she could only say, "I don't know, Jason. Sometimes grown-ups don't pay as much attention or listen as well as they should." Until he admitted it or asked for help, there was nothing she could do.

"They oughta! They *should* know!"

"Yes, they should."

"So I'm gonna ask Em if her nanny'll teach me those good moves. And then I'll kick those droids in their willies too."

His anger had validity, so she let the matter drop.

When they arrived at the house, Jason had his seat belt undone and was out of the car by the time Lucinda pulled the key from the ignition. "Is it ready yet?" he asked as they started up the front walk hand in hand.

"Not yet. It's still a bit too cold for swimming, honey."

"Grrrrr. Not too cold for *me*!"

"While I humbly acknowledge your superhero status, it is still too cold."

"When's it gonna be *not* too cold?"

"End of next week, I hope. Anyway, that's when the pool men are coming. Hungry?"

"What've you got?"

"Let's see. Carrot sticks and celery stuffed with tofu, cherry tomatoes, veggie chips from Trader Joe's, and your all-time favorite beverage, soy milk."

"*Not*! Plain tofu or fancy?" he asked, jumping up the porch steps one at a time.

"I've got plain and flavored."

"What flavor?"

"Sun-dried tomato with just a hint of basil," she lied straight-faced.

"Nope." He shook his head so that his mane of hair flew about.

"French onion?"

"Yack."

"Chive?"

"Double-yack." He made a retching noise as she opened the front door.

"That's what I figured. So I used plain. Okay?"

"Yeah."

"And you know what?" she said, holding the door open for him. "We've got a new kid-flick to review."

"*Way cool*!"

"After your homework. Okay?"

"I hate homework. I'm a *little kid*! I shouldn't *have* homework."

"I agree, you shouldn't. The amount of work you bring home is ridiculous. But you happen to be a *smart* little kid who's the youngest first-grader at your school. So let's get it out of the way, then we'll check out the movie."

"We could check it out while I have my snack and *then* do the homework."

"Not a chance," she said good-naturedly as he flopped into a chair in the kitchen and she went to the refrigerator to get the tray of vegetables and his soy milk.

Jason had a plethora of food allergies and on one occasion when he'd sneaked something not on his stringent list, Lucinda had watched in shock as the boy began sneezing uncontrollably, his face swelled, and for three hours he'd had all the symptoms of the 'flu—running a fever and wheezing like an old man. Then, suddenly, he'd been all right again. Fearful of a repeat of this alarming reaction, she'd stopped buying food he couldn't eat—except on weekends when Katanya and her family were there. If Jason and Renee came to join them for dinner, they'd all keep an eye on him to make sure he didn't casually help himself to any forbidden food. Interestingly, it was Katanya who kept the closest watch and regularly caught him trying to sneak something he wasn't allowed to have.

"Kat 'n' everyone comin' this weekend?" he asked, rhythmically kicking his backpack with one foot.

"Unh-hunh."

"Great! Me 'n' mom invited?"

"Of course. Saturday night, for dinner."

"How come not 'til Saturday?"

"Your mom's taking you to Greenwich to see your grandparents tomorrow night."

"Oh!" His nose wrinkled. He was not fond of the monthly visits. They were stiff, too-formal occasions when he was expected to be properly dressed (in belted chinos, button-down shirt with tie, and polished loafers—the Fairfield County uniform for men and boys alike) and impeccably behaved, speaking only when spoken to. And on every visit he had to defend his right to wear his hair the way he liked it. Impossible. Without exception, the day after the visit, Jason was cranky, rude and noisy, and angry with his mother for not defending his position. He couldn't understand why she never took his side. Privately, neither could Lucinda.

"So," she said, bringing the food to the table, "what kind of homework have you got?"

"The kind that gives me a headache," he said grumpily, grabbing several carrot sticks.

"Are your hands clean?"

"Nope."

"You want to wash them?"

Giving her a sidelong glance, he said, "Nope."

"Want to reconsider that answer?" she asked, amused.

"Oh, o-*kay*!" With a show of sorely tried patience, he put down the carrot sticks, got up and marched off to the hall bathroom.

Lucinda took a Diet Coke from the refrigerator and sat down at the table as Jason came racing back, his huge-looking sneakers squealing on the linoleum as he flung himself into his chair and retrieved his carrot sticks. Chomping away, he asked, "C'n I have a sip of your Coke?"

"Sure. And then I can watch for a couple of hours while you turn into a human tomato with a hacking cough."

"Human tomato." He snorted.

"You and Aspartame are not friends, Soupboy."

Picking up a stick of tofu-filled celery, he asked not for the first time, "How come I can eat this glop but not milk or real cheese?"

"No idea," she answered. "It's one of life's conundrums."

"What's that?"

"It means there are puzzling things we mere mortals can't explain."

"This"—he pointed at the filling in the celery with an accusing finger—"is like eating a foam pillow. Betcha they let tofu get dried out and use it to *make* pillows. I'm prob'ly *sleepin'* on a tofu pillow."

She laughed. "It's very possible."

"Toe-foo," he said. "It's the gunk 'tween your toes when you take your socks off."

She laughed harder.

He nodded, satisfied with her response, again kicking the backpack as he munched his way through half the platter of vegetables, taking special pleasure in bursting the cherry tomatoes inside his mouth.

Lucinda sipped her drink and watched him eat, mindful of how dramatically her life had altered. Agreeing to babysit him had been the first of two major commitments she'd made. The second came about soon after. Out of the blue she was approached via email by Artszine.com, a high-profile online magazine, to write a weekly movie review column. How they'd found her remained a mystery. But Simon Sinclair, the editor, had insisted she was uniquely qualified for the job. After much consideration, Lucinda had agreed to write two columns as a trial run under her old screenwriting pseudonym, Ella Van Dyne.

The first films arrived by courier a couple of days later and she'd watched them, making notes. Then, deciding she had nothing to lose by being truthful, she'd written her column—humorously savaging the big-budget unfunny comedy aimed at the teen audience, and heaping praise on the shoestring independent that had been bought only for limited distribution.

To everyone's surprise, her reviews got thousands of hits as a result of people telling other people via email to check out the column (a phenomenon unique to the web where word could spread, seemingly at the speed of light), and a lot of positive feedback. As well, her praise brought attention to the independent film which moved into general distribution and wound up earning almost thirty million dollars, along with several major awards.

When she'd been sent a children's movie in error some months earlier, she'd decided to let Jason watch it with her. She quoted his comments in the subsequent review, which ran with the now-famous lead line, **Soupboy says, "Yack!"** She was swamped with forwarded emails wanting to know who Soupboy was. In the next column she said simply that he was a young associate who would, in future, offer his response, along with hers, to children's movies. It amused both of them no end to be out together—at the library, say, or at a movie with Elise—and hear kids of varying ages say, "That was a total yack," or, "Oh, yackorama. Soupboy *rules*!"

Initially, Jason was indignant that people were going around using his personal expressions and made-up words and talking about Soupboy as if they knew who he was. But in short order he acquired a satisfied little smile whenever he overheard kids talking what quickly came to be known as Soup-speak. "I rock. I rule!" he would whisper to Lucinda and her grandmother.

Elise invariably responded in her elegantly offhand Gallic fashion, "But of course this is so, *mon petit. Tu es le roi de la soupe.*" This remark sent the two of them into gusts of laughter, while Lucinda marveled at the steadfast connection between a woman and a small boy separated in age by ninety years. Elise and Jason had adored each other on sight. And to Lucinda's initial amazement he made a point of washing his hands carefully before every subsequent meeting with Elise so that, he'd explained, "I don't give her any bad germies and make her sick cuz she's really, really old and old people can get sick way easier than little kids."

"You like her a lot, don't you, Jase?"

"A *whole* lot. She teaches me cool French words. She smells yummy good, she laughs when stuff is funny, she doesn't hate my hair, and when we go out she holds my hand. My *real* gramma doesn't *never* hold my hand. And"—he dropped his voice as if fearful of being overheard—"real gramma smells funny. Like funky doo-doo."

He behaved perfectly when in Elise's company, which was certainly not the case when he was on his own with Lucinda. He liked to try things on, see how far he could go—keeping close watch, trying to pinpoint the precise moment when he crossed the line. But being very young after all, there were occasions when he went too far. And then he would go sober as Lucinda quietly reprimanded him. Sometimes he argued and tried to plead his case; other times, he sobbed sorrowfully. He was an exceptional boy, mischievous and funny, questioning and linguistically inventive.

He had the boundless curiosity and flair of a born writer and she suspected he might well grow up to be one.

After gulping down half his glass of soy milk and making a face, he said, "What's the movie? Not a cartoon thingie, I hope." Jason's dislike of cartoons was equaled only by his dislike of too-cute or new-age feel-good children's books. He preferred authors with some edge like Shel Silverstein and Maurice Sendak whose books had great illustrations, story lines with whiffs of danger and genuine emotions. At his request, Lucinda had started giving Jason reading lessons just before he'd turned four, and she'd begun teaching him to print shortly thereafter. Jason was always keen to learn new words and to read more books. They made trips to the library at least twice a week. And Lucinda regularly scanned reviews for new releases that might appeal to him. Any occasion that called for gift-giving always included books. His interest in new toys, new clothes would be polite but minimal. But he would examine each book with the fastidious care of an archeologist seeking clues to previously unknown cultures.

"It's foreign, but not dubbed," she told him.

"Hate dubbing." He dragged his fingertip through the tofu on one of the remaining pieces of celery.

"I'm well aware of your feelings about dubbing. I hope you plan to eat that," Lucinda said, with a nod at the platter.

He looked over at her. "I have to?"

"You put your finger in it. What d'you think?"

"Krep-*luck*!" he said feelingly, having heard the word spoken one day by a woman in the local supermarket and, thinking it was an arcane swear word, immediately claimed it. Lucinda thought it was so funny that she didn't have the heart to correct him. "Okay." He took the celery and made a morose show of eating it.

Lucinda removed the vegetable tray then picked up his backpack and put it on the table.

"When's Gin gonna be back?" he asked, unzipping the pack.

"Two weeks."

"In time to come swimmin' with me! All *right*!"

Replacing the plastic wrap over the tray, she returned it to the refrigerator saying, "And now for the dreaded homework."

"And *now*, and *now*," he intoned solemnly, dumping papers on the table.

"We zip through this and then it's show time, with popcorn!"

He rolled his eyes. "Who *invented* homework? When school's over it oughta be *over*. We shouldn't have to bring school *home*."

"I agree completely. If school was open all year long and there were no summer holidays, there wouldn't be any need for homework."

"No summer *holidays*? Are you *demento*? No way."

"Okay, then. Homework, sir."

"Grrrrr," he grizzled, settling in to do his printing exercises.

"I'll go cue the tape," she said, patting his arm as she went by. Then, on impulse, she bent and kissed the top of his head. "I love you, Soupboy."

"Me, too. But I'd love you more if you didn't make me do this stupid groanwork."

"Someday you'll be glad I did."

He shook his head vigorously. "Not ever, nope, never."

"Okay. I'll have to live with you loving me less."

He went still for a few seconds, then shifted to look at her, saying, "I didn't really mean it, Luce."

"I know that."

"I love you better than *anybody,*" he declared with brimming eyes. "I didn't *mean* it."

"It's okay, honey. Really."

Relieved, he dragged the back of one hand across his eyes, then turned to his printing, echoing, "Okay. O-*kay*."

Better than anybody. What about his mother? No qualifying: better than anybody. She really had to wonder what went on in that house. From time to time, for no given reason, she wished she didn't have to send him home. Then she told herself she was reading far too much into it. Her reactions were off-kilter from having spent so many years alone.

Chapter Three

Referring to her notes and Jason's semi-approving comments on the kid-flick ("It doesn't suck, but it's not tropendo either!") Lucinda finished writing the reviews for that week's column and attached them to an email to her editor. She shut down the computer, then sat gazing into space, wishing to be able to spend more time with her family, especially her grandmother without having to fight her way past Anne.

She hated feeling the way she did—wanting to take Anne by her scrawny shoulders and shake her until her shellacked hair cracked, or a selfless thought managed to break free and fall into some lucid area in her head. Anne's much-belated territorialism was like a plague, something toxic and highly contagious. As Maddie had warned, her mother's antipathy was the equivalent of an earwig. Insidious and inescapable, Lucinda's brain was being pillaged as Anne slowly chewed a path through it. Oh, sure that story *Boomerang* by Oscar Cook about an earwig penetrating a man's head via the ear was based purely on superstition—and it was a memorable effort, to say the least, given that she'd read it more than thirty years before—but it was a damned good metaphor for the long-term effects of the woman's behavior.

It hadn't taken Lucinda long to discover how Anne always knew her mother's schedule and, in particular, when Elise and Lucinda had something planned. One phone call and she had her answer. Anne was cleverly worming the information out of Gwyn, Elise's assistant ("I was thinking of coming to see Mother this week and wondered what her schedule is like.") and there was nothing to be done about it without putting Gwyn in a very awkward position. She was simply doing her job. How was she to know she'd become pivotal to Anne's scheming? God! It was sickening! And it was Lucinda's own fault. If she hadn't become angry at that first meeting, if she hadn't commented on the knock-off choker or done that riff on snotty salesgirls, Anne would likely have dismissed her. But, no. She'd had to fight back with words—as she always did when something or someone made her angry. Now look where they were! At war.

Her stomach aching, she pushed away thoughts of Anne and looked at the two framed citations on the wall above her desk. One documented Lily's Academy Award for best actress of 1956 in *Street Crime*. The other was Ella Van Dyne's Academy Award for best screenplay adaptation of 1998 for *Flight Plan*. Lily's was real enough. The other felt like the equivalent of one of those *Time* magazine covers you could have made up to order with a photograph you submitted. *Time's Man/Woman of the Year*. Something fabricated to make the recipient feel special. If she hadn't seen the ceremony with her own eyes she'd never have believed she had actually won.

She'd watched the awards show alone that March night a few months before, not for a moment thinking there was the remotest possibility that she would win. She'd been flabbergasted, even, perversely (as if her closely-guarded anonymity were at risk) somewhat chagrined, at being nominated for an Oscar. Winning the BAFTA and Writers Guild awards had seemed reasonable, although she couldn't have articulated specifically why—something to do with distance, possibly. But an Academy Award … It seemed all wrong, even surreal. She hadn't lived that life, hadn't been even a peripheral part of the L.A. scene in more than thirty years. She'd felt dishonest—a new kind of fraudulence—as she'd watched winners go onstage to collect their prizes.

Then, after some dreadfully scripted badinage, the pair of actors presenting the award for best-adaptation category had named the nominees while a camera closed in on the faces that went with the names. There was, of course, no Ella Van Dyne in the audience, not even a photograph to put onscreen. Then, all at once there was some kind of time-lapse. Lucinda blinked several times. She'd missed something, couldn't grasp what had been said. Another camera panned the audience and then fixed on Gin who was moving up the aisle in yet another of her smart little black dresses ("Can't ever go wrong with great shoes, good hair and a little black dress, kiddo. Haute couture looks like hell on short women.") to accept the statuette from one of the actors before moving to the microphone. The applause was tumultuous—or so it seemed to Lucinda—and she thought it had to be in acknowledgment of Gin's nomination for best actress. Everybody loved her. And her performance in *Flight Plan* had been heart-wrenchingly real and honest.

In her husky voice so reminiscent of Lily's, a beaming Gin said, "A few of you here tonight are old enough to remember some movies my friend Ella and I did a couple of centuries ago, when we were kids: *December Blue, Rain Days*, and *Power Play*, to name a few." Explosive applause, cheers and whistling. "Right!" she continued, seemingly unable to stop smiling. "So I'm not the only one who'll admit to remembering drive-in restaurants with waitresses on roller skates and twelve-inch black-and-white TVs." Hoots of laughter, some ear-splitting whistles. "Contrary to certain rumors, my friend was far too young to be blacklisted, let alone hang out with Commie sympathizers. We rode all over town on our tricycles looking, but we just couldn't find them." More laughs. "The truth is, Ella just decided to stop writing. She was busy doing other things. But I've always believed she is one of the finest screenwriters ever, and I begged her to do this script, because no one else could've done it justice. I know she's home tonight, watching, and on her behalf I thank the Academy and the members for acknowledging a truly great talent. Ella, accepting this for you is the proudest moment of my life. I love you, kiddo." She blew a kiss into the camera, waved to the cheering crowd, then sailed off into the wings with the statuette hugged to her breast.

The phone calls started moments later. First was Jeneva, to say, "Lucy, I'm so happy for you, so proud to know you. You deserve that award. It's a wonderful picture. And Gin looked so fine up there, didn't she? I want her to win, I truly do. No one can do what she does."

Next was her grandmother: "Now, like your mama, you have a great prize. It is marvelous, *chérie*. We will celebrate. All the family will come to make a great fuss over you. Now we must watch to see Gin"—she pronounced it Jeen—"receive her prize. *Je t'embrace, chérie*."

All the family. That would include Anne, which would turn the celebration into something else altogether. Lucinda turned off the ringer, letting the machine field calls, while she watched the rest of the show. Like Jeneva and Elise, she wanted to see Gin up on the stage again, accepting the Oscar that was rightfully hers. But it went to a much younger woman who'd given a showy but shallow performance in an otherwise inferior film. Lucinda broke into angry tears at the unfairness of it, the behind-the-scenes politicking that had robbed Gin of her rightful prize.

Glumly, Lucinda watched to the end of the show before listening to her messages. There were better than a dozen calls from her cousins and their children, all of them near-breathless with excitement and filled with plans for the family celebration that was, in no time at all, taking on a life of its own. Naturally, there was no message from Anne. Lucinda was tempted to phone her aunt, make a peaceful overture and invite her to join the celebration. She actually began to lift the receiver but then put it down again. Anne would see the overture as an opportunity to say something hurtful. Lucinda couldn't risk it.

From backstage at *Brown Baby* which was in its final week, after a thirteen-month run, Katanya had left her message between scenes. "I just *heard*. I'm *so* psyched. I'll call you tomorrow after school. Bet your family's freakin' out. I am, for sure. It's tropendo! Love you, love you, *love* you, Luce."

Finally, just over an hour after she'd left the stage, Gin

called. "I had to sneak out to find a pay phone. So is this great or what? Somewhere, Lily's smiling away, happy and proud as all get out."

"*You* should've won, Gin. It's an outrage that you didn't."

"Ah, poo! Who cares? They got one thing right, and that's what matters. You wrote your ass off and you *earned* this. I'll be home in a couple of days with your prize. Gotta scram now before the news hounds get suspicious. Love you to bits, Ella."

Lucinda had turned off the ringer again after that, and tried but couldn't watch the post-show coverage. Her concentration was blown. She'd been too shocked at winning The Big Prize for something that hadn't been very hard to do. Even before she'd completed the final draft, Gin had gone ahead and acquired the rights to another novel, insisting, "Only you can write this. Do it for me, Ella. Please? You don't want me to beg, do you? It's so hard on the knees."

With the award, her profile on Artszine.com had grown in an exponential leap. Suddenly her reviews had the power to lift a film from obscurity or to shift the teenage focus away from a shlocky blockbuster to something more worthy of their time (and their all-important box-office dollars). Since March there'd been many pieces written about her and her popular column. There was considerable media speculation about the true identity of Ella Van Dyne, because the woman didn't seem to exist anywhere, except in her name on some old film scripts, on one new award-winning one, and an online magazine. Sundry journalists did deep research but came up with only suppositions. One enterprising young woman (determined to get a scoop and rise to by-line status) finagled her way into registry information at the Screenwriters Guild, which produced an address for Ella. It turned out to be Gin's old Los Angeles house in Whitley Heights. The new owners had no idea who Ella Van Dyne might be.

It was suggested by the noted film critic of one major weekly magazine that Van Dyne was the pseudonym of a best-selling male novelist. The rival critic at a competing weekly insisted that Van Dyne was actually a producer of some renown who'd written a handful of good scripts in the late eighties and early nineties but who'd been struggling to get another film he'd scripted up and running for the past several years. These suggestions were met with rebuttals by the novelist and the producer, both of whom stated in letters to the editor that they wished they had Van Dyne's talent. But sorry, no. Neither of them was Ella. Throughout the weeks-long frenzy, the Artszine.com staff kept silent, not responding to any form of question—to Lucinda's abiding gratitude.

It was also broadly hinted in the sleazier tabloids that Ella was in fact Gin's secret lover. Rumors had long circulated that Gin was gay. She always dismissed the matter by saying, "Sure. Right. That's it exactly," then emitting her famous infectious laugh. It didn't stop people from trying to out her, but since there was no hidden dirt to be found, Gin just kept on laughing. "Hey, they wanna think I'm gay, fine. Whatever floats their boat."

Lucinda and Gin were the only people still alive who knew about the day when Ginny Holder was summoned from the classroom on the studio lot for a meeting with producer Lloyd Rankin. Lucinda had seen too many kids go for those meetings only to return some time later moving in a glassy-eyed, unsteady fashion, as if they'd been thrown from a tornado-like carnival ride. Even forty-odd years later, recalling that day, Lucinda could feel the heat of Lily's atypical anger as she'd listened to what Lucinda had to say before slamming out of her trailer to go storming across the lot. She could see again the (mercifully temporary) lifelessness of Gin's eyes when she returned to the classroom the next day. And she could hear Gin's sultry voice many years later, floating on the summer darkness as she'd quietly talked about how she'd paid under the table to get a copy of the coroner's report after Lloyd's murder. "I needed to know he was well and truly dead and never coming back, never going to hurt any more kids."

When she got home to Connecticut a week after the awards show, Gin had arrived at Lucinda's door, bundled up in bulky layers of clothing and complaining bitterly. "Dumbest damned thing I ever did, letting you talk me into moving here! I've turned into a human Popsicle just walking from the car to your front door."

"It was *your* idea, not mine," Lucinda reminded her, pulling Gin into the house. "And you liked it well enough during the summer. I seem to remember seeing you here every day, cavorting in the pool with Soupboy."

"He's the only one around here who's my *size*," Gin snapped back. "Here's your goddamned Oscar stuff!" She'd thrust a large envelope at Lucinda before sitting on the stairs to remove her boots. "Even the dogs are cold."

"Knit them some sweaters," Lucinda said mildly. "Coffee?"

"Yeah. Fill the tub with it. I'll sit in it and maybe thaw out."

With a laugh, Lucinda had put the envelope on her

desk—the award itself would arrive in a few weeks, after it had been inscribed—before going to start a pot of coffee.

Padding into the kitchen in her heavy socks, Gin said, "Actually, the dogs are in heaven. They've been running around in the snow like puppies, sniffing out new friends. Me, I've been going through heating oil like you wouldn't believe. I'm thinking of switching over to gas."

"Listen to you," Lucinda said. "You hate it here so much you're considering more efficient ways to keep your nice big Victorian warm and toasty."

"Well, I'm certainly not moving back to the coast after finally finding a house I like. Not to mention having had to buy another car just for winter driving while my poor baby Mustang sits in the garage wearing the equivalent of giant Doctor Denton's. Then there's all the sweaters, the silk undies, down jackets and other stuff I had to get from L. L. Bean—who have the nicest people working their order lines. Ever notice that?"

"Yes, I have."

"And when the hell do we get Spring? It'll be April in a minute. What's with this endless damned cold?"

"I'm sure I don't know. By the way, that was a sweller than usual little black dress you wore to the ceremony."

Brightening, Gin said, "Wasn't it? Told this freelance designer kid who worked in wardrobe on *Plan* what I wanted and she did some sketches, brought over some swatches. At the party after the show, I really put her name out there. If there's a next time, I won't be able to afford her."

"Oh, there'll be a next time," Lucinda had said confidently. "And you'll be taking your own Oscar home. You should've had it, Gin."

Gin shrugged. "I got the Golden Globe and the L.A. Film

Critics award. Losing to someone who's all tissue paper and spangles isn't even worth thinking about. What matters is that *Plan*'s gonna get rereleased, make us more money, and prime the public pump for the new one. I've already got a distribution deal, because you won."

"Really? That's kind of intimidating."

"You just do your thing and don't worry about it. Nothing succeeds like excess, kiddo. Let me take care of the nuts and bolts and get *Exposure* up and running."

Like Jason, Gin was always reading and had great taste in fiction, with an unerring feel for flawed, feisty but sympathetic heroines—perhaps because she herself was flawed and feisty but sympathetic. She looked far younger than fifty-three, and exuded healthy energy without benefit of cosmetic surgery. ("Oh, I don't *think* so. I can barely handle a shot of Novocain. As if I'm gonna have *general anesthetic* and let some overpriced Beverly Hills nutjob snip off bits of my *face*!") A strict exercise regime kept her small body lean and lithe. And genetic good fortune had endowed her with the kind of bone structure that aged well. She had the same Nordic appeal as Lily, with ash-blonde hair, bold wide-set bright blue eyes, a flawless complexion, a go-to-hell carriage that, with the help of the curves built into her onscreen wardrobe and her husky voice, translated into a simmering sexuality undiminished by time. She was living proof that appeal to the opposite sex wasn't solely the dominion of the young. Women adored her; they loved her big grin and gusty laughter and hurried to see her films the minute they were released. Gin still had a lovable presence onscreen, still had box-office clout. And *Exposure* was a terrific study of a hard-edged corporate executive, the sole survivor of an airplane crash, who manages to stay alive for eight days in the wilderness until she's rescued. Afterwards, having had an epiphany, she abandons the corporate world to open a halfway house for troubled teens. It was a great part and Lucinda knew only Gin could play it believably.

"After *Exposure*," Lucinda had insisted, "you'll be going home with the big one."

"Whatever. Hurry up with that coffee. Maybe I'll hook up an IV and let it drip directly to my bloodstream."

Friday evening, after Renee had taken Jason home to get both of them cleaned up before going to her parents' house for dinner, Lucinda drove to the train station.

It still seemed something of a miracle that her property with its overgrown garden had piqued a child's interest, luring Katanya over to admire the tangled flower beds and the white clapboard farmhouse with its deep front porch. She'd turned and beckoned to Lucinda and, surrendering to her own curiosity, Lucinda had responded, going out into the sweltering July heat to make the acquaintance of the sweet-faced enormously gifted girl. As a result, Lucinda's life, that stagnant pond, had been stirred back into motion by an effortless give-and-take of questions and answers—the longest (and by far the most entertaining) conversation she'd had face to face with anyone since her mother's death.

When the train doors slid open and the three of them came into view, Lucinda felt herself grow lighter, as if she were actually physically expanding.

Katanya's mother, Loranne, had the same heart-shaped face as her daughter. She wore clear red lipstick on her perfectly formed mouth, and a hint of bronzing on her high cheekbones. She'd recently had her hair cut into a cap of short tight curls that was most flattering. And Jeneva, an older, slightly shorter and more rounded version of her daughter, wore her straightened hair pulled back in an old-fashioned bun that suited her well, complimenting the high forehead and large eyes she'd passed on to her daughter and granddaughter. Mother and daughter wore short-sleeved, full-skirted, brightly patterned cotton dresses Jeneva had sewn. With her long cornrowed hair in a ponytail, Katanya was in her usual denim overalls with a hot-pink T-shirt and clunky black lace-up Doc Martins that added at least an inch and a half to her height—but she was still only just over five feet tall. The family resemblance each bore to the other was inescapable—the almost-black eyes, the delicately pointed chins, the well-shaped heads and long graceful necks, the dark-coffee tone of their complexions. They were beautiful women.

"You all look so wonderful!" Lucinda declared, embracing each of them.

"You look pretty wonderful yourself," Jeneva told her. "That's a new outfit, isn't it?" she asked of Lucinda's navy linen slacks and matching cotton pullover. "Somebody made a trip to J. Crew," she told her daughter and granddaughter, slipping her arm through Lucinda's as they started toward the car.

"Yes, I did," Lucinda confessed. "I picked up a few things—for all of us."

"Oh Luce!" Katanya laughed, stood on tiptoe to kiss the tip of Lucinda's nose, then, with typical zeal, flew away, doing a series of quick, graceful dance steps across the parking lot that had embarking passengers stopping to watch. "It's Christmas every weekend," she exclaimed as she did several balletic turns, then stopped and flung out her arms, beaming. Several passengers applauded and she bowed and blew them kisses.

"God, she's amazing!" Lucinda murmured, tossing the car keys to the girl who ran ahead to open the car doors. "Anyway"—she turned back to Loranne and Jeneva—"I enjoy buying you things."

"We know that, Lucy," Loranne said, patting Lucinda's arm. "We're long past the point of arguing. We'll just feed you all your favorites tomorrow night, keep on trying to fatten you up some. Mama cooked up a storm."

Jeneva hefted the Bloomingdale's bag, with a dazzling smile. "Oh, say, I finally saw *The Truman Show* and I'm dying to discuss it with you."

"Did you love it?" Lucinda asked, always intrigued by Jeneva's take on movies. Usually they agreed, but now and then Jeneva would raise a point Lucinda hadn't considered, which they'd talk about at length. Jeneva was, to Lucinda's endless delight, a lifelong film buff and a very astute viewer. As a bonus, she was also a fine musician and had passed her gifts on to her daughter and granddaughter.

"That's what I want to talk about."

"I can't wait," Lucinda said truthfully. She relished her late night talks on the porch with Jeneva, when they spoke of films and music, of whatever came to mind. There was rarely a day when they didn't chat on the phone or exchange emails. They had, from the outset, formed a significant attachment. That they were the same age was a part of it; that she was Katanya's grandmother was another part. But, most importantly, she had always accepted Lucinda exactly as she was. So, just as she longed for more time with her grandmother, Lucinda wanted more with Jeneva, too. *Needy*, she thought. Why couldn't she be grateful for what she had, instead of wanting more? Was it a deficiency, a flaw, this unquenchable hunger?

They stopped at the house long enough to drop off their bags, stow the food Jeneva had brought in the refrigerator, and freshen up before going on—as they did once a month and sometimes more often—to Elise's house in Westport for dinner.

The number of family members at these Friday night dinners varied. Usually Anne stayed away—perhaps in the hope that her absence would be conspicuous, worthy of discussion. Or perhaps because she knew it would be impossible to compete with everyone present for her mother's attention. In reality even her children were relieved when she didn't appear. Things always went more smoothly without her.

On this evening, Lucinda's now seventy-five-year-old aunt Adele (who, like Lucinda, suffered from migraines and as a result was thin, but not purposefully gaunt like her older sister) and her husband John were there, along with their son Paul (who was several years older than Lucinda) and his wife Roxanne. Paul's son, Paul Junior, and his wife Annette had brought their two-week-old daughter Amelia, (leaving three-year-old Amanda, who had an ear infection, at home with a sitter). Paul Junior's younger sister Eliza had come up from Manhattan with her long-time partner, Rosemarie.

It was a fine evening, with Eliza and Rosemarie feeding the new jazz CDs they'd brought into the stereo system they and Eliza's parents had given Elise for Christmas the previous year. Elise loved jazz and, from moment to moment, she would pause, listen intently and then say, "Ah, but this is wonderful. Who is this?" Then Rosemarie, who was an executive with a record company and an ardent jazz aficionado, provided the details in her lyrical Alabama accent.

Just as they were about to move into the dining room, Anne arrived in a cloud of cloying perfume. In a puffy-sleeved, full skirted white dress (complete with crinoline) that would've looked more appropriate on a child, her helmet of hair like cake frosting, and spike-heeled white leather slingback shoes, she came mincing across the room accompanied by the jangling clatter of half a dozen bangles on her wrist, to say to her mother, "Sorry to be so late. Traffic was terrible. A big accident on Ninety-five, as usual. Had to get off at exit eight and come up the Post Road. It took *forever*."

It was apparent that Elise hadn't been expecting her. After accepting Anne's air kiss, she slipped away to the kitchen to have a word with Erica, the cook, while Anne went around the room, greeting everyone with varying degrees of civility. The woman was as subtle as a sledgehammer, Lucinda thought, watching. Those with the fairest skin got air kisses, those of color got one of her alarming little handshakes. Anne was a woman of color who not only lived as the white person she appeared to be, she was also blatantly racist, even to her own family. Pointedly, Anne ignored Lucinda until she'd greeted everyone else, stopping to chuck Katanya under the chin, saying, "Don't you look adorable! I could just eat you up with a spoon, you cute little thing." Anne moved on to say a chilly hello to Jeneva and Loranne, and Katanya looked over at Lucinda, crossing her eyes and letting her tongue loll out of her mouth.

At last, as Erica laid another place at the table, Anne doddled over to Lucinda.

"And how are you, Lucinda?" Anne asked, offering neither an air kiss nor a handshake. The coldness of her expression was surpassed only by the enmity in her eyes.

"I'm great!" Lucinda declared, bothered to her very soul by this woman's hatred of her. Anne carried it around like a well-disguised bomb, or a cyanide capsule implanted in one of her teeth. She could either blow someone up or kill herself. She was as transparent and potentially poisonous as a tropical jellyfish.

Startling both herself and her aunt, Lucinda bent and gave Anne an emphatic hug. It was like clasping a bag of kindling, all pointy ends and spindly, brittle twigs. "So glad you could come tonight," Lucinda lied jovially, stepping away, her nostrils clogged with Anne's sickening perfume.

Anne's face was flushed and she seemed thunderstruck, lost for words. Turning away then, Lucinda followed the others into the dining room, repelled by her own behavior. Why on earth had she done that? she wondered, still feeling the impression of her aunt's bony body—like embracing a cadaver. She could hear Lily saying, *If you can't beat 'em, kill 'em with kindness. They never know how to handle it.* No doubt about it, Lucinda thought. Anne had no idea how to deal with Lucinda's gesture of affection. And because Anne was so dumfounded, so plainly at a complete loss, Lucinda felt terrible, sickened both by the horrible perfume and by having hurt the woman. She had never in her life intentionally been unkind to another person. But there was nothing, not a single thing, she could do right when it came to Anne. Were she not such a superficial creature, given to saying and doing such atrocious things, Lucinda might have believed Anne planned these incidents. But she wasn't clever enough for that.

Anne's forays onto the battlefield for Elise's affection were scattershot efforts. She fired away willy-nilly and, invariably, some of the shot made direct hits. There was always wreckage in Anne's wake.

Dinner was, as always, rich with good food, with conversations criss-crossing the table and with periodic bursts of laughter. Anne had been seated well away from Lucinda and looked to be still in a state of shock as she cut her food into tiny pieces, only occasionally putting something into her mouth. She responded with a glacial little grimace meant to be a smile whenever someone spoke to her, but she looked, in fact, like the wrinkled eight-year-old Madeline had said she was. Pouty and disapproving, never once did she meet Lucinda's eyes. Lucinda felt she should apologize. But for what? This was agonizing.

Midway through the meal, slowly looking around, Lucinda studied the other faces, all sound receding as she absorbed the details of these people she'd come to love almost unreasoningly, even greedily. She had the irrational feeling that she might lose them because of Anne; she might be provoked into doing something that would so appall them that they would withdraw their affection and she would be once again alone.

Her uncle John was very black and very beautiful even at the age of seventy-eight. With exquisitely honed Patrician features and a headful of closely cropped white hair that emphasized the precise balance of forehead and chin, the perfection of wide-set eyes and generous mouth, he was still an impressive figure. He exuded a potent aura of kindness and wisdom. The stories he sometimes told of his childhood in the Belgian Congo were powerfully evocative. His voice alone (soft and mellow, with its British inflection as a result of his public school education in England) could soothe a cranky infant to sleep, as he was doing just then—cradling his great-granddaughter Amelia against his shoulder, murmuring into her ear while his grandson Paul Junior and his robust Italian-American wife, Annette, exchanged a smile.

Her aunt Adele (her older sister's polar opposite in affability, personality and natural good looks) was engaged in a lively laughing conversation with Katanya who had changed the blue denim overalls she'd arrived in for a pair of pale pink ones with a white shirt. Worn on a gold chain, Lucinda's Phi Beta Kappa key rested in the hollow of the girl's throat. Loranne and Jeneva—on either side of her in their vivid matching dresses—chatted with Elise at the head of the table. And at the other end, Eliza (a professor of African studies at Hunter College) with flawless black skin, teeth so white they seemed to glow, and bottomless dark eyes like her grandfather's, and Rosemarie, of the fair freckled complexion, unruly red hair and green-blue eyes, were talking to Eliza's parents—Paul, who was a younger, equally handsome version of his father, and Roxanne, a full-blooded Iroquois, who had amber skin, piercing brown eyes, strong handsome features, and gleaming jet hair that fell halfway to her waist.

Filled with dread at the thought of losing these people, Lucinda suddenly had the sensation that she was walled away from everyone—as if she could see them but could not herself be seen. It was a once-familiar, now only occasional, feeling of being so distant in so many ways that it was as if she were drowning in air. Old sorrow, like a stalker's shadow on a night-dark street, was suddenly tracking her.

Her heartbeat became audible in her ears, making itself felt as a throbbing in her wrists and throat, as she tried to breathe steadily, working to conceal the fact that, like an inept student at her first dancing class, she'd lost the rhythm. She looked down at the food on her plate, at the utensils in her hands, and ordered her limbs to perform. They did. Knife and fork worked in unison, mechanically slicing a stalk of asparagus into several pieces, while she told herself to snap out of it; she was being an ass, flailing away in an arcane form of self-pity. No, not that. It was fear, fear that it would never be possible to make up for the lost years; that there would never be a way to satisfy her relentless and mortifying love-hunger. Like some massive sea sponge, she couldn't absorb enough, and was contemptuous of her insatiable need. And as if that wasn't bad enough, her aunt—a woman she'd been prepared to love, simply because they were related—had become not only an opponent but also an obstacle.

Lightly, a hand descended onto her shoulder and she inhaled her grandmother's faint lilac fragrance. "*Chérie*," Elise said softly, "return to us."

A quick glance around the table confirmed that the conversations continued uninterrupted. This exchange, if noticed, was not being acknowledged—not even by Anne who was staring fixedly at her plate. Setting down her knife and fork, Lucinda shifted in her seat, reaching to cover her grandmother's hand with her own as she looked up at her—this small, very erect, white-haired woman with delicate features beneath a subtle touch of color at her cheeks and warm pink lipstick emphasizing her generous mouth. "I feel terrible for doing that," Lucinda whispered, her throat thick.

"You must not allow Anne to have such an impact upon you," Elise said in a firm undertone.

"I keep making it worse," Lucinda said.

"No. What you did, it was brave."

"Brave? It was *crazy*. I can't believe I did that."

"Nor can I," Elise admitted with humor. Then, more seriously, she said, "Before Michael died, she was difficult but not impossible. Since then she has become untouchable. You dared to embrace her and I think perhaps you have reminded her that she is human after all, and no longer young."

"So why do I feel like an ax murderer?"

Elise laughed. "My daughter has this effect. It is an art she has mastered to perfection. She seems, I think, older than me." She looked over at her daughter. "No?"

Lucinda looked, too. It was true. Anne could well have been the mother and Elise the daughter. "My god," Lucinda whispered. "You're right."

"Yes. Bad feelings, anger, they will make one old. I have seen it in others, not only Anne. Eat now," Elise said with a smile. "There is a wonderful dessert, with liqueurs and coffee. And then perhaps, if they will be so kind, Kattie and her m'ma and grandm'ma will make heavenly music for us. We are, when you think of it, very fortunate, are we not?"

"Yes," Lucinda had to agree, stroking her grandmother's delicate hand. "You're right. We are. Thank you," she said gratefully.

Absolution—at least temporarily.

June 2000-July 2001

Chapter Four

On the last day of second grade, a glum Jason came—not running as usual, but trudging—over to Lucinda. Grabbing a fistful of her blouse, he leaned mutely against her as if she were all that were keeping him upright. Thinking it best to let him speak in his own time, she got him buckled up in the car, then slid behind the wheel. When they were several hundred yards away from the school—where half a dozen children ran zigging and zagging directionlessly across the playing field—Jason sighed heavily, then said, "That's not Em's nanny. It's her mom."

"Oh?"

"Yeah. I finally asked Em could she come over sometime and she said she'd ask her mother. And that's how I know."

"You made a mistake. It's okay."

"*No, it's not okay!*" he shouted. Chest heaving, he cried, "I thought her mom was like a *servant* or something. I'm so *stupid!*"

"You are not stupid. A lot of the kids have Filipino nannies."

"I should've *known*. It's just good I didn't say it to Em or she'd've hated me forever."

"If she's as smart as you say, she wouldn't have hated you. She'd have explained."

"She would so have hated me."

"Nobody who knows you could ever hate you, Jason. You're a really nice boy."

"Whatever." He chewed on his lower lip for a moment, then said, "Emma's my *best friend* and she's movin' *away*!"

"Oh, honey, I'm sorry. I know how much you like her."

"*Next week*!" he cried, as if he'd been betrayed. "She didn't even *tell* me 'til I asked could she come over."

"Maybe she just forgot, Jason."

He was in tears now, his face flushed. "I won't have one single friend anymore."

"Oh, you will—"

"I'm not goin' *back* next year! I *hate* that stinkfart school, and all the ratbastards like Tristan."

"There will be different kids next year. You'll make new friends."

He shook his head and turned to stare out the window, saying nothing more.

When they arrived at her house, Lucinda lifted him out of the car and carried him inside, his face hot and damp against her shoulder. Sitting down with him on the sofa, she held him for a time.

At last, she said, "I know you're very sad but you *will* make new friends, Jase. You'll miss Emma, but you know what? You're a lucky boy to have met someone so special. You'll never forget her, will you?"

"No," he murmured. Then he confessed miserably, "I *love* Em."

"I know you do. And in your memory, you'll always love her. That's a wonderful thing. And you never know. Someday you might see her again."

"Unh-unh. She's movin' all the way to Chicago."

"It's not that far. Tomorrow, ask if you could have her new address. And you'll give her yours. Maybe you'll be pen pals."

"What's that?"

"You'll write to each other."

"Yeah," he said, liking the idea. "I'll ask. You gotta help me write down my address so she can read it. You know how crummy my printing is."

"Of course I'll help you. You might even be able to email each other."

"She's not allowed to have email or IM or anything. I asked a long time ago. Her 'puter's only for schoolwork."

"So then you'll write real letters." She got a tissue from her pocket and wiped his face, asking, "Hungry?"

He shrugged. "I guess. Luce? Why do people we really like go away from us?"

"I don't have an answer for that, Jase. But I know it hurts a lot when it happens—sometimes for a long time."

"Yeah." He sighed again.

"How about some lunch?" she suggested gently. "And after lunch, why don't we go to the library?"

"Okay." He remained unmoving on her lap for several moments, then said, "You're not goin' away, are you, Luce?"

"Not if I can help it, no."

"Promise?"

"Yes, I promise."

~

About six weeks later, Jason came flying into the house without knocking, shouting, "I got a letter! Emma wrote me! *Look, look*! I gotta write her back *right away*. I need good paper, Luce. You got any *good* paper?"

"Tell you what, Soupboy. Let's go out and buy you a box of special stationery."

"That's paper, right?"

"Yup. We might get lucky and find some with your name on it."

"Yeah? That'd be way cool."

The letters went back and forth intermittently. Jason carried a small school photo of Emma in his backpack and, occasionally, Lucinda would find him studying it. But he stopped talking about her, and Lucinda thought it best not to mention the black-haired girl with the prepple eyes. Whatever was between them, Jason chose not to share it.

As Lucinda did up his seat belt on Jason's seventh birthday, she said, "We're going to do something special today, Soupboy."

"Yeah? Cuz it's my birthday?"

"Unh-hunh. We're going to open a bank account for you."

He just stared at her, clearly disappointed.

"That's only *one* of the special things we're going to do," she clarified, and he perked right up, giving her a big smile.

Off they went to her bank where Jason signed his name—half printing, half script—on several signature cards. Lucinda showed him how to fill out the slip and they deposited a check for all the money Renee had paid her, plus interest, into Jason's new savings account.

After that, each month Jason filled out the deposit slips

himself, happily complicit in this account, of which his mother was completely unaware. The balance was well over five figures, but its reality meant little to him. He had more interest in the ritual than in what it signified. Money was something grown-ups had, not small children. To Jason, being given the price of an orange sorbet at Baskin-Robbins was a fortune. Nevertheless, his having the account satisfied Lucinda. She felt—an admitted abstraction—that this was a bit of recompense for his father's having emptied the accounts (which had contained primarily his wife's—fortunately ongoing—trust-fund income) before abandoning the family. According to Renee, the man had never once even telephoned to speak to his son. He and his parents had removed themselves completely from Jason's life. She couldn't help thinking that Anne would fit right in with those people—cold, emotionless creatures pretending to be human.

Renee said often that Todd's leaving them the summer of Katanya's Fresh Air Fund visit, when Jason wasn't yet three, had been the best thing that could have happened. Once past the upset of the experience, Renee had turned her attention to Jason—just in time to prevent further deterioration of his behavior (he'd been prone to fiery-faced screaming tantrums). She had resumed her maiden name of Palmer, (wanting Jason to use it, too, but he steadfastly refused and continued calling himself Jason Crane) had gone back to school and started acquiring degrees. In the process, she'd changed from a typical suburban yummy-mummy into a retro-hippie version of her former self. Having given up the unflattering designer clothes and an annoyingly clenched-jaw manner of speaking, she appeared younger and more attractive at thirty-one than she had before. She often wore her long hair in what Gin (who from the outset confided to Lucinda that for reasons she was unable to articulate, just couldn't warm up to Renee) referred to privately as "Princess Leia ear-muffs." Renee dressed in odd clothing—ankle-length flowing East Indian cotton skirts and gauzy blouses, with clunky boots and long sweater vests—that somehow suited her often distracted manner. "Airy-fairy as hell," Gin declared. "She kind of reminds me of street people I've seen trolling the streets, talking to themselves, taking a dump right on the sidewalk, completely oblivious. Not that she's that bad, but there's *something*, kiddo. Definitely something."

Lucinda remained guarded with Renee, mindful of how badly she had behaved during Katanya's Fresh Air Fund visit. It was Lucinda's long-held belief that few people changed as radically as their externals might indicate. Surfaces might get polished, emotions might get unleashed or brought under control, but basic character seldom underwent any significant transformation. People were who they were. Change was only, ever, a matter of degree. There was a strain of self-interest in Renee that kept Lucinda slightly wary of her. As well, she trusted Gin's radar. If Gin didn't feel comfortable with the young woman, there were damned good reasons why. They'd discussed it but had never managed to fix on anything specific. It was, as Gin said, "Just a hinky feeling I get about her. And I think Jase gets the same hinky feeling, but because she's his mother he feels like a traitor, so he buries it."

The kids got out at noon on Jason's last day in the third grade. As she waited for him, Lucinda was thinking about the three weeks she'd have free when Jason went off to summer camp at the end of the month. *Exposure* was in pre-production and Gin was flying back and forth, to and from the coast, up to Toronto (Hollywood North to those in film) to check out locations, then to Boston to schmooze one of the financial guys, then back to Connecticut. When she wasn't approving the final costume and production designs, she was organizing the crew and supporting cast for the shoot which would start late September in Toronto. The final shooting script was done, and Lucinda was sure that at any moment Gin would announce there was another book she wanted to option. Lucinda hoped that announcement wouldn't come until *Exposure* was wrapped and in the can. She was determined to spend as much as possible of the summer months with her family.

She had to stop suddenly, realizing she was operating on pure assumption. Her need had become obsessive, growing like a tumor almost in direct ratio to the number of obstacles Anne managed to put in her way. Anne had even infiltrated her sleep, appearing in nightmares Lucinda had now and then, to do actual, physical battle over who took precedence in Elise's life. In those garishly real scenes, Anne's bones broke effortlessly in Lucinda's hands; she pulverized her aunt's undernourished body with her bare hands, yet Anne could not be stopped. She was like a bad DePalma film that never ended—Anne, supposedly finished, dead and gone, kept reappearing to wreak more and more havoc.

Time was finite for a woman of nearly ninety-eight and Lucinda wanted to share as much of whatever remained to Elise as she could. The only other negative possibility, aside from Anne—one both unnerving and intriguing—was that of her grandmother's internist and friend, Elijah Carter

("Do, please, call me Eli") making another unscheduled appearance.

Eli Carter taught at the Yale School of Medicine and had a private practice restricted to a handful of patients to whom he made house calls because he no longer maintained an office. His only staff was a secretary who made appointments, kept the medical records, and filed the sundry insurance or Medicare claims. When Lucinda had asked about this at their first meeting some six weeks earlier, he'd explained, "The malpractice insurance got so ludicrously expensive that rather than give up practicing altogether, I decided to increase my teaching load and, in the time-honored, old-fashioned way, make house calls on my favorite patients." At this, he'd smiled over at Elise. And Lucinda had wondered if that smiled exchange had contained a hint of complicity. There hadn't seemed to be. Elise's expression was serene, as always. Was it possible that her grandmother was trying to set her up with the doctor? No. The idea was ridiculous. Her nerves were sending error messages—like those incomprehensible alerts that occasionally appeared on her computer screen, just before the system froze.

A man in his late forties or early fifties, tall and solidly built, Eli Carter was visibly of mixed parentage, with a golden hue to his skin, rather blunt features, straight dark hair tidily side-parted, and amused gray eyes. He was intelligent and humorous as well as good-looking. "I understand you did your undergraduate degree at Yale," he'd said to Lucinda, who'd been able only to nod, working to dismiss the idea that this was the equivalent of a blind date.

As if sensing her discomfort, the doctor had, after a few more failed attempts to engage her, shifted his focus to

Elise, turning every so often to include Lucinda, at least visually, in the conversation. Lucinda was able to relax a bit as she drank a cup of the strong black tea her grandmother favored, and followed the exchange, maintaining a casual expression as she took in the telling details about the man: a pleasant cologne whose fragrance was alluring, onyx cufflinks, Cartier tank watch, flawlessly cut custom-made suit with an AIDS pin on the lapel, expensive black loafers. The severity of his apparel was rescued by a pale blue silk shirt worn without a tie and left open at the throat.

He was not only handsome, he also had impeccable taste. She'd admired the look of him, had appreciated his evident sensitivity. But it had been so long since she'd had any interaction with a man that she had no idea how to play this social game—if, indeed, it was a game. And aside from her sense of ineptitude, she couldn't conceive of any man being interested in a woman who, at the age of nineteen, had voluntarily had her breasts removed (in what was then considered to be highly experimental surgery) to save herself from the cancer that had taken her mother, her aunt and her grandmother. All that remained on her chest was the tidy whitened line from the incision. It was an odd sight: the proof of how far she'd been willing to go in order not to die the same agonized death as the other women in her family.

It was her belief, then and now, at the age of fifty-one, that this drastic surgery had forever removed her from the arena where men and women moved about as couples. However, in the months following the operation, she had become less and less able to leave her house, so the issue of men and relationships had become moot. More than three decades later, either fate or her grandmother had conspired to place an appealing man on the scene, and she couldn't forget herself sufficiently even to make small talk.

As he was leaving, Eli had asked, "May I give you my card?"

Knowing she couldn't refuse, she'd accepted it with a murmured, "Thank you."

Then he'd asked, "May I call you sometime?" and she'd floundered, racing through her mental index of acceptable replies but unable to find one suitable to the moment.

Elise had come to her rescue, saying, "If you have no objection, *chérie*, I will give Eli your number."

And how could Lucinda have objected? It would have been unforgivably rude. Instead, she'd managed to smile, venturing to meet the man's clear eyes as she'd shaken the warm, firm hand Eli offered. Then she'd excused herself and gone to the guest bathroom while her grandmother saw the man out.

Lucinda had held her hands under the cold water until they were almost numb, then put her palms to her cheeks for a time, breathing deeply, and battling the cocktail of emotions she was feeling: fear, embarrassment, disability and, worst of all, attraction.

"I did not arrange this meeting," Elise had said upon Lucinda's return to the living room. "Sometimes, Eli comes only to visit. Since the death of his wife, he has been too alone."

"Does he have children?"

"Two sons. They are grown, with families of their own. One lives in the city. The other is in Chicago."

"Oh! How long ago did his wife die?"

"Perhaps it is three years. Eli is a close friend to my grandson, Paul Junior. They attend the same church."

"Oh!" Lucinda couldn't think what else to say.

With some sadness in her smile, Elise said, "You would not have given him your number, would you?"

"No."

"Why is this?"

"I'm not interested."

"*Zut*, Lucinda," her grandmother chided gently. "What is the harm to dine with a very good, very kind man? You think," she guessed sagaciously, "he would care that you have no bosom?" Before Lucinda could respond, Elise said, "He is a professor of anatomy, a doctor. He has seen far worse, I assure you. You, like him, are too much alone. I will say only that it was apparent he was much taken with you. You are a beautiful woman who is young for her years, and you have a good brain. This is not so very common. Most women pay more attention to being pretty than to using their brain. Perhaps you will decide sometime to risk the great danger of a meal with Elijah. Perhaps you will find him to be a good person and you will enjoy his company. Now, I see you are distressed by this, so we will speak of other things."

Eli had phoned a week later. When Lucinda saw his name on the caller ID, she went outside and let the answering machine take over. It was two days before she could bring herself to listen to him say, "I'm sorry to have missed you, Lucinda. I'll try again another time."

The next time he'd phoned, a week or so later, she again let the machine answer for her. He said, "I seem to have bad timing. Sorry I missed you." He left his home number and hung up.

She thought he'd sounded disappointed, which confused her. At last, the following evening she'd called him back. He had sounded genuinely happy to hear from her. But when he invited her out to dinner, she said, "I'm sorry. I just … can't."

"I get the distinct impression that I frighten you," he said apologetically.

"People in general frighten me," she replied. "I'm out of the habit, if I ever had it, of social interaction."

"I am, too," he'd admitted. "After twenty-seven years of marriage, I'm somewhat at a loss." There was a slight pause, then he'd asked if she happened to have read the book he was halfway through. "I'm not sure what I think of it."

"Oh, I loved it," she had told him. "The characters were so well-realized. Stay with it. It's got a great surprise ending."

"I'll trust your judgment," he said.

And they'd been off, chatting away effortlessly.

His voice was low, resonant, a pleasure to her ear. They'd moved on from the book to a discussion of several recent films. As the conversation wound down some twenty minutes later, he said, "I'll call you again, if I may. Or," he'd added quickly, "you could call me. I'm home most evenings."

She often thought of it, but she hadn't called, and neither had he. She decided he'd written her off, and could only conclude that it was for the best. Regardless of his considerable appeal, she felt she had nothing to bring to the table. Besides, women were probably lining up to throw themselves at him. A well-to-do eligible professional man in Fairfield County was as rare and highly collectible as a Fabergé egg. A pathologically shy, no-breasted, quasi-agoraphobic didn't stand a chance.

Perhaps her grandmother would discourage him from visiting if she knew Lucinda was coming to see her.

~

With school over for the year, as a small celebratory gesture, she took Jason into town to the bank (where he matter-of-factly deposited the check she gave him) and then, braving the midday crush, to the diner for lunch. As they settled into a booth, Jason at once asked, "Can I have a burger?"

"Yup, but no bun."

"Grrrrr. What about fries?"

"Yup, but no ketchup."

"What's the point of having fries if I can't have ketchup?"

"People in other countries have them with vinegar," she informed him.

"Hork!" He made a gagging sound. "*What* other countries?" he challenged.

"England, Canada, Australia."

"If they suck, I'm not eatin' them. Okay?"

"Okay."

To the waitress he said, "I want a well-done burger, no bun, fries, with *vinegar*"—he made a face—"and a Seven-Up please."

"Fries are good with vinegar," the young waitress said with a smile.

"Yeah, sure," he said disbelievingly, sweeping his hands back and forth across the tabletop.

"Home fries and coffee, please," Lucinda said.

The waitress went off and, as if he'd been saving it up for quite some time and couldn't wait a moment longer, Jason said in a rush, "I'd rather stay with you than go to summer camp, Luce."

"You'll have the time of your life." Lucinda gave him an encouraging smile.

"Yeah. I'll get bitten by snakes and bugs, and be stuck with a cabinful of loser-creeps."

"Now that's interesting. You know what, Jason? In most circles *I'd* be considered a loser-creep."

"*No way*!"

"Yes, way. It's not fair to judge people without taking the time to get to know them."

"*Who'd* think you're a loser-creep?" he persisted.

"Lots of people."

"*Why* would they think that?" he asked angrily.

"Because I'm old and I'm different, because I'm not married, because I don't go out very much, because because because."

"You are *not* old!"

"I am, but that's beside the point. The thing is, you know me so you don't think I'm a loser-creep. Do you?"

"No way, *no*!"

"So maybe the kids you meet will be different, too, but cool in their own way. If you give them a chance and find you don't like them, don't hang out with them. But even if you don't like them, it *still* doesn't mean they're loser-creeps. It just means they're different. *You're* different, too, you know."

"Me? How?" he said warily.

"Well, you're a superhero, for one thing—the one and only Soupboy." She smiled again. "And for another, you make up good words. You're also probably the only kid movie reviewer anywhere."

"Cuz I rock, I rule," he said, without conviction.

"Yes, you do. And therefore you're *different*. Different isn't bad, honey. Would you *want* to be like every other kid in your school?"

"Not!"

"So okay. Give the kids at camp the benefit of the doubt, and see how it goes."

He shrugged, unconvinced.

"Here ya go!" The waitress slid one platter in front of Lucinda, the other in front of Jason.

"Grrrrr. A naked burger. It oughta come with underwear or something."

She laughed. "Decorate it with some mustard." She handed him the squeeze bottle and watched as he drew a mustard face on the burger, then used two fries to create a mustache. "Burgerman!" he declared without his usual élan.

"Very clever."

"Three whole weeks." He gazed down at his platter. "I *really* don't want to *go*, Luce," he said mournfully.

"Have you told your mom?"

He shook his head.

"Why not?"

He shrugged helplessly. "Cuz she *loved* summer camp when she was a kid, so she thinks *I'll* love it, too. I can't hardly stand *school*, and camp's just gonna be school with bugs and boats."

"If you honestly don't want to go, tell her."

"She'll be mad."

"Not if you give her good reasons," Lucinda said. "Have you got good reasons, Jase?"

"I'll be lonely," he said almost inaudibly. "I don't wanna go someplace where I don't know anybody. I wanna stay here with you and Gin and your gramma. I wanna see Kat and her moms and gramma when they come up. Wouldn't that be okay?"

"It'd be fine with me," she told him, thinking her hope for family time was about to disintegrate. "But you have talk to your mom and tell her how you feel. She'll understand."

"But she *paid*!" he said, his round brown eyes all at once tear-filled. "What if she can't get her *money* back? She'll be so mad at me."

"She won't be, honey. And she won't care if she gets her money back. She wouldn't want you to be miserable for three weeks."

"You think?"

Lucinda hoped that would be the case, but it was impossible to predict how Renee would react. "If you like," she offered, "I'll stay with you while you talk to her."

"Would you, Luce?" he asked plaintively. "Please?"

"Sure. Now you'd better eat Burgerman before he morphs into Iceman."

"I'm not hungry anymore," he said, eyeing her as if afraid he'd now make her angry, too.

"When I get upset, I never want to eat," she told him. "So why don't I get the waitress to wrap up our food and we'll eat it at home? Shall I do that?"

He nodded, still very worried. Was he afraid of his mother? Lucinda wondered. No, that couldn't be it, she decided.

"Things'll work out, Soupboy. I'm sure they will," Lucinda said, an idea taking shape in her mind.

Leaving Jason listlessly watching the Discovery Channel (he was too upset to read), Lucinda put in a call to Loranne at her office. "I'm sorry to disturb you at work," she apologized.

"No, no," Loranne said quickly. "It's fine, Lucy. How's everything?"

"Good, good. Listen, I wanted to run something by you, Lorrie. You know Renee's been planning to send Jason off to camp."

"Unh-hunh."

"Well, he just told me in no uncertain terms that he doesn't want to go."

"Uh-oh!"

"He *really* doesn't want to, but he's been afraid to tell her."

"Poor Soupboy. He thinks she'll pitch a fit. Right?"

"Exactly. So I was wondering if Kat would be interested in coming to stay here for those three weeks and baby-sit Jason—a kind of holiday with pay. I'd be able to spend extra time with my grandmother, take her out for lunch, see some new movies; just be with her. Plus, I rarely get to spend any time with Maddie and she's dying to have a hen party at her place with me and Roxanne, Annette and Eliza and Rosemarie."

"I'll talk to Kat when I get home. But you and I already know she'll do it. She dotes on that boy. Far as she's concerned, he's her kid brother."

"I know. Would you have her call me later with her answer?"

"She'll be on the phone to you about ten seconds after I tell her." Loranne laughed softly. "Count on it."

"Wonderful. And we're still on for Friday?"

"You bet. After the lunatic week I've had here, I'll be ready to float in that pool and stare into space for about ten hours straight." Lowering her voice she said, "I have to get another job. Remind me to give you all the gory details when I see you."

"I will. Thanks so much, Lorrie."

"No, thank *you*. It's a terrific idea. You're too good to us."

"That's not possible. I can't wait to see you. It's dinner at Elise's Friday night."

"You think your aunt Anne is going to put in another unscheduled appearance?"

"God," Lucinda said fervently. "I hope not."

"Me, too. She does that chin thing again to Kat, Kat's liable to haul off and wallop her. And she was downright rude to my moms, all but ignored her. She's like that again, *I* might be the one to haul off and wallop her."

"She's a deeply unhappy woman," Lucinda said pleased by Loranne's opinion of her aunt yet assailed by a potent sense of disloyalty. As always, when it came to Anne, Lucinda couldn't win.

"What's with her always trying to one-up you, getting in your face?" Loranne asked.

"If I had the answer to that, my darling, I might be able to deal with her. As it stands, if I were Catholic, I'd be spending my life in the confessional, doing penance and begging forgiveness for the way I feel about her."

Chapter Five

Lucinda went to the kitchen to make coffee—giving mother and son some privacy—while Renee tried to talk to Jason, who'd managed to get himself so worked up that he went completely to pieces and couldn't stop sobbing. He kept repeating ever more loudly how sorry he was, the depth of his emotion sending his voice out of control. Renee's tone remained low, and gradually Jason's declarations began losing volume. When it sounded as if matters had reached the consolation stage, Lucinda returned to the living room carrying a tray with coffee for herself and Renee, and a glass of apple juice for Jason.

On his mother's lap, his head against her shoulder, he was still whispering, "I'm sorry, I'm sorry," while Renee insisted, "Jase, it doesn't matter. I just wish you'd told me sooner. That's all."

"I was scared you'd be *mad* at me," he said miserably.

Handing mother and son their drinks, Lucinda said, "I

spoke to Lorrie this afternoon and invited Kat to come up for the three weeks Jason was supposed to be at camp. I thought she could baby-sit him—"

"*Yeah*!" Jason jumped in. "That'd be so"—he hiccuped, his breathing still ragged—"so … so cool. Mom, please, can … can … Kat sit me?"

"We don't know yet that she'll be able to do it—" Lucinda began.

"But if she *can*, please? I'd be so *happy*! I *love* Kat. You know I do. And Kat loves me, too. Please say yes, mom!"

"If Kat agrees," Renee said, looking oddly satisfied, "I don't see a problem."

"Oh, *thank you*!" He clutched a handful of his mother's skirt and pressed himself closer to her. His relief was such that within a minute or two his eyes fluttered closed and he fell asleep.

Half an hour later, Katanya phoned. "I'd *love* to do it, Luce. I'm so ready for a break. This semester was brutal, hours of homework every night, plus all the rehearsals for the end-of-semester showcase. Soupboy and I could do the pool thing, ride our bikes into town, catch some movies, hit the library. It'll be da bomb, tropendo to the max."

"Wonderful! Why don't you tell him yourself? Hold on a second." Lucinda beckoned a now-awake Jason to the telephone.

"Kat? You gonna do it?" he dived right in, his previous misery gone as he listened.

"Will you lose the fees?" Lucinda asked Renee in an undertone while Jason talked to Katanya.

"I don't know," Renee answered, eyes on her son. "I don't understand why he was afraid to tell me."

"You still want your parents' approval, don't you?"

Her eyes shifting to Lucinda, Renee said without hesitation, "I want them to think I'm the greatest human being who ever lived."

"Most of us spend our whole lives trying to please our parents. We want them to adore us, to think everything we do is brilliant."

"But Jason *knows* I ..." Renee stopped. "You're right. I could have it tattooed on my forehead how much he means to me, and he'd still worry. How did you get to be so smart?"

"It's not about being smart. It's just that I spent a lot of years closed up inside this house, thinking nonstop about issues like that."

"But you said your mother adored you!" she said, frowning, as if she'd caught Lucinda in a lie.

"She did. But I'll always wonder whether or not she'd approve of something I do. Jason's that way too. He's brighter and more sensitive than most kids; he takes things more to heart."

Renee gazed at her intently. "You're a wise woman."

"Let's just agree that what I said is true."

"You can't accept a compliment, can you?" Renee asked almost angrily.

"I lack skill in that area." Lucinda smiled. "It's a major deficit of mine—one among many."

"Oh, bullshit!" Renee said abruptly, then glanced over to make sure Jason hadn't heard, but he was too involved in his conversation with Katanya.

Lucinda couldn't help but see that Renee actually was angry for some reason. Anxious to move on to less fraught territory, Lucinda said, "Just know that to Jason your approval is everything."

Still looking over at her son, Renee merely nodded.

That night, standing in the living room Lucinda studied the photographs of her parents, stricken by the sympathy for Jason she hadn't dared display until things were settled for him with his mother. He was a boy whose feelings ran deep and strong. When he cared, he cared completely, without reservation. And when he was afraid, his fear was so immense that it blocked everything else from his view.

The trio of school bullies who took a quite evil pleasure in tormenting the younger and smaller kids, the kids with talent or those without, gave Jason a hard time every day of the school year. He'd stopped talking about Tristan, Rory and Aidan by the end of the first grade, and he'd exacted Lucinda's promise not to tell Renee. But Lucinda knew that it gnawed at him, very possibly in the way Anne's combative behavior ate away at her.

On top of that, she knew Jason wondered why his father and his father's parents had failed to evidence any interest in seeing or talking to him. Once, in reply to Lucinda's casually asking, Jason had said, "They've got other grandkids. It's not like I was special to them or anything." But plainly it wounded him to have been summarily cast aside. And she herself wondered how anyone could have dismissed such a special child from their consciousness, without so much as a backward glance.

Lucinda's childhood experiences couldn't have been more different from his. Her world had been—until Gin entered it—an exotic, solitary but not lonely life, filled with an intriguing combination of bizarre sights and behaviors.

Actors were forever making overblown displays for anyone within viewing range. Temperamental directors and didactic producers with their edicts, their mandates, their rules and tickish mannerisms, their fearsome power, ran the world she and her mother knew. Lucinda had accepted as a matter of course the endless fake-front small towns and big-city streets on the back lot, the meticulously created ceilingless rooms inside the sound stages—gaffers shouting orders to their crews rigging the lights, and grips laying dolly tracks or shifting flats; riggers erecting scaffolding; the second and third assistant directors; wardrobe people and makeup assistants and still photographers. They were simply the people who worked where her mother did.

Away from the studio, Lucinda was endlessly fascinated by Lily's pragmatic lack of pretension, and by her ability (exactly like Gin's) to don when necessary for the public a glamour that radiated sexuality as if it were merely a cumbersome but significant part of her wardrobe. Being the daughter of a movie star was just a fact of her life.

Lucinda knew very early that her mother was rare and special, someone unique in that make-believe world. Lily always knew her lines, was always on time; she didn't throw tantrums or make unreasonable demands. She treated the crews with respect and always gave them personally selected gifts (she and Lucinda had great fun shopping for these items) at the wrap parties at the end of a shoot. As a result—the highest of filmdom accolades—they loved her. Several techs and a couple of make-up artists she'd worked with ten, even twenty or more years before had traveled from California as a group to attend her funeral. Those unable to attend had sent flowers and telegrams and letters filled with grieving affection. For weeks after her death, the mailman had staggered to the door carrying sacks of mail from bereft fans. Because it summed it up so succinctly for her, what Lucinda had kept was the issue of *Time* with the Hurrell portrait on the cover and, beneath it, the words:

Lily Hunter 1925-1969. Gone Too Soon.

The week she died, Lily's image was on the cover or front page of every major newspaper and magazine in the world. All of them carried lengthy obituaries that chronicled her career and included her filmography, her awards, brief mention of her only child, adopted daughter Lucinda (which was how Lily had presented her to the world) and the scant biographical information Lily had permitted to be made public. Unlike so many of her peers, Lucinda had never felt a need to profit from or share in her mother's celebrity in any way—especially not by penning one of those dreadful tell-all books that depicted a beloved public icon as a private monster.

Living in rented houses and eating out because Lily couldn't cook, and attending school on the lot was ordinary life for Lucinda. But not being an ordinary child, the details of what went on around her were noted and absorbed and analyzed. (Ultimately her comprehension of the dynamics at play were reflected in her scripts. She had, she knew, a particular ability to transpose behavior from life, or a book, into a visual medium.) As a small child a considerable amount of Lucinda's time was spent with her mother's publicist Eddie and his wife, Estelle. Childless, the Rifkins had doted on Lucinda. Their kindness and overt approval of her most minor accomplishments, along with Lily's assurances of her love, were the cushion against which she could rest when things around her were worrisome or confusing.

She had had a most unusual childhood. Yet she'd thrived in that esoteric environment, in large part because Lily had never treated Lucinda as if she were less than a complete person merely because she was a child. It had been an exceptional gift. As long as Lily was alive, Lucinda had had her mother's approval. And that had given her the confidence in her early teens to concoct half a dozen film plots with her girlfriend Ginny Holder and to write the scripts which transformed Ginny to Gin and moved her to stardom. That confidence had sent Lucinda sailing through Yale, making Phi Beta Kappa, and graduating in three years. But just at the point when Lucinda was ready to confront a world of possibilities, Lily had atypically confided she wasn't feeling well. Four months later she was dead. Lucinda then found the photograph of her father and her life fell inward, like a slow-motion film of a high-rise demolition. That was the beginning of her intimate relationship with fearful bereavement: a death, a photograph, and a life put in storage.

Leaning against the wall, looking at the images of her parents, she could hear again Jason's sobs, the cadence of his fear. She knew how it felt to love a mother that deeply. Renee was the focal point of Jason's life, just as Lily had been hers. *We need our mothers,* she thought, growing aware of a gradual tightening at the back of her neck, the slow needlelike penetration of pain into her temples, and a rising nausea.

Still hearing the echoes of Jason's sobs, with a sympathetic ache in her chest, she went to the kitchen. Leaving the lights off, she got her medication from the cupboard.

She had to struggle to get the cap off the Evian bottle and spilled water on herself as she washed down the capsule. The wetness of the shirt against her skin made her shiver and she moved unsteadily down the hall and up the stairs to her bedroom. This was the worst possible time to fall into the grip of a migraine. She didn't want to lose entire days in a state of drug-induced lassitude when Renee would be dropping Jason off first thing in the morning, and tomorrow evening Katanya, Loranne and Jeneva would be arriving for the weekend.

Struggling out of her clothes, the shivering getting worse and playing hell with her coordination, she managed to pull on a sweatshirt, some drawstring pants and a pair of heavy socks. Then, teeth clenched, holding on to the banister, she returned downstairs to the kitchen where she mechanically chewed several wheat crackers and drank some more Evian to combat the nausea before heading to the living room. She dragged a pillow and the afghan from the sofa and lay on her back on the floor, waiting for the meds to kick in and for the room to stop its tidal surging.

She was awakened by the ringing of the doorbell—Jason's signature triple ring.

Lucinda went creaking to the front hall and opened the door, the daylight stabbing into her eyes.

Renee took one look at her and said, "Go back to sleep. I'll take Jase with me today." Picking up the newspaper from the doormat, she passed it over with what was unmistakably a look of annoyance.

"I'm sorry," Lucinda murmured.

"We'll come by after my classes."

"Feel better, Luce," Jason said, taking his mother's

hand and looking back at Lucinda over his shoulder as they went down the porch steps. "Love you," he mouthed.

"Love you, too," she mouthed back, then closed the door and returned to the living room. Cautiously bending to pick up the pillow and blanket, she crawled onto the sofa and was asleep again in moments.

She went from sleeping to wide awake all at once. Without moving, she took a mental inventory and decided she'd managed to stop the migraine before it had had a chance to sink its claws too deeply into her skull. Her head seemed pain-free, and she was hungry—a positive sign.

After starting a pot of coffee, she put a slice of bread in the toaster. It was almost one o'clock. She'd slept for close to thirteen hours. She needed a shower, badly. A migraine always heightened her sense of smell, and right then she could scarcely bear the smell of her body. So she'd eat, then wash from head to toe. She'd still have plenty of time to cut flowers for the bedrooms and take the groceries she'd picked up the previous morning over to the barn before Jason and Renee got back from New Haven.

It was going to be a good summer, she thought, pleased with how things were shaping up. Katanya would look after Jason while Renee worked on her doctoral thesis. Lucinda might just get to have precious additional time with her grandmother. And when she wasn't flying all over the place, scouting locations, making nice with the financial backers and doing the dozens of other things involved in getting the new film into production Gin would be home—less than two miles away.

Lucinda poured herself some coffee and settled at the

table with the *Times* and her toast. Things were falling into place. And maybe, just maybe, Anne would decide to take a cruise around the world or go on Safari in Africa. "Sure! That'll happen," Lucinda said aloud, and laughed. Like it or not, the war was nowhere near over.

Chapter Six

Things were going wonderfully well. For almost two weeks, (with no sign of Anne) Lucinda had been able to spend time with her grandmother almost daily—an hour to have a cup of tea and a chat, or an entire afternoon or evening, to go out to lunch and a movie, or to dinner. They were catching up. Lucinda's memory bank was filling steadily with tidbits of family history, anecdotes, facts and events. It was obvious that Elise was as anxious to close the historical gaps as Lucinda was.

Sometimes, Katanya and Jason came along on their outings. Elise had a splendid way with the children, entering gleefully into their humor, yet taking their thoughts and observations seriously. She was never condescending, never patronizing. And, as a result, both children adored her. Jason clamored daily to come along on Lucinda's visits but Katanya knew how to divert him, interceding to suggest some alternative that at once captured his attention. Several afternoons a week, Gin came to spend a few hours in the pool with the kids, and she let Katanya help her run her lines for the forthcoming shoot—which the girl did with serious enthusiasm.

At least once a week, Lucinda's young cousin Annette would bring two-year-old Amelia and five-year-old Amanda to visit. Jason was, surprisingly, captivated by the toddler who was a languid, cuddly child. He would sit in the shade with Amelia on his lap and study her, beaming when she played finger games with him, or peek-a-boo, or simply nestled contentedly in his arms. He'd speak to the chubby child as if unaware that he could be heard by anyone but her. "I want a baby like you one day, *just* like you," he'd say, or, "What are you thinking? Do you wish you could really talk? I do. You like me, don't you?" He'd nod, as Amelia laughed up at him and gabbled incomprehensibly. Amused and moved by his engagement with Amelia, everyone observed him but refrained from commenting in his presence. There was something about his engagement with the toddler that was considerably deeper than mere boyish curiosity, something that gave hints of the scope of his private cache of hurt.

"That boy will grow up to be a good father to some lucky child one day," Jeneva observed late on a Friday night as she and Lucinda, Loranne and Katanya sat on the front porch. "He has a tender heart."

"Too tender sometimes," Lucinda said. "I worry about how much he keeps buried inside. He saves things up. Then they come flooding out and his emotions go out of control."

"He hates his father," Katanya said. "Calls him a stinkfart and a ratbastard for going off the way he did and never once calling or coming to visit."

"He might *say* that," Loranne said to her daughter, "but it doesn't mean Jase wasn't hurt that the man took off and never looked back. That's a serious ratbastard in my books."

Lucinda kept silent, knowing that not one of them knew the whole truth.

"We could write a book," Katanya suggested, "and call it, *Ratbastards We Have Known*. Moms can do a chapter on my dad. Jason will do one on his. Who will you guys write about?" she asked Lucinda and Jeneva.

The two women laughed. At once an image of Anne hobbled across the interior landscape of Lucinda's mind, in too-high heels and some typically ill-chosen, overpriced outfit and, immediately conscience-stricken, she said, "Your grandmother and I reserve the right to invoke the Fifth Amendment."

Later, when the others had gone to bed Jeneva said, "One of these days, you're either going to have to reconcile your feelings or do something about your aunt."

"Like what?" Lucinda asked her.

"That I don't know. But you've got to find a way to settle this, for your peace of mind. She's nobody's favorite and that's a fact. Even her own children shy away from her. But she's seventy-eight, Lucy. At this stage of the game, it's not likely she's going to change. So maybe you're the one who'll have to do some changing."

Lucinda sighed. "You're probably right," she allowed. "Let me ask you something. What's your impression of Renee?"

"The truth? Strictly between you and me, I think she's a few bricks short of a full load."

"Me, too."

"And you know what else?" Jeneva said quietly. "I think Jason's afraid of her. Can't tell you why. It's just a feeling I get, watching the two of them together. Far as I can tell, you're the only person in his life he can be himself with."

"I wish I knew why," Lucinda said. "Sometimes, I have the impression that it's all a performance; she's in a play and the rest of us, including Jason, are only part of the audience."

"Uhn-hunh." Jeneva nodded. "Exactly. As if there's lights and a heavy curtain between her and the rest of us."

The following Monday morning, Lucinda was just getting out of bed when the phone rang. It was six-forty. She was instantly fearful when her aunt Adele said, "I'm sorry to call so early."

"No, no. I'm an early-riser," Lucinda said, heart racing, breathing shallow, hands suddenly damp. "How are you, Aunt Adele?"

"I'm well, but I'm afraid I have some distressing news, Lucinda."

God no! Please! "Oh?"

"I just got a call from Madeline. It seems Anne's had a stroke."

"Oh no!" Lucinda said, so relieved to know that her grandmother was all right that it took a few moments to get her thoughts aligned and she was able to say, "That's terrible. How is she?"

"I'm not sure. Neither was Madeline. The paramedics think it was a stroke but they weren't sure. Anne's in Greenwich Hospital. Gwyn's on her way to Westport to pick up Mother and take her to the hospital. John and I are just leaving but it's going to take us at least an hour and a half. We'll probably get caught in the morning rush-hour traffic in Hartford. But I thought you'd want to know."

"Of course. I'll head down there as soon as I'm dressed. Thank you for letting me know, Aunt Adele."

While she showered quickly, her thoughts were chaotic, flying off in all directions, with her emotions following suit. Her immediate reaction to the news was a grim satisfaction. Anne was the beneficiary of cosmic payback for her horrible behavior. Put enough negative energy out there and one day it'd come back to smack you down, feed you a shockingly huge slice of humble pie. Then shame followed, and Lucinda wondered how she could think such a thing. However Anne might behave, she was, at worst, childishly insensitive, even cruel, but not evil. She'd never, after their first meeting, actually said or done anything unforgivable. And no one deserved to have a stroke. Elise would be so distressed. No matter how awful she might be, Anne was her child. Few things were more painful for a parent than to have an ailing child—regardless of its age. The immutable fact was they were mother and daughter. It was a bond forged, in most cases, from steel. Why hadn't Anne ever understood that? After all, she, too, was a mother. But some people, and she strongly suspected that Renee was one of them, always had to come first—ahead of even their children. She'd encountered these people, primarily women, regularly throughout her childhood. California seemed to be a fertile breeding ground for them.

Pulling on a dress while stepping into her sandals, she was moving so fast—her heart still in overdrive—she nearly tripped over her own feet and had to pause to take several breaths, trying to get herself under control. This was terrible! What if Anne died before Lucinda had a chance to make things right? And just how was she supposed to do that? She didn't believe people suddenly had epiphanies as death drew near and they saw, all at once, with terminal clarity the error of their ways. No, in her opinion people went out in the same fashion they'd behaved all along. Anne was ill but that wouldn't prevent her from ordering the nurses about and being disdainful of the doctors.

But strokes could be evil. Anne might be trapped, mute, inside the cage of her own maltreated body, unable to make herself understood. She might be damaged beyond repair yet still have a Timex heart that would keep on ticking and ticking while she struggled to speak comprehensibly. *God*! This was truly awful.

She debated whether to slide a note under Katanya's door or to wake her. Five to seven. She knocked lightly on the door, then opened it and walked over to the bed to lay her hand softly on the girl's arm.

"What?" Katanya murmured, eyes closed.

"Kat, I've got to go to Greenwich Hospital. My Aunt Anne is ill. I don't know how long I'll be."

Katanya sat up, instantly alert. "Oh, no! I'm sorry, Luce. Is she gonna be okay? Is it serious?"

"They think it's a stroke."

"That's not good. But maybe it's only a little one and she'll be okay."

"Let's hope that's the case. Will you take care of Jason when he gets here, until I come home?"

"For sure. Take your cell phone so you can call and let me know what's happening."

"Good idea. I will. Thank you, honey."

"Be careful driving. Is it okay if I call and tell my moms and gramma?"

"Of course." Lucinda kissed the top of her head and hurried out.

"Don't forget your cell!" Katanya called after her. "And take a sweater. It'll be cold there!"

She couldn't stop the parade of images that marched through her head as Anne, in varying costumes, appeared to disrupt one planned event after another: Lucinda arrived at the Westport house to have lunch with her grandmother only to find Anne smiling happily as if she'd won first prize in some arcane contest, ensconced on the living room sofa, artfully positioned to show to advantage an ugly, printed-silk Dolce & Gabbana suit in liverish colors, her feet contained by yet another pair of very high heels, these in dried-blood red; saying hello in a cheery voice while her mouth seemed to be at war with emotions seething behind her eyes. Or Lucinda arrived with Kat and Loranne and Jeneva for a Friday night family dinner and there was Anne, posed before the fireplace, decked out from head to toe in black leather (including needle-toed, stiletto-heeled glove-leather boots), looking like nothing so much as an elderly dominatrix who enjoyed her work rather too much. Hilarious and horrifying. Lucinda could remember perfectly Jeneva's little gasp of surprise, Katanya's trying to contain a snigger and Loranne's open-mouthed gaze. Then there was the afternoon when Lucinda arrived to have tea with Elise—the British tea complete with *petits fours* and crustless sandwiches Elise loved—and there was Anne, rigged out all in white silk like a fallen Mother Superior who'd surrendered to a lifetime secret passion for makeup, seated at the piano, playing a Chopin étude and playing it very well. When Lucinda said, "That's wonderful," Anne had abruptly stopped and, despite Lucinda's entreaty that she continue, Anne acted as if Lucinda had interrupted a command performance. When Lucinda had looked to her grandmother for some cue, Elise had rolled her eyes and murmured, "*Il n'y a rien à faire*. It cannot be helped."

There were so many occasions, too many to enumerate, when Anne had forced her presence because she'd known Lucinda would be there. When it was only the three of them, Anne never attempted to monopolize the conversation, never inflicted her opinions on whatever was said. Her presence alone was sufficient to suck most of the air from the room and, each time, make Lucinda feel clumsy and very weary. What, she'd wondered, was it all in aid of? Aside from taking advantage of the opportunity to display a wardrobe of singularly expensive, singularly ghastly clothes, Anne never seemed to derive any specific pleasure from her efforts. She simply appeared, spent an allotted amount of time, then drove off with remarkable ease—shifting gears with the aplomb and confidence of a rally participant—in her late-husband's 1954 dark green Jaguar XK120 sports coupe.

When Lucinda had complimented her aunt on the car, Anne had said, "Take it for a drive," and held out the keys.

"No, thanks very much," Lucinda had demurred. "I'm afraid it's too much car for me." Then, thinking of Gin and of Katanya's young neighbor, Hernan, who both had a passion for rare old cars, she'd said with a smile, "I have friends who'd kill to drive it. It's a beautiful machine."

With a brief softening of her tone, Anne had looked off

into space, saying, "It was Michael's dream car. He took better care of that car than he did of himself." Then, grounded once more in the present, she'd tossed the keys into her Prada handbag, saying, "Oh, well. Never mind."

Because it was so early, the traffic was light and Lucinda made good time getting to Greenwich, through town to the hospital and into one of many vacant parking spots. As she navigated the route, she had visions of Anne with one side of her face downpulled, her left arm useless. Or she might have none of those classic impairments but instead have suffered severe brain damage. As Lucinda approached the information desk she wondered how Katanya had known it would be cold inside the hospital. Lucinda was already shivering and thinking longingly of a hot cup of coffee. She put on her cotton cardigan as she asked where to find her aunt.

The woman typed Anne's name into her computer, leaning in close to read what it said on the screen, then gave Lucinda directions.

It seemed to take forever as she made her way through the corridors, her thoughts on the days and nights she'd spent with Lily as her life trickled away, and of her own hospital stay some weeks later when all she'd wanted was to be strong enough to leave the place and go home. She'd been unable to sleep for more than an hour or two at a time and unable to eat the trays of bad-smelling food that kept appearing with hateful regularity. She'd managed to drink the beverages—juices, coffee and tea, sodas—and nibbled at the bread and rolls accompanying every meal, but each time she'd lifted the lid on another plate of lunch or dinner the smells had sickened her and she'd had to replace the lid, then push the tray as far away as possible.

Anne would loathe hospital food, Lucinda knew, and would make a great to-do about it. Even though she scarcely touched the marvelous meals Erica prepared for the Friday night family dinners at Elise's house, Anne was very fussy about food, highly complimentary always to Erica, even venturing out to the kitchen to ask about recipes. According to Madeline, her mother spent a fortune on esoteric items, ordering from specialty stores in Manhattan. But she rarely consumed more than a few bites of anything. Nutrition wasn't high on Anne's list of what was important, if it had a place on the list at all. Clothing, cosmetics, hair-care, accessories—these were the list-toppers.

God, hospitals were scary places. Births were the only good things that took place in hospitals. Everything else was sickness, debilitation, death. And yet there were people who turned up repeatedly in ERs, desperate for attention of any kind. What kind of life experience turned a person so needy that they'd feign illness and spend hours in a featureless, plastic waiting room just so an ER team would satisfy his or her craving with a few minutes of their valuable time? Lucinda knew from her reading that often these people had families and weren't depressed loners. They were souls adrift, unanchored by the weight of love they required.

There was a small waiting area where Madeline stood with her husband Steven and her brother Michael. Their faces were a script Lucinda read in an instant—fatigue and shock. It was not good. Madeline turned, saw Lucinda, and came over to her. Automatically, their hands joined and, looking down at the connection they'd made, Madeline said, "Thank you for coming."

"I wouldn't not come," Lucinda said.

"She's not going to make it." Madeline's green gaze lifted to meet Lucinda's. "They've got her on all kinds of machines. You can scarcely see her, for all the machines. But she's not breathing on her own and they say there's no brain activity."

"I'm so sorry," Lucinda said. "Do you know what happened?"

"A massive stroke. She's always had lousy circulation, never moved a muscle if she didn't have to, didn't eat enough to keep an infant alive. Vanity really can kill you." Her mouth curved into a small smile. "Fashionably thin, fashionably brain-dead. I don't know if Grandmother ever told you, but my mother was top of her class at Vassar. Hard to believe, isn't it? My father wouldn't have tolerated a stupid woman, so she had to stay alert. She was never going to make mother of the year, but at least her intelligence showed. Then Dad died and, almost overnight, she turned stupid. Her life became an endless shopping expedition and she began to shrink, getting thinner and thinner. She just roared around in Dad's Jag, buying ugly clothes and delicacies she never ate. Such a goddamned waste!"

"Yes," Lucinda agreed. "Terrible. Sometimes, when their partners die, people can't remember, if they ever knew, how to live alone." She remembered vividly how diminished Eddie Rifkin had been after Estelle's death. He'd still been the Eddie who'd run the high-powered engine of Lily's PR machine, the same man who'd been the closest thing to a father Lucinda had ever had. But Eddie after Estelle died was almost a silhouette of his former self—the resemblance in outline was there, but details and color were missing.

"I think that's it. I honestly don't think she could remember how." Madeline paused. "Michael and I are getting ready to tell them to pull the plug. We both agree it's the right thing to do. We're just having a hard time actually doing it."

"I truly am sorry, Maddie."

"You know what *I'm* sorry about, Lucinda? All her incomprehensible games and conniving. She just refused to see how wrong she was to do that to grandmother and you."

"No, no—"

"Every one of us tried to get her to back down, to see reason, but she wouldn't budge."

"It's okay, Maddie. Really. I brought it on myself. I shouldn't have smarted off at her that first night we met. If I'd just left it alone, she probably would've dropped it."

"No. It was never okay and you certainly did *not* bring it on yourself. We all know how hard it was for you, trying to get to know the entire family after so many years. And there was Mother, like General MacArthur on maneuvers, plotting her campaign, using Gwyn the way she did. It was horrible to watch. And yet, in a way, I felt sorry for her. I couldn't tell you why. I just did. I'm considered a smart woman, a good defense attorney. But my smarts failed when it came to my mother. Now it's all coming to an end, and I feel so shaky. I mean, you think about it, you know. Your mother's seventy-eight. She's not going to live forever and, frankly, you think maybe that's a good thing because she's done a lot of damage—mostly to herself. But it's still a tremendous shock to get the late-night call."

"What was it?" Lucinda asked.

"Her neighbor in the condo complex noticed that the curtains hadn't been drawn and all the lights were still on, which wasn't typical. So Mrs. Findlay got her husband and they went over and knocked on the door. No answer. They looked in the window and there was Mother on the living room floor. Mr. Findlay called nine-one-one on his cell phone." Madeline emitted a sad little laugh and shook her head. "She was dressed to the nines. That would've pleased her—not being found in her nightgown, without her hair done and a full face of makeup. So, all things considered, it's a good exit for her."

Lucinda freed one hand and wrapped her arm around her cousin, saying, "Whatever I can do to help, I will."

Stepping away, Madeline said, "Thank you. If I think of anything, I'll take you up on that."

"I really am sorry and I will help in any way."

Madeline's hand slid free and she seemed to drift backward into the circle of her husband's arm. Michael Eye Vee approached and wordlessly hugged Lucinda. Then he and his sister went into a corner of the room to talk.

Looking bleary-eyed and disheveled, Madeline's husband Steven approached Lucinda saying, "I'm going to the cafeteria. I need coffee in the worst way. We've been here most of the night. Could I get you something, Lucy?"

"I'll come with you," Lucinda said, following him out of the room. She was very fond of balding, slightly overweight Steven, with his tidy features and cupid's-bow mouth. He wore red suspenders over a custom-made white shirt, a subtle red on navy silk tie, with gray flannel trousers, highly polished lace-up oxfords and fine black socks. He'd made senior partner at one of the most distinguished law firms in the city by the time he was thirty. St. Paul's and Harvard Law, he wore his Phi Beta Kappa key on an old-fashioned watch fob with his three-piece suits. Soft-spoken, innately gentle of manner and incisive of intellect, he'd given up corporate law at thirty-five to become one of the earliest (and now one of the most noted) practitioners of environmental law. "How are you holding up, Steven?" she asked him.

"The truth? Aside from being sleep-deprived, I'm fine. Actually, to be candid, I'm relieved—more for Maddie's sake than my own—that this part of our lives is finally over. I've maintained a discreet distance from her mother since Maddie's and my wedding day. The only reason Anne didn't make a scene at the reception was because Michael headed her off at the pass. It's a shame you never knew him. He was a wonderful man, a great father. But Anne? I'll be charitable and just say she wasn't easy."

"No, she could be difficult," Lucinda agreed. "What did she try to do at the reception?"

"Her usual nonsense, wanting to call the shots. It's not as if we were kids. Maddie was almost thirty and I was thirty-four. But there was Anne, treating us like small, not especially bright children, trying to tell us what to do, and where and how, and being unbelievably rude to my parents."

"I can imagine."

"You probably can," he said. "I'm well aware of her endless surprise visits to Westport when you just happened to be there."

"I was thinking about that on my way down here."

"I'll bet you were. Anyway, poor Maddie and Michael have to shut down her life support. No matter how we might feel, she's their mother and I wouldn't want to have to do that. The weird thing is, Anne has had everything planned for years, with very explicit instructions about what she wanted done after her death. No viewing, no service. Cremation followed by a party, quote, to celebrate her life, unquote."

"A party? A *party*?" Lucinda couldn't quite take that in.

"Yep. Everything's been prepaid, including the so-called festivities. Nothing in her life was ever left to chance. I'll give her points for that. Maddie won't have to do much more than call the Sally Ann or Goodwill to come clear out the condo. Anne got rid of the valuable pieces when she sold the house. She even had me draft instructions about which consignment shop was to get her clothes. Can you believe it?" He laughed. "What a piece of work, that woman!"

"I'm kind of surprised," Lucinda said. "I wouldn't have thought she'd be so organized, so pragmatic."

"You have no idea," Steven said, grinding a fist into his eyes as if he could physically rub out his fatigue. "The only reason I acted as her attorney was because Maddie asked me to. Otherwise, I'd have stayed well away. If I had allowed it, Anne would've been changing her will every other month. From the outset I told her she could only make annual changes. She didn't like it, but she agreed. And now, Maddie and I get to be her executors. I'm probably out of line, but who's going to care if I talk about the terms of her will?" he asked rhetorically. "You're mentioned in it, by the way."

"You can't be serious!"

"Yessiree. Half the estate is divided between Maddie and Mike. The other half is equally distributed among the rest of the family, except for Elise of course, who has a sizable fortune of her own."

"But … Anne made it seem as if she didn't believe I was who I claimed to be."

"I know. But she *did* believe it. She was positively giddy when she got the news. Crazy, huh?"

"Completely." *Giddy? Anne?*

"She had me print out your online columns so she could read them, never missed one. She loved them, raved about you to all and sundry, saved the reviews in a special folder."

"I had no idea." She felt terrible, guilty and deeply sad.

"Well, no. How would you? So, we're going to have a 'celebration of her life,'" he said with mild amusement. "It'll be one hell of a party. I can promise you that. Nothing but the best for Anne. The Homestead Inn, here in Greenwich. Prepaid, of course, to avoid taxes. I'll make the reservation later today. There's to be Dom Perignon, Beluga caviar, fresh lobster, imported fois gras *with* truffles, of course; the works, including live music—provided I can pull it all together quickly enough."

No one was ever just what their surface might lead you to believe, Lucinda thought. Anne in particular. If she'd accepted that Lucinda was who she claimed to be, why had she gone to such lengths to make everything so difficult, so unpleasant? What had all that plotting and planning really been about?

As if reading her mind, Steven said, "The way I see it, she loved dissension, Lucy; she positively thrived on it. And, by god, she was very damned good at creating it. I'm in the will, too. Even Rosemarie gets a bequest. Go figure. She made such a show of her disapproval of Eliza and Rosemarie. Two women in a long-term committed relationship? Scandalous, an abomination. Not as bad as being a gay man, but *bad*. I wonder if they'll sell me a whole carafe of coffee. Everybody's going to want some."

"I'm sure they'll sell you as much as you want," Lucinda

said, trying to absorb all he'd said and wondering how Elise would handle this.

Elise was sad but philosophical. "It is better this way. Anne would prefer to die than to find herself in a nursing home. It is just so sudden, so unexpected," she told Lucinda as they sat together, holding hands, in the waiting room. Madeline and Michael and Adele had gone to the room to bear witness to the life support systems being shut down. Elise had gone earlier to look at her daughter, but had chosen not to be present for the end. "I would find it difficult to see such a thing," she'd told the others. Now, to Lucinda, she said, "I prefer to think of Anne as she was, a very, very long time ago—a lively, pretty child, quick and bright. So loving, so good-hearted, so *engagée*. It is how I wish to remember her."

"Even when it's expected, it's unexpected," Lucinda said. "I knew Lily was dying, but I didn't truly believe it until it actually happened, until she was gone."

"That is how it is, precisely. It was this way with my Guillaume. One wishes not to believe the finality, yet we have no option but to accept the ending. But *this*." Elise's shoulders lifted in a slight shrug. "It is not the natural order of events that a child should die before her parent. With Adam, your papa, it was a war. That was a justification of sorts. He chose to be a pilot. It was his joy. But Anne, she had no joy, even with Michael, although she adored him. It was plain to see." She paused, thinking.

"Once she was beyond the age of eight or nine, life was a grim affair for her. I have believed, always, that something happened. Someone was unkind or racist; cruel words were spoken—perhaps about her papa or her brother with their dark skin—and nothing for her was ever the same. She changed. That child disappeared and never returned. I have mourned her for almost seventy years. Today is an ending to what occurred a very long time ago—the death of *ma jolie fillette*."

Lucinda sat, stunned, continuing to hold her grandmother's hand, thinking she would have to go through the old family albums and look more closely at the children—the two fair girls and the dark boy—to see if their lives were in any way foreshadowed in their captured images.

The party five days later at the exquisite Victorian mansion-turned-hotel was a huge success. After conferring with Rosemarie, Steven hired a jazz quartet she recommended highly, and they came up from the city for the evening. Elise was enchanted, repeatedly drawn close to the musicians to stand, swaying to the music, aglow with pleasure. Live jazz was something she hadn't heard in a very long time. Giving in to impulse, Lucinda danced her grandmother around the room, both of them near delirious with champagne, transported by the music and the general mood.

"Do you miss her?" she asked her grandmother as they moved.

"I miss the child. The woman she became was beyond my comprehending. I am sad for her because she was so hollow, so absent."

"I feel very badly about how I behaved with her," Lucinda confessed.

"But you must not," Elise declared. "You must remember that at a certain point she chose who she became. We all choose who we are to be."

"That's true," Lucinda said. "It is true. Thank you for saying that."

"But it is only the truth, *chérie*."

There were bursts of laughter; conversations flowed steadily—loudly at moments, quietly at others. Elise went on to dance with John and then Paul, with Paul Junior and Michael and Steven. Everyone was impressed by her energy, affected by her delight in the music.

Watching her grandmother dance with Paul Junior, admiring how graceful they both were, Lucinda thought that Anne would have done her damnedest to be the center of attention—even if it meant doing battle with her own mother. This was her party, the celebration of her life, and yet it wouldn't have been anywhere near as much fun if she'd been there. Ironic, Lucinda thought. And then she wondered if, after all, she'd seriously underestimated her aunt. Certainly, she'd discounted the woman's intelligence—principally because it had never been on display. But perhaps what had fueled Anne's discontent for so long was her knowledge of what she'd lost (or had had taken away from her, possibly by an unfeeling classmate) and her inability to find her way back to the heart of the family. Perhaps she'd hungered after the love of her parents and siblings, of her husband and children with an appetite as large as Lucinda's but with a fear so ingrained that it eradicated any possibility of her ever being able to attain it. Knowing as she did of Jason's constant harassment by the school bullies, Lucinda couldn't help thinking that for some people there were lifetime consequences from suffering such casually administered childhood torments.

And all at once, things clicked into place and made sense. Anne's seeming battle with Lucinda hadn't been for her mother's attention but for Lucinda's. *My god*! she thought, suddenly stricken by sadness. *She wanted me to love her*! *Not Elise, but me.* Why hadn't she *seen* it? She'd have given it freely, whole-heartedly, if Anne had only allowed herself to receive it. It was too sad, Lucinda thought. Locked inside that pinch-faced old woman, unable to get free, was the little girl who had been, as Elise so lovingly recalled, lively and pretty, quick and bright. *I would have loved you*, Lucinda thought, an ache at her core. *But you didn't believe you were lovable.* Rather than permit anyone, ever, to reject her, Anne had made it nearly impossible for anyone to accept her.

Looking around, she realized there was no one here with whom she could share her conclusions. She would come across either as egotistic as Anne had seemed, or self-serving, or simply mistaken. But Lucinda was convinced she had unearthed the truth. From clues and comments she'd collected and analyzed, she knew she was right. She had, at last, come to know what had driven her aunt. All those foolish costumes, the vastly overpriced, inappropriate garments had done the opposite of what Anne had hoped for: instead of drawing to her those she'd loved in her crippled, stunted fashion, she'd driven them away. It was exactly as if Anne had, for years and years, been speaking some foreign language—one nobody understood, least of all herself.

Stepping outside, Lucinda walked into the moonlit garden, away from the music and, breathing in the fragrance of night-blooming flowers, she wept in sorrow for her aunt and her untranslated, lost life.

Chapter Seven

The following Thursday Lucinda went to Westport to take her grandmother out to lunch. As she and Elise were getting out of the car in the parking lot that ran behind the shops and restaurants on Main Street, Lucinda saw Eli and a woman standing beside a late-model Lexus parked half a dozen cars away.

"Look," Elise said with a smile, waving. "It is Eli."

Eli looked over, smiled, waved back, and started toward them.

Lucinda's composure at once began to crumble. As she'd guessed would happen, Eli had found someone fearless—at least that was the impression she had as the emaciated, expensively dressed, darkly tanned, fortyish blonde came smiling toward them at Eli's side. *God*! she thought despairingly. *I'm not up for this*. She had the same style, the same brittle, nervy aura, the same imperious quality Lucinda saw so often in the women who frequented the upscale shops in the area. Obvious wealth and a certain ferocity made a combination that Lucinda found intolerable. A streak of ruthless self-absorption gave these females a dangerous demeanor. You could feel it even from a distance.

"Elise!" Eli exclaimed happily, exchanging kisses on each cheek with the elderly woman. "What a treat! You look wonderful, as always." Lowering his voice, he said, "I was so sorry to hear about Anne." Elise thanked him, and there was a brief visual exchange of mutual understanding that made Lucinda understand that this man and her grandmother were not only doctor and patient but also close friends. Then, offering his hand with a smile, he said, "Lucinda, it's so good to see you again. This is Peg Bowen. Peg, Elise Franklin and her granddaughter, Lucinda Hunter."

The woman's hand was thin, cold and hard and there was a deadness to her glacial pale blue eyes ("Murderer's eyes," Lily used to say. "Never trust anyone with 'em. They'll kill you, one way or another.") as she shook first Elise's hand, then Lucinda's. "Don't I *know* you?" she asked Lucinda, head tilting slightly to one side as she adjusted the heavy gold-link bracelet on her wrist. The massive diamond solitaire on her ring finger threw off needles of light and Lucinda instinctively turned her head to avoid them. Many, perhaps most, divorced women of a certain age in Fairfield County—and Lucinda would've taken it to the bank that this one was of their ranks—seemed to wear these ostentatious rings as proof of their previous, hopefully continuing, desirability. Someone had once cared enough about them to present them with large, flawless, round or square-cut emblems of their affection. Therefore, someone else was also bound to care for and desire them. It was, they believed, inevitable.

"I don't think so," Lucinda said. The sun was lasering into the top of her head and she wished she'd remembered to bring her hat; wished she'd chosen some other restaurant so that this encounter could have been avoided. "It's really very hot," she began, "and we have a reservation—"

"Oh, *I know*!" Peg Bowen declared in the horribly affected clipped manner of speech so common to females of her type (known to many as Long Island Lockjaw) and a smile that was positively malevolent. "*You're* the one who runs that … What? Is it a *halfway* house?"

"I beg your pardon?" Lucinda said, glancing at Elise who was now studying the woman with confusion, then at Eli whose expression mirrored Elise's.

"*You're* the *one*! You've got that di*vine* old farmhouse on *acres* of property. And there are always odd children running about, people coming and going, night and day. I'm in real estate in Darien. I know my office has called you tons of times about listing that place. We've had so many queries about it. You *are* the one, aren't you?"

"*Odd children*?" Lucinda's mouth had gone dry and she could feel her pulse pounding in her throat. *Ratbastards We Have Known*, she thought, trying to imagine what possible reason Eli might have for being with this odious middle-aged anorexic.

"Oh, you *know*. Every age and color, people coming and going at all hours," she repeated. "Everyone at the office assumed it must be a halfway house." Peg Bowen laughed and looked up at Eli, as if for approval. He stood perfectly still for a second or two, then took a step away from her. The woman seemed unaware of the significance of that step away, and sailed right ahead. "I've always thought you must have the patience of a saint, to endure so much *traf-*

fic. No offense intended," Peg Bowen said, again offering that dead-eyed lethal smile to Lucinda.

Unable to stop herself—the restraints previously in place with Anne (who had deserved respect, at least) non-existent here—Lucinda said in a voice gone deep with indignation, "Are you on drugs or are you simply stupid?"

The woman's smile shattered like a store window hit by a brick.

"We must go," Elise said, slipping her arm through Lucinda's and urging her away. "*Au 'voir*, Eli."

"*Au 'voir*," he repeated, appearing to be immobilized.

As they neared the door to the restaurant, Lucinda realized that her grandmother was trying, and failing, to suppress laughter.

"You thought that was funny?" Lucinda asked.

"What you *said* was wonderfully funny," Elise said. "A horror, that female. I cannot think what Eli would be doing with such a woman."

"That makes two of us."

"Put it aside," Elise counseled. "We will have a lovely lunch and think only of pleasant things. They make a very fine crab salad here. The dressing is especially good, with fresh dill."

"I'm not sure I could eat."

"But of course you will eat. You must have a reward for such a brilliant remark. 'Are you on drugs or simply stupid?' Marvelous!" she declared. "I will pray for an occasion when I may use it."

"She was a goddamned idiot," Lucinda fumed.

"Oh, absolutely," Elise agreed as the hostess found their reservation in the book, picked up two menus and began to lead them to their table. "It is remarkable, what stupid things people will say. My Anne had a positive genius for it."

"Poor Anne," Lucinda said. Then, indignation rushing back, she said, "A halfway house? People of every age and color? Good grief! And she's in real estate? Who'd be willing to sit in a car with her, let alone go looking at houses while she played tour guide?"

"Ah, she is one of those who is bored at home with no husband, no children, nothing to do, so she has a little job," Elise said, donning her reading glasses and opening the menu. "We will have some wine, I think. Yes?"

"Sure, why not. I need *something*." Lucinda turned to look out the window which offered a view of the river that was, unfortunately, obstructed by the parking lot. Rows of cars sat baking in heat that shimmered like waves in a funhouse mirror. "What makes you think she's divorced?"

"But it goes without saying," Elise said. "She has that hungry look."

Hungry. Lucinda smiled. "You think she'd like to dine on Eli."

"*Mais certainment*!"

The waitress was approaching as Eli appeared and made his way toward them. "I wanted to apologize," he told Lucinda. "That was—unbelievable."

"Indeed, it was," Elise agreed.

"Who *is* that fool?" Lucinda asked angrily, inhaling the wonderful scent of his cologne with her next drawn breath.

"She's the daughter of one of my patients," he explained as the waitress said, "Hi, Doctor Carter. Shall I bring another setting?"

"If you have not eaten, Eli, please dine with us," Elise invited.

"Lucinda, if you'd prefer to be alone with your grandmother, just say the word and I'll be on my way. I don't want to make you angrier than you already are."

Lucinda said, "I'm very specific with my anger. I tend not to misdirect it." Seeing that he was beginning to smile, she said, "Oh, sit down, Eli. And tell me what you were doing with that mouth with feet."

He broke into booming laughter that had people at nearby tables turning to look over. He laughed so hard that tears started in his eyes. Pulling out a handkerchief, he blotted his face and with a shake of his head, declared, "We should keep you angry all the time. You're fabulously articulate when you're angry."

"Yes, well, unlike certain stick creatures with jewelry that weighs more than they do, I actually do have functioning intelligence."

Eli emitted another booming burst of laughter.

"Could I get you something to drink?" the waitress asked the table with a smile, as if voluntarily participating in their jollity.

Quite merrily, Elise ordered a bottle of French Merlot and when the waitress had gone to get it, she asked, "Eli, you are involved with this Peg?" The woman's name came out sounding distinctly like pig.

Startled by it, but pleased by her grandmother's directness, Lucinda waited for his answer as he refolded the handkerchief and put it back in his pocket.

"Oh, not *involved*," he answered. "We've had lunch a couple of times. In fact, we were on our way here when we … ran into you."

"And where is she now?" Lucinda asked.

"We came in separate cars," he said, looking somewhat uncomfortable.

"So she went off in her 'separate car'?" Lucinda said.

He nodded as a busboy came over with cutlery and a napkin and placed them on the tablecloth in front of Eli.

"Tell me you didn't explain anything to her," Lucinda said.

His eyes fixed on hers for several beats. "Do you think I'm stupid, Lucinda?"

"Men have been known to do remarkably stupid things, Eli, when it comes to women."

"Maybe. But I'm not one of those men."

"So what did you say to get her going off in her separate car?" Lucinda persisted.

His eyes went to Elise who was following this exchange with an expression halfway between amusement and concern. His gaze again on Lucinda, he said, "I told her I found it a bit surprising, given her obvious racial prejudice, that she was willing to be seen in public with me."

"Oh, very good!" Lucinda said approvingly.

"Well, it was the truth. I mean, seriously. I suddenly realized that she was willing to overlook the fact that I was someone of color because it was important to her to be seen in public with a man—any man. She was pleasant enough company but I certainly wasn't in love with her. Nothing like that."

"Good, because I'd have to question your sanity if you were," Lucinda snapped.

Keeping his voice down, he said, "I did ask you out, Lucinda. You were definitely not interested."

"I didn't *say* I wasn't interested. You asked if you frightened me and I said everybody did. You just *assumed* I wasn't interested—" She stopped abruptly, feeling heat rush into her face.

Elise was smiling again. "I must go to the W.C.," she announced, and was up and moving away before Lucinda or Eli could react.

"This is mortifying," Lucinda said in an undertone.

"Don't feel that way. Maybe 'Pig'"—he pronounced the name as Elise had done—"did us a favor. I wanted to phone you again, but I don't want to be responsible for putting anyone on edge. I have my own problems with that."

"Are you telling me that woman didn't put you on edge?"

"Lucinda, we had lunch a couple of times. That's it. I don't have to justify myself here."

"If you hang around with women like that, you certainly do."

"I don't 'hang around' with women like that. Look, this is silly. Could we drop it?"

"I'd love that," Lucinda said.

"Good."

"Good," Lucinda echoed, then looked again out the window, thinking that if she wrote this dialogue into a script people would stay away from the movie in droves.

"So," he said, "we'll have lunch now. Next time I phone and ask, will you have dinner with me?"

"I don't know." At any moment she was going to start hyperventilating.

"What's the matter with you?" he asked interestedly. "I'm missing something here. This isn't about me really, is it?"

"It is a bit," she said, unable to look at him. "But primarily it's about me. I have something of a ... problem."

"Tell me, before your grandmother gets back."

She turned and looked at his clear, non-judgmental gray eyes. "Something like agoraphobia," she whispered.

His eyes stayed on hers for what seemed like a very long

time. At last, he said, "After Maria died I needed something to do with my evenings. So you know what I did?"

She shook her head.

"I took a cooking course."

"Really?"

"Really. So how about this? I will telephone you and we will talk about books and movies, and then we will pick an evening for dinner. And on that evening, I will come to your house and bring the dinner with me. Would that work?"

"I have a teenage girl staying with me."

"Does she eat?"

Lucinda laughed. "Yes, she eats."

"Would *she* be afraid of me?"

"Hell, no."

"So, fine. I will bring dinner for three. Okay?"

Elise was on her way back to the table.

"Okay?" Eli asked again.

"Yes, okay."

"See! That wasn't so hard, was it?"

"Are you crazy? That was murder."

Eli started laughing again.

"Are we friends now, *mes enfants*?" Elise asked, sliding back into her chair. "Because I am very hungry and it is time to order our food."

"Okay, so why the panic?" Gin asked.

"Having a man come to my house for dinner. It isn't something I do," Lucinda answered, looking up at the stars. It was a very clear night, with a full moon that seemed to light up the entire pool area and everything beyond.

Gin finished her Diet Coke and lit a cigarette before saying, "Once upon a time, it *was* something you did. You didn't have a problem then. So, aside from being out of practice, what's the problem now?"

"Cort was easy. I mean, we were kids, we were at school together. It was the sixties, peace and love and all those good things. It was *easy*."

"He was a nice boy," Gin said.

"Yes, he was."

"He loved you."

"Yes, he did."

"Did you love him?" Gin asked.

"Yes, I did."

"But you pushed him away."

"I had to. I wasn't very nice about it, but I had to."

"I know this kind of stuff throws you into a certified tizzy, but did you sleep with him?"

Grateful for what darkness there was, her face afire, Lucinda said, "Unh-hunh."

"Did you like it?"

"God!"

"Just answer the question."

"Yes. I liked it. Is this your personal remake of the Spanish Inquisition?"

"I'll ignore that. Point is you're functional."

"I *was*."

"If you were once, you can be again," Gin said reasonably.

"Who says I *want* to be functional?" Lucinda argued.

Swinging her legs over the side of the chaise so that she was facing Lucinda, Gin said with tried patience, "Kiddo, could we just agree here that you do? After schmoozing with cigar-smoking creeps for weeks on end, smiling and playing sweetness and light to get their bucks on the table for the new picture, I'm not in the mood to cha-cha with you. You met a decent-sounding guy and he's not only coming for dinner but he's actually bringing the meal. What? You think he's going to expect to get laid for dessert? Never happen. You're forgetting that the connection here is Elise. This guy's got to be able to show his face to her again. Nope. This is purely greet and eat, make nice. Plus, Kat's gonna be here to keep things kosher. So, I ask again: Why the panic?"

"I worry about people's expectations," Lucinda confessed.

"Why are you assuming the man *has* expectations? Maybe he's just after some company."

"I'm the wrong person for that."

"No, kiddo. *I'm* the wrong person for that. I don't *do* company. You, on the other hand, have decent skills."

"Not with men."

Stubbing out her cigarette, Gin said, "Ella, this is ridiculous. Really. I love you more than life, but this is completely, absolutely, utterly ridiculous. Worst case scenario, the two of you will discover you're not compatible. Best case, you'll make friends. So you're shy. Big deal. Are you gonna drop this before I whack you one?"

Lucinda backed down, saying, "I'm sorry."

"Don't be sorry, just stop giving yourself ulcers over something that, on a scale of one to ten, is maybe a four." Settling back on the chaise, Gin said, "Look at that moon! Can you imagine going there? Can you imagine standing on the moon and looking back at earth and thinking, So, people, what's the big deal?"

"You sound tired, Gin."

"I'm very tired. I'm thinking of pulling a Lily and walking away after this picture's in the can. Only problem is, I'd die of boredom without my career. On top of that, because

I won't have to anymore, I'll stop working out and then I'll pork up and despise myself. Remember how gorgeous Tuesday Weld was? Married that divine violinist Pinchas Zukerman, ultimately quit working and for a while now she's been up there size-wise with Rosemary Clooney and Shirley Knight. Mind you, those two are still working, and god bless them. They're talented ladies. But Tuesday kissed it off, said bye-bye to the biz. Me? I'd have to stick my head in the oven because much as I hate doing it, I need the workouts. I need the discipline to keep any respect at all for this body."

Lucinda looked at her friend's figure, tiny and taut, in white jeans and a pale blue T-shirt. At fifty-five, she was in peak physical condition. To maintain that condition took ninety minutes of hard work every day, that got done no matter where she was. When she traveled, she always stayed in hotels with a pool or a gym area so she could put in those ninety minutes, even if she had to get up before dawn to do it. Her discipline was rigid, ingrained. She'd been acting in movies since the age of ten. It was all she'd ever known or wanted to do.

"Do you really think you could walk away?" Lucinda asked her.

Gin shrugged. "Probably not. But I think about it, more and more these days. Lily had the right idea: Quit while you're ahead. Thing is, I'm still ahead. That makes the quitting tricky. It's not like writing, something you can do all alone at home. Trust me, if I had any other talent, I'd be using it. This is getting old. The only good part of it is that it's my show, my production. I don't have to kiss some fat bastard's ass to get a halfway decent role. I can pick my own. But I need you on my team."

"You've got me on your team, always."

"So I won't have to beg if I happen to have another book I like?"

Lucinda erupted into laughter.

"You are *such* an actor, *so* damned *devious*," she accused her now-beaming friend.

"Hey! It's why they pay me the big money."

"What is it this time?" Lucinda asked.

"You'll love it," Gin promised enthusiastically, with no hint whatever of her former mood. "I'll drop a copy by tomorrow when I come to swim with the kids."

"You played me like an accordion."

"Please! That is so Lawrence Welk, so down-market. No, Ella darling. I played you," Gin said, "like the Stradivarius you are. I'm going home now. You be sure to phone me the minute this Eli goes out the door. Okay? I want to hear every last detail."

Chapter Eight

"You're so jumpy, Luce. I've never seen you like this. Maybe you should just call and tell him to forget it."

"I couldn't do that, Kat. It would be—" Lost for an adequate word, Lucinda gave up and looked with dismay at her reflection.

"Let me do your hair," Katanya volunteered. "A French braid would look good." Grabbing the hairbrush, she said, "Come sit down. I'm gonna do your hair."

Too agitated to argue, Lucinda sat in the slipper chair (one of the few items of Lily's that, despite its ugliness—even reupholstered and with chintz fabric in keeping with its style—she'd kept for purely sentimental reasons) and Kat smoothed out Lucinda's hair, then began to brush it.

"It's getting really long again," Kat observed. "This'll be great, Luce. The longer the hair, the better the braid. And you've got good hair for it, nice and thick. Skimpy hair looks yack in a French braid."

The motion was soothing, and the tension began to ease out of Lucinda's shoulders as the girl pulled the brush through her hair. Lulled, she remembered countless times when Lily had handed her a brush, saying, "Do my hair, will you, hon?" and then she'd closed her eyes and sighed contentedly as Lucinda had gently brushed her mother's baby-fine, wheat-colored hair. Now, all these years later, Lucinda understood the act from within its unique intimacy.

She looked at the girl in the mirror, admiring her beautiful features and the style so typically hers: Gap overalls with a pale pink T-shirt, bare feet in clunky white sneakers that looked overly large. She positively glowed with energy and intelligence. "You are such a kind girl, Kat."

"Don't be silly," she said with a grin. "I just want you to look nice."

"My mother used to get me to brush her hair all the time. I never understood the point of it, but I was glad to do anything that brought me close to her. Now I know why she loved to have me do it."

"Didn't anybody ever brush your hair for you?" Katanya looked at her in the mirror.

Lucinda shook her head.

"Get *out*!" the girl said in disbelief. "Never?"

"Hairdressers, when I was young and there was going to be a photo shoot for one of the fanzines."

"Fanzines? That's like, what?"

"There used to be dozens of movie magazines, honey. Articles on the stars, photo layouts of so-and-so at home, phony gossip and advice columns."

"Oh! Like *Movieline*?"

"Not really. Most of the material was bogus, total hokum tailored to make the fans think so-and-so was just the girl or boy next door who got lucky. The subtext being that if they could get lucky, so could you. As far as I can see, *Movieline* is reality-based. The interviews actually reveal a lot about the subject—depending on how incisive the questions are. I like the magazine."

"Okay. I get it. So back when you were a little kid was the only time anybody did your hair?"

"I had regular haircuts when I was at Yale. I was a regular kind of person back then."

"You're *still* a regular kind of person. I hate when you get all down on yourself. You shouldn't do that."

"It's a habit."

"I know," Katanya said sympathetically. "But Luce, that is so *sad*. Remember way back, when the wheels came off with Renee and her husband and I came to stay here with you, and one day I taught you how to do my hair?"

"I remember."

"The truth is, I could've done it myself. But I was missing my moms and gramma so I asked you to do it cuz it made me feel … like I was home, kind of. You know? You were so nice to me and everything but I felt sorta blue, so I pretended I couldn't do it to get you to. And it made me feel better." As she spoke, she continued to draw the brush through Lucinda's hair. "You follow that?"

"Yes, I do. It made me feel better, too, Kat, to do it for you."

"Yeah? I never thought of that. Cool. Then I'm glad I asked you. Anyway, when me and Moms first came to live with my gramma when I was little, Gramma was always brushing our hair, 'specially my mom's."

"To comfort you," Lucinda said softly.

"Yeah."

"And now, here you are, comforting me."

"I guess, cuz you're so freaked. It's just somebody coming to dinner, Luce. He's even bringing the food. It's a no-brainer."

"Part of me knows you're right, but a bigger part is what you'd call freaked."

Putting the brush aside, Katanya started separating sections of Lucinda's hair, her eyes now on the task at hand. "Did you ever want to get married and have kids, Luce?"

"Once upon a time I was engaged."

"You were?" Surprised, Katanya's eyes went again to Lucinda's reflection. "What happened?"

"My mother died, and everything changed."

"Oh! That's so too bad. Was he nice?"

"Very. But I would've made him unhappy, so I broke it off. Would *you* like to get married and have kids?" Lucinda asked.

Her attention back on the complicated braid she was fashioning, Katanya said, "I don't know about getting married. I'd like to have kids, though. At least one, for sure. I think I'd be a good mother."

"So do I."

"Yeah? Thanks, Luce." Katanya sighed. "Thing is, the boys I know at school are either screaming queens from the dance programs or psychodweebs from advanced music. I like them. I mean, those're my friends, you know? The theater guys are so completely boring, so full of themselves. The girls are, too. So far I haven't seen one single boy I'd even want to kiss, never mind getting naked with."

Lucinda laughed.

"I'm not kidding," Katanya said. "Back in the day, didn't you check out guys and decide whether or not you'd want to get naked with them before you'd even, like, go for coffee?"

"Yes, I did," Lucinda admitted. "That's just not quite the way I thought of it."

"Well, what else would it be? You have to get naked to do the deed. So every new guy you meet, you put the picture up inside your head and see if it's possible, not disgusting, or if it makes you want to heave up your heart."

"True." Lucinda was smiling.

"So okay. I have not yet met one boy who doesn't activate my gag reflex. The gay guys are my girlfriends and we hang together. Which is not an altogether terrible thing because they're better girlfriends than my girlfriends. They don't have hidden agendas, not about me anyway. About guys they like, that's a whole other thing. So tell me about this dude coming tonight."

"It's *doctor* dude," Lucinda corrected her. "He's my grandmother's internist."

"And?" Katanya prompted.

"I sort of got railroaded into inviting him."

"You, railroaded? Unh-unh. I so don't believe you. He's nice and you like him. Right?"

"Kat, he's nice and I like him, but just so we're clear on this: I'm not interested in getting naked with *anyone*."

"Gramma always says: never say never. Give me that band, please." Katanya extended her hand. "Okay, done! Check it out." Stepping away, she got the mirror and passed it to Lucinda. "Look at it from the back."

"Wow, Kat! That's really something. I love it."

"Suits you," the girl said judiciously. "I knew it would. What time's Doctor Dude coming?"

Lucinda looked at the time and her stomach lurched. "Any minute."

"You gonna hurl? You just went a really spooky color, like green."

The doorbell sounded. Lucinda stared at Katanya, then said, "You get it. I need a moment."

"Okay, but you better not bail. I will be *really* mad if you do."

"I won't bail."

Lucinda stood breathing deeply, listening to Katanya fly down the stairs. The door opened and the girl said, "Hi, I'm Kat. Come on in. Luce'll be right down."

Godohgodohgod. Why was she putting herself through this? Lucinda asked herself as she wiped her damp hands on her skirt and headed downstairs, following the voices to the kitchen where Eli was putting an insulated bag on the counter and Katanya was saying, "... so I'm the chaperone." Eli emitted one of his booming laughs as Katanya asked, "Would you like something to drink?"

"Hello, Eli." Lucinda took a few steps into the room and stopped. He was dressed tonight in relaxed, much-faded jeans and a bright yellow polo shirt, his bare feet in loafers that were practically falling apart. The sight of those shoes was reassuring. A man who dressed casually but wore new shoes was sending a message she didn't want to receive. It was, as Katanya would have said, indicative of a hidden agenda.

"Hello, Lucinda." Eli smiled. "I like your hair."

Lucinda didn't answer, her eyes still on his shoes. She had the arbitrary notion that a chunk of the man's history could be read in that shabby footwear, if she only had the particular skills necessary to decode the clues of their travel.

Katanya filled the lengthening silence. "Doesn't it look fanticulous?" she said.

"If that means great, yes, definitely. You look very nice altogether."

"Thank you," Lucinda spoke, finally, glad she'd decided not to dress up but to wear her old, short-sleeved sun dress and sandals.

"Blue is a good color for you. Is there wine?" he asked.

"Is there wine, Luce?" Katanya repeated.

Lucinda again couldn't speak for a moment, trying to get her mind around the fact of this man's presence in her kitchen. He seemed perfectly comfortable and she wondered how that worked, how you could be someplace you'd never been before and not display the least bit of nervousness. Confidence, she answered herself. He was a confident man. What an enviable state of being!

"I could run out to the local boozeteria, pick up some," Eli offered into the silence. "Unless you'd prefer something soft."

"Boozeteria!" Katanya repeated. "Too great! You make that up?"

"I must give accreditation where it's due. A wonderfully mad, former patient of mine made it up. I stole it."

"I would've too. It's excellent. Fanticulous is a Jason word. He's wonderfully mad, too. We have wine, Luce?"

"We do," Lucinda said, recovering her voice and her mobility. "All colors and flavors. What's your preference, Eli?"

"Red, please. Jason?"

"Red, please," Katanya parroted, with a big smile. "Yeah, I baby-sit him. He's one scary-smart little dude."

"You are allowed to have any beverage in the house that doesn't contain alcohol," Lucinda told her, getting a bottle of red wine from the rack under the far counter. "My grandmother's been educating me about wines," Lucinda explained, showing the bottle of 1962 Margaux Bordeaux to Eli. "Is this okay?"

"This is better than okay," he said. "It's probably too good."

"Really? I've got others."

"I'm teasing. I'll gladly have some of that. Shall I do the honors and open it?"

Katanya scooted over to the counter, pulled open a drawer, got the corkscrew and scooted back to give it to him, saying, "I'll get the glasses. Luce, you're supposed to ask about the food and if the oven needs to get turned on."

"She thinks I'm socially backward," Lucinda said.

"You are, a bit," Katanya said with an encouraging smile.

"It's true, I am."

"Merely rusty," Eli said graciously, opening the oven door to remove the broiler pan before setting the temperature. "You need a little practice, that's all."

"I need way more than a little," Lucinda said, watching as he next turned his attention to the wine bottle, removing the cork with surgical efficiency, then sniffing it.

"Why're you doing that?" Katanya asked.

"If the wine's off, you can smell it in the cork. Save yourself a nasty taste sensation."

"I'll remember that," Katanya said.

"I'm of the opinion," he said to Lucinda, "that Kat should be the official taster. If she keels over, we'll know it's not safe to drink the wine."

"Yeah!" Katanya got another glass and before Lucinda could protest, Eli poured about an inch of wine into it, then said, "Take a good sniff, see what you think of the bouquet."

"Wine's all about sniffing?"

"When you open a bottle of this caliber, yes indeed."

"Bouquet? Like flowers?"

"In a sense."

Katanya lowered her face to the glass and inhaled deeply. "Smells good."

"Okay, a decent sip now. Let it sit on your tongue for a second or two before you swallow."

Katanya followed his instructions.

"And the verdict is?" he asked her.

"The verdict is yum. It's dee-vine."

"Make it last," Lucinda cautioned her as Eli half-filled the two other glasses before giving one to Lucinda.

"God, it *is* yum," Lucinda said with a smile after taking a sip.

"Your grandmother knows her vino," Eli said.

"My grandmother knows more than just her vino," Lucinda said. "She's one of the most amazing people I've ever met."

"I'll drink to that." Eli clinked his glass against hers.

"This is fun," Katanya said. "I've only had wine once before. That stuff tasted b-a-d, like vinegar."

"Cheap wine," Eli said. "And it was probably white, right?"

"Yup. Nasty."

"There's a school of thought that believes real wine connoisseurs only drink red."

"I'd enroll in that school." Katanya laughed.

Eli reached out and patted the girl's cheek. "Beautiful *and* smart," he complimented her.

"I don't know about the beautiful part, but I'm not too bad in the smart department. I'll be a senior in September."

"I'm impressed."

"Oh, I'm impressive as anything. Everybody says so." She made a face, then laughed self-mockingly.

"Everybody can't be wrong," Eli said, obviously entertained.

Lucinda followed their banter, feeling herself beginning

to thaw. Katanya had finely tuned instincts about people. She liked Eli. That could only be seen as a good sign.

"Let me just put these pans in the oven," he said, setting his glass on the table, "then we've got about forty minutes before we eat."

"What is it all?" Katanya asked as he removed foil-covered baking dishes from the insulated bag.

"It's all dinner," he said, teasingly. "If I'd known I was dining with a celebrity, though, I'd have made something special. I saw you in *Brown Baby*."

"Get *out*!" Katanya lit up. "I only had one solo number. You recognized me from *that*?"

"Your one solo number," he said seriously, "was a heart-stopper. I got so choked up I missed the next three scenes."

"Me, too," Lucinda said softly, amazed at his willingness to admit this.

"Luckily," he went on, "I was with my son and daughter-in-law. They're used to seeing me blubber. Otherwise, it might've been embarrassing. You are a wonderful, wonderful singer."

Katanya threw her arms around him and hugged him hard. "Thank you. You are a very, very nice man." Stepping away, she said, "I have to set the table now."

"Come to the living room," Lucinda invited.

He stopped on the threshold, his gaze on the portraits. "Lord, lord," he murmured. "Look at that! They're so beautiful the two of them, so *young*."

Beside him, Lucinda, too, studied the portraits.

"Does everyone look too young to you these days?" he asked.

"They do. I feel as if I've lived a thousand years when I

look at kids and see how untouched their faces are, how scarcely lived-in they are."

"Me, too. Was she as good a mother as she was an actress?"

"Better."

"That makes me glad. And you never knew your dad?"

"No."

"Sad for all of you. What an incredible heritage, Lucinda. No wonder you can come up with quips like 'a mouth with feet.'"

"According to Elise, I inherited that talent from my mother and," she joked, "my blindingly high IQ from my father."

"Blindingly high, huh? You and Kat obviously have a lot in common."

"We do, actually. But our roles are reversed. She's the grownup and I'm the child."

"I can see how that works."

They found themselves seated together on the sofa, in the brief lull hearing Katanya humming softly as she set the table in the next room.

"Am I still frightening you?" he asked.

"Off the charts," she admitted.

"Drink your wine. I get less scary in direct proportion to the amount of alcohol consumed."

"I hadn't had a drink in over twenty-five years until I found Elise," she said. "My capacity is extremely limited."

"All the better. It won't take too long for me to lose the red suit, the tail and the horns."

She laughed again and took another sip.

"It's mildly intimidating," he said, "drinking a three-hundred-dollar bottle of wine."

"I've got a six-hundred-dollar bottle of Mouton Rothschild, and some California red that cost nine ninety-five. We can either go up from here or way, way down, so don't be intimidated."

Katanya came in, picked up a CD and slid it into the slot. "You forgot the music, Luce," she said. "I have to remind her of everything," she told Eli.

"I can see that."

"So," Katanya said, sitting cross-legged on the floor opposite. "You have kids?"

"I do. Two sons."

"Are you a grandpa, Eli?"

"Not yet," he said. "I'd like to be. I love kids."

"I can tell," Katanya said.

"So, Kat, you're the parent and Lucinda is the child."

"Only in special circumstances, like tonight," Katanya said. "Most of the time, Luce is my fairy godmother. And she can be v-e-r-y funny."

"I've noticed. When she's angry, she says some amazing things."

"Oh boy! Did you see Luce lose it?"

"I did. It was spectacular."

"Yeah," Katanya said. "A little scary too."

"Excuse me," Lucinda interjected. "I am sitting right here."

Katanya said gently, "We're cool, Luce." Turning back to Eli, she explained, "This one time, when I was first here, like five years ago, Lucinda pitched one at this fat lady who worked at the post office, cuz I couldn't get waited on. It was amazing and scary, because she was defending me and at the same time outing herself as African-American by saying she was my grandmother. Back then, I was kind of scared. But when I think about it now, I feel so proud of her. Luce forgets to be shy when she's angry."

"I have noticed that," Eli said. "So I guess the plan is to keep her a little tipsy and a little angry, and everything'll be perfect."

There was a moment of silence as they waited to see how Lucinda was going to respond. She burst out laughing. Seeing the relief on their faces, she realized Gin had been right—functionality was within her grasp.

Chapter Nine

Diplomatically, Katanya excused herself after dinner, saying, "I have to go check my email, see what's up with my moms and gramma." She hugged Eli and said, "Dinner was fabulous. Thank you. I hope we see you again really soon."

"I hope so too," he replied. "It was such a pleasure to meet you."

Lucinda's nervous system started cranking itself up into overdrive the moment Katanya left the room. But as if he'd guessed this might be her reaction, Eli looked at his watch and said, "I should be running along," and she was, perversely, disappointed.

"It's still early," she said, caught by the notion that he'd had a less than wonderful time and that she should make some effort to entertain him, to be what Lily used to refer to scathingly as "a good hostess." God, this was awful! She was behaving out of character and couldn't seem to center herself.

"I've got housecalls to make first thing in the morning. I get the impression you're a night owl, Lucinda."

"Pretty much," she said. "I only sleep through the night when I have to take my migraine meds. Then I'll be out for ten or twelve hours and wake up feeling as if I've been run over by a truck."

"Migraines are terrible," he said sympathetically. "Your cousin Paul suffers from them and so does his mother. But you probably already know that."

"Yes, I do."

She walked outside with him, maintaining a distance that was beyond arm's length but not so far away as to appear rude. The air was still heavy with heat and she felt as if she were moving through bathwater. As they walked down the driveway toward his car, she said, "The dinner really was splendid. You definitely didn't misrepresent your culinary skills."

"Next time, if I'm not being presumptuous in assuming there'll *be* a next time, I could bring the ingredients and cook from scratch. You could even help." He smiled over at her.

"That would be fine," she said stiffly, thinking that if he wanted to come back he couldn't have had a bad time. But why did she care? She hated feeling so uncertain, so unlike herself.

They arrived at his car, a sedate dark blue Infiniti, and he turned to her. "I'd invite you to my place but I suspect you'd refuse. Anyway my condo is nothing special, except for the view of the marina from the deck, which is very nice at night. Otherwise, it has about as much charm as an Amtrak waiting room."

"Is that self-deprecation or fact?" she asked.

"Fact. I sold the house after Maria died, let the boys take whatever they wanted, kept a few things and sold the rest. I've had the condo for almost three years and there are still boxes I haven't unpacked because I can't be bothered. So could we do this again?"

The original three weeks already having stretched to four, Katanya would be leaving at the end of the following week. Lucinda wasn't sure she was up to dealing with Eli on her own, without the girl's intuitive knowledge of when to step in to fill any awkward pauses.

"What? Am I so scary you need extra time to think it over?" He smiled and leaned against the car door.

"I need more time—for just about everything—than most people are willing to give."

"Oh, I'm the patient sort. I can give you all kinds of time," he said. "A lot of things worry you, don't they? I couldn't help noticing you were aware of how much wine I drank. So let me tell you up front that my limit is two glasses of whatever's going. I'm not a big drinker."

"I'm sorry," she said, appalled at the idea that she was so transparent. "It's just that I grew up in an environment where people got falling-down drunk and did awful things. Please don't think I was … I'm sorry," she repeated. "I thought I had more subtlety than I obviously do."

"As I said"—he smiled again—"a lot of things worry you."

"What else did you notice?" she couldn't help asking, curious about the extent of his powers of observation.

"Well, I know you don't want to entertain me here alone, without reinforcement of some kind, and I'm not going to take that personally. You mentioned the other day you had something like agoraphobia. I'd really like it if you could elaborate on that. It might help us both." Neither his tone nor facial expression indicated anything other than interest.

She was surprised to find that she was willing. He seemed entirely open and uncritical. "I had a lot of trouble leaving the house … until Elise and I found each other. To be honest, the only places I went were the library and the post office. And it sometimes took several days before I could even start the car. I'm getting better," she said, folding her arms over her chest and looking down at her feet. She considered inviting him to sit on the porch with her but was reluctant to break the flow of the conversation. "I'm light years beyond how I was before. But I'm nowhere near—adjusted, for want of a better word."

"Were you ashamed when you learned your father was a man of color?"

"Oh, not at all!" She raised her eyes to his. "It was about my not knowing *how* to be someone of color, about feeling fraudulent. I wasn't white, but I wasn't black. I had nowhere to stand, no history to follow as an example of how to *be*. Lily wanted to protect me from any sort of stigma, and she did. But the end result of her protection was a horrible ignorance, a corrosive kind of fear. I became more and more convinced that people would know I was fake, that I was pretending to be something I wasn't—no matter how I tried to proceed. So, gradually, I took smaller and smaller steps until, finally, I could scarcely move at all. Which meant that I very rarely left the house. Even when I wanted to, there were times when I simply couldn't."

"It must have been very difficult for you, and for Lily, too," he said thoughtfully, folding his arms across his chest so that their postures mirrored each other. "My mother was estranged from her family. When she married my father, she never saw them again. Not one of them even came to her funeral."

"Your mother was white?" Lucinda asked.

"My mother was Siamese—the country became Thailand in nineteen thirty-nine, long after her family emigrated, first to England and then to the U.S. My maternal grandfather was a very successful importer who, on the one hand, took great pride in sending all five of his children to college, yet on the other was determined to prevent them from intermarrying—despite having pushed his children deep into the American culture. My father had a Jamaican mother and an Italian father. His family came here from the Caribbean in the twenties. My paternal grandfather took over his family's construction business and turned it into a major conglomerate. Later on, not a week after he graduated from Princeton—which is where he met my mother, who was also getting her MBA, with the plan that she would work for *her* father—my dad went into the family business. I think her father disowned her, in part, because he was so pissed off that she took the degrees he paid for and went to work somewhere else."

"Where?" Lucinda asked.

"Wall Street. My mother had an absolute genius for making money. My dad was a sharp guy but a dim bulb, compared to her. She loved the market and was always making charts and graphs, tracking this and that, doing projections on some stock offering, studying the merits of a bond issue or analyzing the earnings of a company whose stock she considered to be overpriced."

"She sounds remarkable."

"Believe me, she was. Anyone who can make the market sound exciting and get a small boy worked up to the point where he's saving up his allowance to buy stocks and bonds is a very smart cookie. Every single investment I made as a kid under her tutelage was solid gold. You know, one of the reasons I've always been drawn to your family is because it's so mixed, just like mine."

"How do you get to be Italian with a name like Carter?"

"Oh, it was Cartierri and got Anglicized into Carter several generations back. Probably by one of those impatient people at Ellis Island who loathed foreign names because they were too hard to spell, and so gave every arriving family a good, solid Anglo-Saxon moniker."

"But you always knew your background, didn't you?" she asked.

"I did. I can understand, though, how devastated you must've been, finding out who your father was."

"Devastated is precisely what I was," she said, appreciating his incisiveness. "When Lily died, I had no one left, except for Gin, and a few friends who gradually gave up and went away over time. I tried so hard to find ..." She stopped and again looked down at her feet. "Sometimes I can't believe I finally found them. And now I'm afraid there won't be enough time."

"Yes, there will," he said reassuringly. "Anne's death was sudden but not surprising, at least not to me. One look at her and I could tell she was in terrible shape—undernourished, hypertensive; too little food and a few too many pills of one kind or another. It's surprising she lasted as long as she did. But Elise is in great condition and has a lot of years left. Live in the moment, Lucinda. If you worry about what's to come, you'll lose out on what's happening now."

"I know. I tell myself that every day. But I can't help having this sense of urgency, this recognition that I have to value every moment and yet, at the same time—like a Greek chorus—there are whispers constantly reminding me how much was lost and how little remains." Meeting his eyes again, she said, "Tell me more about your family."

"Okay," he said. "Here's the short version. My mother and little sister died in a car crash when I was eleven. A year and a half later my father married a woman who didn't like children and I got shipped off to boarding school. It was the end of my world." He gave her a sad smile. "I couldn't believe he chose her over me. But he did. He was a man who had to have a wife—someone to tell him what to do. When I think about it now, I pity him, and the boy I was, too, because our shared history became mine alone. We could hardly sit and reminisce about my mother and sister with Elizabeth scowling at the very mention of their names. Bad enough that I had to come home on school holidays and disrupt her well-organized household. The very sight of me annoyed her. I went back to school early every single time because she made it so obvious how much she disliked having me around. By the time I was fifteen, I stopped going home on school breaks. I'd either go stay with my Jamaican grandmother who was more than a little crazy but who always made a gratifying fuss over me and cooked me curries and roti and gave me a lifelong passion for spicy food." He smiled again. "Sometimes I got invited to spend the breaks with friends, but if I didn't, and I didn't feel up to dealing with Granny's nuttiness, I just stayed at school with a couple of other kids who had nowhere to go. I never lived at home again.

"I was furious with my father for years, primarily for his refusal to stand up to Elizabeth; for not telling her where to put it, because I was his son and I would always be welcome in his home. If she didn't like it she could take a hike. But he never said a word; he just let me go, and salved his conscience by sending me more and more money—as if I were a pint-sized remittance man." He shook his head and rolled his eyes. "Most of all, though, I was angry with him for leaving it to me to keep the memory of my mother and sister alive. The last time I went home, I noticed several cartons in the garage, next to the bins, waiting to be put out on trash day. Curious, I opened one of the boxes. Inside were all the framed family photos. In the other boxes were the photograph albums."

"Oh my god!" Lucinda exclaimed. "That's *horrible*!"

"Sure was," he confirmed. "I carried the boxes up to my room and that night when he came home, I got my father alone and told him to have the albums and photos sent to me at school. He simply nodded and said he'd take care of it. Not one word about how he felt at having that monster he'd married consign our former life to the garbage. I was so outraged and hurt that I packed my bag, phoned a cab, got on the next train, and went back to school.

"During my first year as an intern, several major things happened one right after another. My loony Jamaican granny died, which meant I had nowhere at all left to go when I wasn't at school. Then, very suddenly, my father died—just fell over dead at the office. Within six weeks, Elizabeth sold the house and disappeared. No heartbreak there, that's for sure. A month or so later, I met Maria and fell in love with her on the spot. Once she was in my life I didn't have the time or the energy to be angry anymore. I was euphoric, anxious to be with this electrifying woman who had an effect on me like a tsunami—just washed the ground right out from under my feet. All I could think of was being with her and creating a new family, with children who would never be displaced by anyone or anything else. I was just too happy to waste any precious time being angry about the past.

"Over the years, Maria and I had the usual disagreements, made the usual compromises, but no matter what else happened, we had a great, great friendship. And I miss that most of all. After almost thirty years of knowing someone nearly as well as you know yourself, it's hard to stop thinking, 'Oh, wait till I tell Maria this!' Or I see something in a shop window that I know she'd love—a dress or a piece of jewelry or a pair of shoes. There's a moment or two of such excitement, and then ..." He stopped, frowning. "I think about death sometimes, you know, and examine it the way a researcher studies a renegade cell. I gaze into the microscope, turning the slide, adjusting the focus, looking at it this way and that, trying to get a sense of it as an entity. But I can't. It's just not possible."

"No," Lucinda agreed softly. "It's too enormous to view in its entirety, like standing at the base of a mountain and trying to see all of it—top, bottom, its entire circumference. Can't be done."

"Good analogy. And still," he said, "we keep trying to comprehend its terrible totality. So." He cleared his throat and shook his head. "Maria died of breast cancer, like Lily did."

How did he know that? she wondered, then realized that most everyone knew how Lily had died. It was one of the first times that breast cancer got major news coverage. Not for long, but it did heighten women's awareness, and their fear.

"It happened," he went on, "in a kind of extreme slow motion. First the tiny lump, followed by a partial mastectomy, chemo, radiation. Then six years of remission. We were flying; we'd beaten it. Then one day it was back to the oncologist for tests and x-rays, and we were grounded, hard. It had migrated into her bones.

"For a while, maybe a couple of years, it wasn't too bad. Then one night she was undressing for bed and, just like that, her arm broke. Scariest damned thing I've ever witnessed. The bone just snapped. I actually heard it. That was the first of so many trips by ambulance to the ER that we got to know the paramedics on a first-name basis.

"She was left-handed and had to learn how to use her right hand because the bone never did mend properly. They did surgery after a few months, put titanium struts in to support the bone. She made jokes about setting off metal detectors, and carried on. Then, some months later, she caught a cold, coughed hard and two of her ribs broke. The chemo was evil but she never complained, not even when everything smelled and tasted like toxic waste and her hair came out in handfuls. She'd have a few months after the chemo when she'd hold her ground. But that third year after the cancer moved into her bones, every so often I'd look at her and she'd be focused inward, completely oblivious to externals, as if she was seeing something incomprehensible, and trying to get a grip on it—as if she could *think* her way out of it. It was the pain, of course, the unimaginable, relentless ferocity of it.

"She'd laugh and say she had moths in her bones, making holes. Another five months of this went by, until it took an almost superhuman effort for her to tear herself away from that inner view, to look out at the boys and me. Then she'd be ashamed and guilty, tearful at neglecting us. But ten minutes later, her attention was gone again. That's when I started hoping it would end for her soon, that she'd die and get free of it. Her life was narrowed down to something too small to be seen by the human eye. All she could do was lay perfectly still, while the meds washed over the pain—like waves on a beach. I could literally see it. There'd be this superficial relief when her features would relax and she'd lose that fierce, awed expression, but, underneath, it was still there.

"Finally, *finally*, when her morphine intake was at an astronomical level, she just went out on one of the waves. I was so glad for her and so instantly bereft and lonely, knowing I'd never again hear her voice on the telephone, never have her blow up over something stupid I'd said or done, and hurl Spanish epithets at me." He laughed. "She had one hell of a temper. Like a flash flood. The boys are just like her, except for the Spanish epithets. They swear like white boys, like the preppies they were taught to be at Andover: as if the words are hot, like my old Granny's curry, and might burn their mouths."

Lucinda laughed. "What do they do, your sons?"

"They're both lawyers. My oldest, Emmanuel, is corporate counsel for a group of hotshot equity traders in the city. And Rafael works for the ACLU in Chicago. They're polar opposites. Manny is a typical avaricious yuppie, and Raf is a true, open-hearted liberal."

"Did Maria have a career?"

"Sorry. I guess I thought you knew. She was a pediatrician, adored children. She worked until the year before she died. Let all the kids sign her cast when her arm broke, then afterwards wore a sling to the office so that her damaged arm wouldn't get in the way."

"She sounds wonderful—brave and funny and clever."

He looked as if she'd given him an unexpected present.

"She was exactly like that," he said. "You couldn't be more different, yet in some ways you remind me so much of her. Your humor and your generosity, your intelligent skepticism."

"I'm not good at accepting compliments. But thank you. I must agree with Kat. You are a very nice man."

"Thank you. How about we strike a deal, Lucinda? I won't make any sudden moves that might startle you. We'll visit, cook and eat and talk, get to know each other."

"I'd like that," she said truthfully.

"Good. So what night next week works for you?"

"Thursday?" she suggested, thinking she'd have Katanya's presence as a buffer at least one more time. It was cowardly but, much as she liked him, she wasn't ready to be alone with him.

"Thursday would be good."

"If you tell me what you need, I'll do the shopping," she offered. "I can't let you do everything."

"Fair enough. You have email?"

"Absolutely. How's your memory?"

"Flawless."

"Okay. It's my full name at cableline dot net."

"I'll email you a shopping list. Okay?"

"Perfect."

He held out his hand and she put hers in it, at once returned to awkwardness. "Thank you for this evening," he said. "I like the way you listen. It's a rare talent. Since Maria died, I've found that most people only pretend to listen while they're actually thinking about what they want to say when you're finished. And they most definitely do not want to hear about my late wife. I am truly tired of people telling me to get over it."

"That's so stupid," she said angrily. "As if the death of someone you loved is a virus, or you're being boringly self-indulgent. I liked hearing about her. I like the way you talk. You have a writerly way of expressing yourself."

"I'm flattered. I used to think I'd like to write but, in truth, I knew I didn't have anything special to say."

"Most people have the idea that since they can read, they can write."

"I'm not one of them. I'll just stick to reading."

"I only have one question," she said. "I know it's none of my business, but I'd really like to know."

"Okay," he said. "Fire away."

"What were you doing with that awful Peg person?"

His booming laughter echoed into the night. "I was waiting for that. What *was* I doing with her? Aside from listening to her extol the virtues of sundry cosmetic procedures and the efficacy of laxatives as a way of maintaining weight without the evil necessity of doing any exercise, not much. We had lunch twice. There wouldn't have been a third time but she just *happened* to be there when I went to see her mother."

"I see. She had her cap set for you. It's amazing how she managed to hide her racism."

"That shocked me," he confessed.

"It made me very goddamned mad. Are all your patients elderly?"

"My practice now is elder care. I like old people. They're living lessons for us to learn, if we take the time. Aside from my house calls, I'm the attending for a nursing home. And that's where I'm headed at seven tomorrow morning. So I'll say good night now, Lucinda. Thank you for one of the nicest evenings I've had in a long while."

"It was my pleasure," she said.

He opened the car door and slid into the driver's seat.

She stood and watched him reverse out of the driveway, then she went back into the house, thinking of how lovingly he'd spoken of his wife and how, when he'd talked about her inward gaze, his, too, had turned inward.

The next afternoon Renee phoned. "Could I talk to you, away from the children?"

"All right." At once, Lucinda assumed there was something wrong.

"So you'll come?"

"You mean now?"

"Yes."

"I'll be right there."

Lucinda went out to the pool where Katanya and Jason were playing some peculiar word game they'd made up. "I have to do a quick errand," she told them. "I'll be back in half an hour."

"Okay, Luce." Katanya smiled over from the side of the pool, then returned her attention to the stopwatch in her hand. Jason (his nose white with zinc oxide) was jumping up and down in the water, and waggled his fingers at Lucinda without looking over, shouting out a string of words that seemed to have no logical connection to each other. "Weekend, cucumbers, Saturday, radish ..."

Perhaps it was the equivalent of a verbal Rorschach test, Lucinda thought, heading down the driveway. She was apprehensive about Renee's atypical request and hoped she wasn't about to be presented with a problem.

Renee was waiting in the doorway as Lucinda came up the front walk. "I thought it'd be better not to discuss this in front of the kids," she said, standing aside to let Lucinda pass.

At the time of Katanya's Fresh Air Fund visit, the four-bedroom three-bathroom colonial had been traditional, almost impersonal, looking, to Lucinda's mind, like an expensive hotel suite. Now it could have been a loft apartment in Manhattan. Renee had returned most of the furniture her parents had taken it upon themselves to provide along with the house as a wedding present for their daughter. Gone were the wall-to-wall carpeting, the chintz-covered Tuxedo sofa, the overstuffed armchairs and formal dining set complete with massive sideboard. Now, two large, very worn antique Persian rugs in time-muted red and blue designs lay on the bleached oak floors. The living and dining rooms, separated by a broad archway, had been painted a rich burgundy color, with white ceilings and trim. The matte black wood dining suite was Italian and more comfortable than the clean straight lines would have led one to expect. In the living room two enveloping black leather armchairs were paired opposite a matching sofa, separated by a low five-foot-square white-lacquered Parson's table. The trio of front windows was concealed by silver verticals. Here and there were accents of chrome, black or red. A scattering of Jason's toys lay on the floor near the white marble fireplace, and sections of that morning's *Times* sat on the coffee table next to a shallow glass bowl filled with fresh-cut flowers. The effect of the place was unexpected and pleasing, reflecting the excellent taste of the designer Renee had hired—a woman infinitely more sophisticated than her employer.

"Would you like a Diet Coke?" Renee offered, leading the way into the living room.

Lucinda declined, then said, "I do love the look of this place."

For a moment or two, the younger woman looked around as if seeing it for the first time. "It's nice," she said at last, slipping into one of the armchairs as Lucinda sank into its companion. "I never knew this would be what I wanted. I thought I'd spend my life with the same stuff that's in my parents' house. But one morning about six months after Todd did his disappearing act, I came downstairs, looked around, and decided I wanted my own place, not a newer version of the Greenwich house."

"That can happen," Lucinda said. "Is there a problem, Renee?"

"What? Oh, no. I just wanted to run something by you. The thing is, I'm making good progress on my thesis. In fact, another three or four weeks and I'll have it finished."

"That's great." Lucinda was on edge and wished Renee would come to the point. Her tendency to digress and her distracted air—very much in evidence just then—irritated Lucinda. Why have her come rushing over if there was nothing urgent?

"I remember Lorrie saying she couldn't wait to get her diploma and start working. I feel the same way now ... which is why I wanted to ask you kind of a huge favor."

"Let me guess," Lucinda said, relaxing. Why did she invariably anticipate bad news, especially when it concerned Renee? "You'd like to find out if Kat would be willing to stay on to look after Jason so you can finish. Right?"

"It's nervy of me, I know—"

"I'll have a word with Kat this evening. If she's willing, so am I." Why, Lucinda wondered, did she get the feeling that this wasn't about finishing a thesis but about not having Jason around? At that moment, she had a powerful impression that, regardless of her protestations to the contrary, Renee didn't care very much about her son. At once, Lucinda told herself she was wrong, that it was terrible of her even to think that.

"It would be a big help," Renee said.

"I understand, Renee."

"So you don't mind?"

Lucinda said, "Actually, I can't imagine Kat'll turn down a chance to stay. She's already stayed an extra week and has been dropping hints, talking about how much she hates summer in the city. No, this will work out perfectly, I'm sure."

As she walked back home on the side of the road, Lucinda couldn't help being pleased by the way things were unfolding. Katanya's staying on would mean not only that Lucinda would have even more free time to spend with her family, but also that she'd get to have Jason with her every day. And, humiliating as it was to admit it, she wouldn't have to worry about being alone with Eli.

Chapter Ten

She had no idea what prompted her to do it, but she didn't stop to question the impulse. It simply felt right. When Eli's email arrived that night with the shopping list, she wrote back at once.

Dear Eli,
You used water metaphors when speaking of Maria and I found that touching and most profound. Water is the essence of life and, clearly, Maria was essential to your life. I understand that depth of loss. It's something that goes beyond pain, something that almost requires anesthesia. But we have to stay conscious in order to do what must get done. And somehow we stagger through day after day, until the weeks begin accumulating in spite of our desire to stop time.

Finding those cartons in the garage waiting to be put out with the trash is one of the most terrible things

I've ever heard. I can't understand how someone could be so heartless, so unfeeling, particularly for a child who'd lost his mother and sister. Yet I couldn't help noting that you placed no blame. Only truly reasonable people recognize that blaming others for the conspiracies of fate is pointless. Yet so many go down that road. Perhaps it's easier to disallow personal responsibility. I don't know. I've never been able to fault others for my own failures. If anything, I am rather too good at assuming the wrongness—in any circumstance—is mine.

Thank you for telling me about your family. I'm still thinking over everything you told me.

I look forward to seeing you next Thursday.

Best, Lucinda.

She hit the Send button and the email disappeared from the screen. Then, concerned that she might come across as affected, or worse, she went into the Sent folder to reread what she'd written. No, it was all right. It was what she'd wanted to say.

Just as she clicked back to her Inbox a reply came in.

Dear Lucinda:

You pointed out something that's never occurred to me before. But you're absolutely right. Maria was essential, she was water; she was my sustenance for a very long time. You're very perceptive. That email and your observation of the metaphor was a gift, and I thank you for it.

You listen hard and you listen well. You also have an exceptional talent for language. Conspiracies of fate. That tastes almost as good as the three-hundred-dollar wine. I don't think I've ever known anyone, except a few pretentious cigar-smoking jerks, who would spend that much money on a bottle of wine. The difference is that the jerks buy it as an investment. You bought it for consumption. I admire that. The result for the jerks is their investment usually turns to something sour and unpalatable instead of the gold they'd hoped for.

It's a shame you would assume you're always in the wrong. But I understand the tendency. I have it myself. For a beautiful woman, you appear not to see yourself—particularly not as anyone else might see you. I like that about you. You have trouble with compliments, and I like that about you, too. I'm not very good at that either. But then again, I don't get all that many.

One thing I wanted to clarify. I didn't phone again after that first call because I got the impression that I'd made you uncomfortable. I did think of trying again, actually quite a few times, but decided to respect your feelings and step back. So even though our chance meeting in the parking lot last week was considerably less than a shining moment, I'm glad it offered us an opportunity to connect. I can't tell you how appalling I found that scene with "Pig" as Elise called her. In the circumstances, I thought your comment was hilarious and wonderfully fitting. I've always wished I could come up with something brilliant to say when a situation called for it. Usually, after going over and over the event in my head for hours, those brilliant somethings occur to me at three in the morning, when the only one who can appreciate them is me.

I, too, look forward to next Thursday.

My warmest regards, Eli.

Smiling, she shut down the browser, thinking—as she often did—that email was a great tool when used properly. It allowed people to express themselves in a manner they couldn't necessarily strive for or achieve in person. Face to face, there were inevitably too many distracting gauges to read: facial expression, tone of voice, physical stance. But in email the language was made to work for you. And language, as he'd noticed, was her water.

Every evening after that there was an exchange of emails. She looked forward to it with progressive eagerness. Sometimes when she opened the browser there'd be an email from Eli waiting for her. And with an inner lift, she'd read his thoughts, then respond. Sometimes she made contact first and his prompt replies led her to believe that he was not only waiting to hear from her, but also enjoying this as much as she was. It made her less fearful, more predisposed towards him, because he was so unafraid to reveal himself. She'd never known anyone like him. And when she commented on his willing openness, he replied:

… I've traveled too far along the road to fear revealing myself at this point. I'm fifty-four years old. What would be the point in hiding behind untruths, after all the trouble I've gone to to learn about myself?

In a way, our writing back and forth puts me in mind of an era when people used pens and ink and blotters, then carried their letters to the post office, returning home to wait for the arrival of the mail. Granted, this is a hell of a lot faster than any postal service. But it has that feel to it. It makes me want to reread Dickens and Wilkie Collins. I've always enjoyed those long, convoluted stories that require you to set aside the pace of the present and take the time to absorb the settings and exhaustive details that are pretty much left out of contemporary fiction. Everything's got to be fast today—our food, pop music, books, even our behaviors. Foreshortened attention spans. My elderly patients can't get enough of the big, fat books. And most of the women love Taylor Caldwell, for reasons I will probably never understand. Then again, I don't know why men so enjoy Tom Clancy. I guess I'm a closet purist.

What I've been wondering since we started our "correspondence" is whether or not you're satisfied with the status quo. I'm aware that you wrote a number of screenplays some years ago (I've seen most of those movies and have to say they were damned good scripts). With a talent like yours, I would think you'd feel compelled to write. At least, I've always understood it to be a compulsion …

She thought about it, decided there was no risk involved, and wrote back:

… a closet purist. Very nice. You're pretty good with words yourself.

There are only a few people who are aware of my second persona. But since you raised the subject and have been so complimentary about those old screenplays, I think you deserve an answer. If you click on this link you'll see some of my writing. Granted, it's not, perhaps what you had in mind. But this combines two of my greatest pleasures: film and putting words together. You haven't yet met Soupboy but I'm sure you will. Kat is staying for another month, to continue baby-sitting him while his mother, Renee (my neighbor), finishes her doctoral thesis ("Crisis at the Core"—her degree is in urban planning). He's a lovely, moody, highly imaginative boy who adores Kat (but then everybody does) and who, I have no doubt, will grow up to be a most interesting man.

I consider myself blessed to have these children in my life, in my house every day. Where before there was just the hollow sound of my footsteps echoing through an empty house, now there's little-boy laughter and Kat singing to herself in the shower (she claims the guest bathroom has perfect acoustics and much prefers it to the one in the barn where she stays on the weekends when her mother and grandmother come up from the city). Sometimes I stop and look at their so-young faces and have to wonder why I didn't go completely mad during those twenty-seven years of hiding ...

"Are you doing another web editing job?" Katanya asked, coming into the living room with a small bottle of Evian for Lucinda.

Lucinda thanked her, then said, "What makes you ask that?"

"Well, every night you zoom in here right after dinner and then you're back and forth for an hour or two. So are you?"

"No. It's … uhm … Eli and I have been emailing."

"Get *out*!" Katanya grinned. "That is so cool, Luce. I *knew* you liked him!"

"Well, I'm beginning to."

"You're like a kid," Katanya said, sitting cross-legged on the sofa. "It's sweet. Really, Luce. I could tell he liked you."

"How?" Lucinda asked, crossing the room to sit next to her, perpetually taken with Katanya's awareness of what went on around her.

"For one thing, the way he looked at you—like you were candy and he had a sugar jones."

"A sugar jones," Lucinda repeated, much amused. "Funny, but an exaggeration. We're just friends." Lucinda opened the bottle and drank some of the water.

"I was only teasing," the girl said, sliding over to give Lucinda a hug. "I should know not to. You always think I'm serious."

"That's because I'm socially retarded," Lucinda said, resting her cheek against the top of Katanya's head. "Everybody knows that."

"Go on back to the computer if you want to. I won't tease you about it anymore."

"I'm enjoying the emails, Kat. But I have no illusions. He's very bright and we're exchanging *thoughts*, not promises. This is something different for me. The last time I had any kind of an exchange with a man I was nineteen years old."

"What happened?"

"I broke off my engagement."

"Yeah, you told me you bagged out? *Why*?" Katanya asked.

"Because my mother had just died of breast cancer. I'd just discovered that I was a person of color. And I was scheduled for surgery to have my breasts removed. I didn't feel it was fair to inflict all that on my fiancé."

"Whoa! That's a whole lot of information. Let's talk about the first thing. Did he try to make you change your mind?"

"The probability that I was part black didn't matter to him. But the surgery … That shook him. Cort wasn't shallow, but he was very young and I think the idea of living with someone disfigured was more than he could handle. Basically, I painted a lot of ugly pictures and drove him away. I was trying to spare him. Instead I wound up being cruel."

"Cuz you were scared. Right? How it works is you hurt someone before they can hurt you."

"In a way," Lucinda said. "Have you done that, Kat?"

"Nothing that harsh, but yeah. Some geek at school thinks you're a hottie and has eyes. You don't want to hurt him but you've got to point him in another direction. It's no fun, but sometimes you have to. Did you have cancer, too?"

"No, I didn't."

"So why did you have to have your breasts removed?" Katanya asked a bit fearfully, one hand automatically going to her own dainty bosom.

"It was considered a radical procedure at the time, something they weren't sure would work. But I went ahead with the surgery, hoping that it would, so that I wouldn't die the way my mother and aunt and grandmother did. The way Eli's wife did."

"His *wife* had it, too?"

Lucinda nodded. "Eli and I have a lot in common, Kat. You do understand I'm not telling you this to upset you."

"No. You're telling me so I'll know why you're nervous with him. Right?"

"Right."

"But Luce … Why should that matter? I mean about your surgery and the rest of it."

"I don't know, honey. It just does. As much as we think we know people, they can always surprise us. Like my aunt Anne. She seemed so awful."

"That's for sure."

"I think the truth is she was unhappy and wanted everyone to love her. But she didn't know how to make that happen."

"You think?" Katanya looked unconvinced.

"I've given it a lot of thought and I do believe that. I wish I'd figured it out sooner, although I doubt it would've made any difference. It's one thing to want to be loved. It's something else if you don't know how to accept it, when it's offered."

"I guess that could be true," Katanya said.

"Anyway," Lucinda went on, "I don't want to let myself in for any unpleasant surprises at this stage of my life. So I'm somewhat overcautious. There's an expression: Old habits die hard. This is an old, old habit of mine."

Katanya hugged her again, murmuring, "I love you, Luce, and I wish you didn't worry so much about stuff like this."

"To be completely honest, I find it kind of scary to have someone interested in me. You saw what a dolt I was at dinner last week."

"You were okay, just nervous. And he's nice, *really* nice."

"Yes, he is. In a way, that makes it worse."

"Maybe. It's not the greatest feeling shutting down a geek. I have to say, though, there's zero geekiness about Eli. But if you like the man and he likes you, I guess it's tricky cuz you don't want to get your hopes up."

"No."

"But I *know* you guys'll be good. I absolutely know it."

"Honey, we'll be good because the only thing on the table is friendship."

"Okay. I hear you. I'll drop it. But can I ask you one thing?"

"Of course you can."

"This probably sounds stupid, but all the time I've known you I thought you were just flat-chested. And that was cool. Big bazongas are a nightmare for some of the girls in the dance program. In the 'hood, that's a whole other story. Big tits, big ass and you're a magnet. But at school, the guys are drooling, they're practically doing the bad 'nads boogie, and the girls ignore them or flip them off. All they talk about over lunch is breast reduction, which gets v-e-r-y tired after a while. Now you tell me about the surgery, but you don't wear bras or like that. I've seen ads for those things you can wear that make it look as if you've got a chest. So my question is: How come you're not into any of that?"

"After the surgery, I thought about it. I finally decided that my wearing bras with prosthetic breasts would be dishonest."

"How so?"

"I was already on shaky ground, not knowing how to be a person of color, not knowing how to *be,* period. To pretend to have breasts when I didn't ... Anyway, there was no one to see, so what difference did it make?"

"I can get with that," Katanya said thoughtfully. "You're very honest and really brave."

"Oh, I'm not, honey. I'm the biggest coward you'll ever know."

"You're not. And I won't listen." Katanya put her fingers in her ears and started singing, "Lalalalala."

"Okay," Lucinda said, tugging at the girl's arm. "I've got a couple of videos to watch. Interested?"

"Sure. Uh-oh!" she said, hearing the chime from Lucinda's computer indicating the arrival of email. "You go see what Eli has to say. While you do that, I'll go check *my* email, then come back and we'll watch a vid-flick. Okay?"

Dear Lucinda,

I'm flabbergasted. You are Ella Van Dyne! I'm a big, big fan of the column. Am I correct in guessing that Jason is Soupboy? If so, I can't wait to meet him. He's got quite a gift for coining words. My personal favorite is "gorpo." I've encountered a lot of people who fit the description perfectly. The incredible thing is, I always look to see what you've said about a movie before I'll go see it. If you say it's a stinker, I give it a miss. There hasn't been one where you haven't been right on the money.

And if that isn't enough, you're an Academy Award winner! Flight Plan was a terrific movie. I thought that Gin (I just now clued in to the fact that the Gin you spoke of the other night is The Gin) should've had the Best Actress award. She was robbed. Her performance was heart-rending, without once being "actory"—if there is such a word.

I'm honored that you'd trust me with this, Lucinda. I'll keep it to myself. In fact, I'll probably horde it and gloat, like a miner who's found the mother lode. Just one question. Where did the name Ella Van Dyne come from? Was it something you just made up, or is there a subtext? If I'm overstepping the bounds of polite curiosity, just say so.

We are going to have a lot to talk about Thursday. It's great to know that your obvious talent is being put to such good use …

Dear Eli,

Kat's upstairs checking her email, then we're going to watch a video, so I'll make this short. I met Gin when we were kids at school on the studio lot. First she nicknamed me Cinders, then it evolved into Ella. As you may know, Ella Cinders was a comic strip character way back—as Kat says—in the day.

When we started working on the first of our screenplays, we put our heads together to come up with a name we could register with the Screenwriters Guild. Gin and I both liked the Philo Vance novels by S. S. Van Dine. We also liked the name, so we decided to change the spelling and use it. And that's how Ella Van Dyne was born.

Gin alternates between calling me Luce and Ella. Luce when she's serious; Ella when she's in a playful mood. Kiddo when she's either one. You'll get to meet her; she is my oldest, dearest friend and one of the best people ever.

It makes me both happy and mildly daunted to know that you make decisions on which films you'll see based on my reviews.

I hear Kat galloping down the stairs so I'll say goodnight now.

My best to you, Lucinda.

"Done?" Katanya asked from the doorway.

"All done. Just shutting down."

"What're we watching?"

"We've got three. You pick."

"Popcorn?"

"I'll nuke it while you cue up the movie. Okay?"

"Yup. Good e from Eli?"

"The man gives great e, Kat."

"Ooooo, you wicked, girlfren!"

"Yo, yo, yo. I be wicked." Lucinda was laughing as she started for the kitchen.

Thursday evening when Eli arrived, Lucinda had to resist her immediate impulse to hug him. She smiled, abashed, and finding her voice, she said, "Hi. Come in, Eli."

"I'm really enjoying the emails, Lucinda," he said. "Please don't regret whatever prompted you to write to me."

"No, I'm enjoying them, too."

"This is for you," he said, handing her a small box.

"Should I open it now?"

"Only if you can't contain your curiosity."

She studied him for a long moment, then lifted the lid. Inside the box, resting on a bed of tissue paper was a sun-bleached sea urchin shell. "This is beautiful. Thank you."

"From the sea," he said. "Water."

"It's beautiful," she repeated softly, running her fingers over its pebbled surface that had once been covered with black spines. At last, she said, "Everything's ready for the chef." She started toward the kitchen then turned back. "Eli, you smell delicious. What is that scent?"

"It's Joup." He pronounced it yoop.

"Joup," she repeated as they came into the kitchen.

"Hey, Eli!" Katanya came dancing across the room to hug him. "What's a yoop?"

"My aftershave."

Katanya sniffed at him. "That's a yoop? It's dee-vine. What've you got, Luce?"

Lucinda handed her the box. "It's a sea urchin."

"It's so pretty. Don't I get a present, too?" she asked with a laugh.

"Right here," he said, pulling a small paper bag from his pocket.

"I was only kidding," Katanya said, taken aback.

"I know, but I wasn't. This is for you."

"Junior Mints and Nibs! My faves! Thanks, Eli!" She gave him another hug. "How'd you know?"

"My faves, too," he admitted.

"I think," Lucinda said, "tonight we'll open the six-hundred-dollar bottle of wine."

"Are you sure about that?" Eli asked.

"Oh, yes," Lucinda said, setting the box with the sea urchin on top of the refrigerator, out of harm's way. "Don't you, Kat?"

"Definitely!"

"Okay!" Eli said, studying the ingredients Lucinda had assembled on the counter. "Let's get this show on the road."

"This is so fun!" Kat declared, getting the corkscrew.

Lucinda got wine glasses from the cupboard, set them on the counter, then, giving in to another impulse, she kissed Eli's cheek. "Thank you," she whispered, and felt her ears turn hot.

"That was a sudden move!" Eli accused happily.

"You said *you* wouldn't make any," Lucinda said boldly. "I didn't say *I* wouldn't."

"You guys," Kat said, shaking her head. "You are such *kids*."

That was it, Lucinda thought light-headedly: the feeling of being young again, of having a good time and not being preoccupied with surfaces; of being susceptible to possibility.

Chapter Eleven

Dear Lucinda:
I thought it only fair to warn you that Elise has invited me to come to dinner on Friday evening. I know this is usually a family affair but Elise has assured me that I fall within the rules of exception. Still, I'd like to be sure that it's not a problem for you. I hate the idea of upsetting you and this comes perilously close to our sudden moves agreement ...

Dear Eli:
Actually, Elise had already told me that you'd be coming. Gin will also be there, so you'll finally have a chance to meet her. I appreciate your concern for my feelings, but it's perfectly fine with me. In fact, I'm looking forward to it. You must be, too—a dinner you don't actually have to prepare. I'm sure you must know how wonderful Erica's cooking is. She and Elise

plan meals as if they're organizing a military operation. It's quite something to watch. They go through Elise's three-ring binder of recipes and deliberate over everything from the appetizers to the dessert.

Perhaps living alone for so long warped my ideas about cooking. I could never see the point of going to all that trouble just to make a meal for myself. Luckily, since Trader Joe's came to the area, I've been able to stock my freezer with really good frozen food. But before '97 when the store opened, I have to confess I ate a lot of sandwiches and cereal. If you tell anyone that, I'm afraid I'll have to kill you ...

… Lucinda, you do make me laugh. You'll have to kill me? Me? Sandwiches and cereal have been the mainstays of my diet for a few years now. Nobody likes cooking for one; it's too much of a bother—which is why I've been so happy to try out my cooking-class skills on you and Kat. Anyway, I hope the playing field has now been leveled and you won't have to kill me.

I'm relieved to know my coming to dinner Friday night isn't a problem for you. I was hoping it wouldn't be. I know you don't like "surprises," (which skirt too close to being sudden moves) so I'll do my best not to spring any on you. I can't wait to meet Gin. I will try not to act like the fawning fan that I am. I'd have said groupie, but I'm too old to qualify as one of those.

I had a great time at the pool with the kids. Being with Jason took me back to when Manny and Raf were little; it's almost a sense-memory—that rowdy, endless energy small boys have, their coppery little-boy smell and the amazing clarity and directness of their eyes. Kat is great with him. She's a great girl altogether. When she suddenly breaks into song, I swear I get goose bumps. If you hadn't, in an early email, told me about her singing in the bathroom I don't know what I'd have thought. It was certainly unexpected and my heart paused for a few beats. Clearly, singing is Kat's instinctive way of expressing joy. We should all be so gifted, so unrestrained. I hope you'll invite me again before Kat goes home.

Just one question. Why did you stay in the shade and watch, instead of coming into the water?

She sat and stared at the computer screen, trying to think of how to answer his question. She'd been prepared to swim, her suit and T-shirt at the ready. Then, suddenly, she had imagined Eli seeing her wet—the T-shirt highlighting her obvious lack of breasts—and she couldn't do it. Instead, she'd kept her dress on and sat at the poolside to watch Eli with Kat and Soupboy. No matter how often she told herself it shouldn't matter, it did. And it was too late in the day to go down the road of buying bras and the forms to stuff into them. She'd never liked confining undergarments in any case, so in a way it would've been hypocritical. But that was a side issue. The point was that she was disfigured, and it was one thing to get into the pool with the kids, or Gin, or her cousins. It was another thing altogether to reveal herself to Eli.

... I did intend to swim but in the end I was glad I didn't. It gave me a chance to enjoy the three of you. You were lovely with the children, Eli. I have to believe you're a very good father. So many people say they like children but few really do. The ones who do, like you and my grandmother, Jeneva, Lorrie and Gin, don't place artificial barriers between themselves and children. They interact on the same level as the one in place when they deal with adults. I've found that to be rare. Growing up in Hollywood, there were so many people who left the care and feeding of their children to employees. The children were grief-stricken when the employees left, and the parents were shocked and indignant at the unwarranted (to their minds) affection the children had for their nannies, and so treated the kids like traitors. They were even more shocked when as teens the kids went bad, got into trouble and often bottomed out. Or worse, their kids went into the business and wrote tell-all books that distorted the truth of their experiences. But you can't turn the care of children over to others and not expect the children to bond with the caregivers.

I'm rambling and off topic. I can't give you a direct answer, Eli, about why I didn't get into the pool. I'm not there yet. But I'm looking forward to seeing you Friday evening ...

She shut down the browser and sat looking at the computer screen, thinking there were all kinds of barriers. Some were self-imposed, like hers, and grew from fear like city tree roots forcing themselves upward through the cracks in sidewalks, causing the pavement to buckle and heave. She had no idea if her particular fear was surmountable. Katanya was upstairs, singing in the shower, and her voice wafted down through the house like a caress. With a slow exhalation, Lucinda turned off the computer but continued to sit at the desk, wondering. If fear kept you from having what you wanted, did that mean you didn't want it badly enough?

She got up and walked over to the bookcase to look at the photograph that had arrived earlier in the week. It had come by courier, carefully enclosed in bubble-wrap, with a note from Madeline that said, "In a final codicil, Mother left instructions that you were to have this. I truly cannot fathom why, but perhaps you can. Probate continues to drag on, but I couldn't see any reason not to send this to you now. Much love, Maddie."

It was a black-and-white studio portrait of Anne, taken when she was perhaps seven or eight. And it was proof that the conclusions Lucinda had drawn were correct. Anne *had* wanted Lucinda to know and love the beautiful little girl Anne once had been; she'd wanted Lucinda to see past the foolishly decorated surface, past the wreckage, all the way back to the time when, her heart undamaged, Anne had been a happy child, her eyes alight with mischievous energy, love, and hope.

Lucinda loved the portrait and wanted to believe that somewhere Anne knew that she had a place of honor in Lucinda's home, and in her heart.

"They have made a friendship," Elise observed happily.

"It's amazing," Lucinda said. "Gin is almost never comfortable with men, except for her gay friends."

"I have seen this in her," Elise said. "Something—a very long time ago, I think—has damaged her, made her very cautious. She is not what she would seem in films."

"No," Lucinda agreed, perpetually in awe of her grandmother's astuteness, "she isn't. At all."

"She reminds me very much of Lily. They are different, yet in many ways the same."

"I think so, too. They seemed more like mother and daughter than Lily and I ever did. When we were kids, people who didn't recognize them—because neither one of them, as you know, ever played 'movie star' in public—they automatically assumed Gin was Lily's daughter and I was the friend."

"And how was that for you?" Elise asked with keen interest.

"I liked it," Lucinda said. "Gin's always been far more than just a friend. Her mother was an *awful* woman, who really didn't care what happened to her daughter, as long as she kept on making money. The ironic part of it is, Gin was the one who wanted to be in movies. Her mother wasn't one of those terrible stage mothers who push their kids into the business. She was just deeply stupid, uncaring, cold. I've never been able to understand people who don't care about their children."

"I think the same," Elise said. "And you like it now that Gin is making a friendship with Eli?"

"Of course," Lucinda said, surprised but also pleased by the question. "Gin's my barometer. If she had a problem with Eli, I would, too. Her friendship is more important to me than any man could ever be."

"This is wise," Elise said approvingly. "So many women put aside their friends if a man appears. When the man is gone, there are no friends. Have I told you that Gwyn will be leaving me?"

"When? Why?" This was a surprise. Lucinda had assumed that Gwyn, in her capacity as Elise's personal assistant, was, like the cook, Erica, a permanent fixture.

"Her husband is to retire. In October they will move to Arizona. After sixteen years, it will be difficult without her."

"Do you plan to hire someone else?"

"I must consider it," Elise said. "It will not be easy to find someone who suits me so well."

"You know who'd be perfect?" Lucinda asked, with sudden inspiration. "Jeneva. Mrs. Weinburg has been very lonely, very unhappy since her husband died. Her son would like her to sell the apartment and come live with his family."

"Yes? And when is this to happen?"

"I don't know. Would you like me to ask Jen if she'd be interested, or would you prefer to ask her yourself?"

"You think she would come each day from the city?"

"She might. Shall I ask her?"

"I would adore to have her here. And so would you, I think, hmn?"

Lucinda laughed softly. "I'd adore to have all three of them here, to be honest. But Lorrie's got a great new job and Kat's got one more year of high school. Otherwise, I'd be trying my damnedest to get them to move to Connecticut."

"I will speak with Jeneva," Elise said. "It is a brilliant idea." She patted Lucinda's cheek before making her way over to the sofa where Jeneva and Paul Junior sat chatting.

Lucinda glanced across at the sound of Gin's laughter and saw her friend punch Eli lightly on the upper arm. All at once, she wanted to go over and lean against the man the way Soupboy so often leaned against her. She had no doubt that it would be immensely comforting. Also immensely embarrassing. Smiling, Lucinda went to join them.

~

"That is one of the nicest, funniest, best-looking guys I've ever met," Gin declared, taking a drag on her cigarette. "If they were all like him, I'd be able to recommend the species."

Lucinda laughed. "When you punched him in the arm, I knew it was okay."

"Yeah. It's not as if I punch just anybody."

"No. I know that. You're very discriminating about who gets to be punched."

"Damn right, kiddo. So what's up with the two of you?"

"Nothing's *up* with us. We're friends. He's good company."

"*Please*. He's a hell of a lot more than just good company. He's crazy about you. And what, you're scared of him? What's with you?"

"I'm not scared of *him*, Gin."

Gin stared hard at her for several seconds, then said, "My god! Are you going to let that surgery ruin things a second time? Do you know how nuts that is? You really think a grown-up, decent guy like that is only thinking about sex? Or that it would matter to him?"

"It matters to me," Lucinda said quietly.

Gin took another drag, then stubbed out her cigarette and put the ashtray down on the terrace wall next to where she and Lucinda were sitting and said, "Listen good, kiddo. Two things. First, you just admitted you're interested in more than friendship. Second, this is coming from me, from someone who never had any breastworks to begin with. Okay? The only person who cares about your chest is you. *You are the only one*. Wanna do that thing where we put our shoes in the pile? Wanna run a comparison check? 'Cause we can do that and you're going to be happy to take your shoes back and wear them home."

"I know."

"I don't think you do. So let me refresh your memory. I'm the one who's had body doubles for every single skin scene in any film I've done, ever. I don't do the pasties and the gauze undies. I don't show *anybody anything*. Ever seen me without clothes on?"

"No."

"Right. I'm the one who has to run to the nearest bathroom to throw up, then gargle with Listerine after shooting close-up kisses where you can't cheat the scene. Okay? The crews have always covered for me, thank god, because I treat them right, with respect. I'm the middle-aged sex symbol whose PRs have, from day dot, had to warn every arranged date not to touch me, unless we were in front of the public. You wanna take back your shoes yet? Or should I go on?"

"It's different—"

"Fuck that, Lucinda! It's *way* beyond just *different*. It's honest-to-god genuine impairment, versus your self-induced whatever it is. Nobody ever *harmed* you. Nobody. Not ever. And I would *kill* anybody who ever tried. What I'm saying is, your memory's a clean slate in the harm department. I'll swap you, right now, right here. Your memory for mine. I really would, you know. I'd give anything to feel normal—or whatever passes for it—just once, for even an hour. I'd give anything to meet a guy as terrific as Eli and not shrivel up at the thought of him coming anywhere near me. I've got an actual reason, as you very well know. The things that sick bastard *said*! I still have nightmares where he's whispering to me, and I wake up sweating and shaking. All these years later and I can't get the son of a bitch out of my head. You saw him in action for years, Luce. You know Lloyd Rankin ruined lives. Not one of those kids at the studio ever got over what he did to them. Okay, I didn't let him ruin my career, or my brain, but he sure as hell ruined my life as a woman. So I didn't get over it either. Listen to me! Don't let the surgery you had done to keep you alive spoil your chance with this man, Luce. You had a good reason. It was the *smart* thing, the *right* thing to do. You wanted to live, so you did what had to be done. And here you are, alive. You're out in the world again, you've got your family, and friends. You've got a *life*."

"Yes I do," Lucinda said quietly, grieved always by the enormity of Gin's losses.

"It's still early in the day," Gin said, her calmly. "Give this an honest chance, kiddo. Don't kill it because you *think* what worries you would worry him. It's just so lame. You're way too smart to let that get in the way of something that could be great—for both of you."

"I can't promise you I'm going to flick a switch and get past how I feel, Gin."

"I know that. All I'm saying is keep an open mind. Don't do the man's thinking for him. He's not rushing at you, is he?"

"No."

"So okay! Allow for the possibility that he's grown up enough to care about the person you are. We're getting old here, for crying out loud. Nobody over fifty has one of those tight little bodies the twenty-year-olds have. Nobody who hasn't been surgeried within an inch of their lives, that is. I mean, jeez-*us*, would you want to look like Cher? How scary would *that* be?"

They both started laughing.

Slinging her arm around Lucinda's shoulders, Gin said, "Be happy, Luce. I'll enjoy it vicariously, the way I always have, and be happy as hell for you."

"What're you guys laughing about?" Katanya asked, coming over to sit on the wall beside Lucinda.

"I'm giving Luce a little pep talk," Gin told her.

"Yeah? What about, Eli?"

"God! Did all of you have a conference or something?" Lucinda said nervously.

"Who all?" Gin asked.

"First Kat, then Elise, now you," Lucinda explained. "Message received. Okay?"

"Everybody likes him," Kat said reasonably. "You should like him, too."

"I do. Please let's drop it now. I'm starting to feel bruised from getting beat up one way and another."

"Hah!" Gin scoffed. "I'll give you bruises," she said, and punched Lucinda's upper arm. "You and your mom gonna sing, cupcake?" she asked Katanya.

"Sure. You comin' back in?"

"We are. Gin just needed a cigarette."

"Smoking's gross," Katanya said, getting to her feet.

"Tell me about it!" Gin said. "You think I'd have started forty years ago if I'd known I'd wind up a nicotine junkie?"

"Forty years? That's older than my moms."

"Yup, started when I was a year old," Gin said, then laughed madly, grabbing Lucinda's hand and pulling her upright. "Come on. There's gonna be Taylor Family music. Can't miss that."

"Hurry up, you guys," Katanya said over her shoulder, hurrying back inside through the French doors.

"We'll be right there," Lucinda called to her.

"You pissed off?" Gin asked.

"At you? Never. At myself? Always."

"Get over it! Seriously. I happen to be very damned glad you had that surgery, Luce. I would've been lost without you. I'd never have made it this far."

"You would—"

"I would *not* have made it," Gin insisted. "Even locked up in that goddamned house, you kept me going all these years. Just knowing you were alive in the world was enough, even if it took you months to pick up the phone. You and Lily were the ones who believed in me, no matter what. Your writing got me to the top, and it's keeping me there. Now enough of this maudlin shit. Gimme a hug, then we'll go inside. I wanna hear those two sing." She wrapped her arms around Lucinda. "I love you, Luce. If you're happy, I'm happy."

"I love *you*. I'll try," Lucinda promised. "I will try."

"Try hard!" Gin said, releasing her.

As they stepped back into the dining room, Eli came over, saying, "Were you out there swapping war stories?"

"Depends on what you mean by war stories," Gin said, eyebrows lifted.

"It was a pep rally," Lucinda told him.

"I'm not going to ask." Eli held up both hands palms outward.

"Wise man," Lucinda said.

"Nope, chicken," he corrected her. "I'm not about to take on the two of you."

With a laugh, Gin left them to make her way over to the group gathered around the piano. And, at once, Lucinda was sober and alert. *Why was she fine with Eli when other people were around, and hopeless when it was just the two of them? He wasn't going to say or do anything that might upset her. She knew that.*

She studied his face, the humor that illuminated his eyes, and without knowing she would, she let gravity prevail. As if gently pushed by an unseen hand, she leaned against him and closed her eyes, breathing in the now-familiar scent of Joup. He kissed her forehead, then whispered, "That was another sudden move."

"I know," she whispered back, absorbing his warmth, the solid mass of his body for a moment longer before stepping away. "Jason does that to me almost every day. I wanted to know how it feels."

"How *did* it feel?" he asked.

"The way I thought it would," she answered enigmatically.

He frowned. "Are you telling me something, Lucinda?"

"I don't know what you mean."

"Kat's going home on Sunday. I thought maybe this was your way of saying goodbye."

She'd forgotten that. Her heartbeat accelerated and she chewed on her lower lip for a moment. "I don't think that's what I was doing," she said uncertainly.

"I've been expecting the invitations to stop once she leaves."

She shook her head. She'd also failed to take into account that he might have fears of his own. Was she self-absorbed to the point of ignoring other people's feelings? Was she, like Jason, someone whose fear could—like a one-way mirror in a bad TV cop show—block out everything but her own reflection? "I would miss you, Eli."

His brow smoothed and he smiled. "That's the nicest thing you've ever said to me. So we're on for next Thursday? I don't have to cook. We could go out."

"Let's play it by ear. Is that okay?"

"That's fine. I'd miss you, too, you know."

"Would you?"

He smiled indulgently. "I would, more than you might think."

"Sometimes," she said slowly, "my thinking is like an endless loop. It just goes around and around, circling the same points repeatedly."

"I've been there. Just pull the cord and the conductor will stop the train."

It was her turn to smile. "Nice," she said. "Maybe you should reconsider your writing career."

"I don't think so. Come on," he said. "They're starting," and took her hand to lead her back to the living room.

Chapter Twelve

Dear Eli:

If the offer is still good, let's go out to dinner. Not because Kat isn't here but because I'd like to. Symbolic, perhaps. Stepping out on the high-wire without a net. I'm bored with the inside of my head. It's like the attic of this house—filled with dusty boxes of things that have value only to me and to collectors, film buffs and dealers. Heaven knows, there's not a big line of people waiting to collect anything stored upstairs in my head.

It's your call. We can go to a place of your choosing; it can be dress up or dress down. Let me know. As you've noticed, dressing down is what I do best. But I think I remember how dressing up works.

I have to confess that I miss Kat terribly. The house seems very vacant and I feel like an apparition, drifting through the rooms, unintentionally alarming the new occupants who bought the place, never dreaming it was haunted ...

Dear Lucinda:
Very gothic imagery. Less than a week alone and you're feeling like a ghost. That's not good. So my idea is we dress up and go to La Crémaillère in Banksville. I'll make a reservation, provided you're willing. If you've never been there, you're in for a treat. They even have wines in that stratospheric price range you enjoy, as well as the best ice cream and sorbets anywhere outside of Paris. (The one time Maria and I were in Paris, I kept buying lemon sorbets from street vendors. I had dozens of them over the course of a week and finally couldn't _think_ about having one more. I swear my entire body shriveled from the acid content and my mouth was pursed like an old-maid school teacher's. The upside was the impossibility of my ever contracting scurvy.) The only wrinkle to dinner on Thursday is that we'll have to be there on the early side because they take the last dinner orders at eight. It's only a thirty or forty minute drive, just over the New York line, so we should leave at six-fifteen, unless that's a problem, or if your preference is for dressing down.

I'll go give my good shoes a polish right now—on the off chance that you'll want dig out your glad rags. I'm really looking forward to this. Assuming you agree with my suggestion, shall I drive, or would you prefer to chauffeur us in, gulp, The Bentley? I have to confess I am deeply in awe/envy of that car ...

Dear Eli:
In awe/envy of the Bentley? You sound like Hernan, a sweet young neighbor of Kat's whose dream is one day to own a service center for foreign cars. Right now, he's working as a mechanic for a BMW dealership in the Bronx (which he hates, but he wants the certification; he's already certified for Benz and Jaguar—which he claims is ridiculous because the late-model Jaguars have Ford engines) and he takes care of the Mulsanne for me on his own time.

I am willing to play dress-up, and will go in search of my ancient glad rags. If you're serious about your awe/envy, I'll be happy to let you drive the Bentley. I tend to be rather a nervous passenger, but you probably already guessed that—given how obvious it is that almost everything makes me nervous. I didn't used to be this way. Sometimes I look at the girl I once was from the distance of time and I can see all she had that is now gone forever. Do you do that, look backwards and remark upon the young you?

Doesn't it seem that summer went too quickly? Or is that another age issue? When I was a child, summer stretched off into infinity. Now it seems to come and go in hours. I won't miss the heat but I do miss Kat—terribly. I miss her suddenly breaking into song, and the sound of her and Soupboy splashing about in the pool—his occasional squeals and shouts, his calling for Kat to, "Look! Look!" while he cannonballs into the water or does a particularly well-executed dive (he practiced endlessly). It's already August 30th and the kids go back to school next week. September's upon us and what I've always thought of as "the sad season" begins (leaves and flowers all darkening and dying, the days getting short). Of course, my usual routine with Jason will begin again on Wednesday—which is a good thing. I need to have a destination. It's important for my personal momentum.

As well, my former anxiety and ambivalence are down to a manageable level, having had the chance to spend extra time with Elise and the rest of the family during the past few months.

I tell you so much in these emails; sometimes it amazes me, and I wish it were as effortless to communicate face-to-face, but so many things get in the way—particularly those dusty items in my mental attic … I must go examine the contents of the closet, to see if I own anything that hasn't long-since decayed like Miss Havisham's wedding dress.

"I was right," she said. "You are a good driver."

"Thank you." He glanced over at her with a smile, then returned his attention to the road. "If it's okay with you, I'm going to get off at the next exit and take the back roads. The Merritt might have been high-tech back in 'thirty-nine when it opened, but at night it's just scary."

"That's fine. It's a little strange sitting over here. No one else has ever driven this car—at least not with me in it."

"I am honored. It's a thing of beauty. Not maybe what Keats had in mind, but definitely by my standards."

"You're honored and I'm impressed," she said. "Quoting Keats. You're full of surprises."

"All those school vacations when I didn't go home, I spent a lot of time in the library. I've always been a bookworm."

"Me, too. That was a wonderful, wonderful dinner, Eli.

If I kept a diary, I'd go home and write an entry about the goat cheese and beet gateau, and the *crême brulée* ice cream. Thank you again."

"My pleasure. An evening entirely of firsts."

"I know," she said quietly. "I'm amazed I'm still coherent."

"Did you think this outing would turn you to stone?" he asked with a laugh.

"I used to be a very social being, believe it or not."

"I believe it. Just because you're shy doesn't mean you're incapable of social interaction."

Every so often he'd make an observation like this and she'd be taken aback by his understanding.

"You're very kind."

"So are you." He signaled and slowed as the next off-ramp came into view. "Someday they'll put lights on this parkway. When they do, I'll reconsider my feelings about it."

They were silent for a time and Lucinda gazed at the road ahead, with the odd sensation that the car was driving them. She wondered if it was how Lily felt whenever she'd climbed behind the wheel of the old Cadillac, which would explain why she had disliked driving.

As the car traveled the back roads, she reviewed the dinner—the lovely eighteenth century farmhouse and attentive staff, the charming *sommelier* presenting Eli's selected bottle of Bordeaux, the flowered Provençal tableware. She thought of her parents in France, awaiting her birth, dining in some *auberge* where the staff saw nothing extraordinary in a mixed-race couple out for a meal. "I'd like to go there someday," she said.

"Where?"

"To the south of France where Adam and Lily lived, where I was born."

"Then you should," he said. "I'd want to see the place, if it were me."

"Have you traveled a lot, Eli?"

"Quite a lot. Maria loved to travel. I didn't much like the hassles of getting there—cabs and check-ins, crowded airports and all that—but once we arrived wherever we were going, I loved it. Our last vacation, we drove around Europe. It was the strangest thing. As long as we were in the countryside it was clear we were somewhere foreign. But we couldn't help noticing that most of the big cities—this was in the late eighties—had become interchangeable. It was scary. American chain restaurants on the main drag of every city: Pizza Hut, McDonalds, Burger King; franchise stores of all kinds: Benneton, The Gap. Lots of loud rock music, lots of neon. We could've been anywhere, suburban Chicago or Oxford Street in London. The only difference was the architecture of the buildings, the houses, once you got away from the city center. We stuck to small towns after that. They gave us more of a sense of place. It was disturbing, though. I couldn't stop thinking about that moment in Amsterdam when we found ourselves in a sea of tourists from all over the world, most of them flocking into American fast-food outlets, and I realized we could be anywhere. There was nothing to distinguish that street from any other."

"When Lily and I moved here from California, there were lots of small bookstores, shops. One by one they all shut down and the chains came. I miss those shops and the bookstores most of all."

"Me, too. Shopping on Amazon is expedient but not satisfying. Neither is going into one of the superstores. Sometimes, when I need a bookstore fix, I'll go into the city to one of the few surviving small independent bookstores with an old-fashioned cash register and a cranky owner who actually knows the stock and has read most of it."

Lucinda laughed. "Let me know and I'll go with you."

"You're on. I dreamed of you the other night."

"You did?" At once, she was apprehensive.

"It was strange," he said, then quickly added, "nothing sexual," and glanced over at her, then back at the road.

"Oh! So I'm not an object of lust," she quipped, then was shocked at herself.

He now laughed. "Don't be so sure of that," he countered. "Depends on the interpretation you put on lust. I like your brain."

"Should I be disappointed?" she asked, grateful for the darkness of the car's interior.

"Never! Seriously, it's the highest compliment I can offer. 'The sad season,'" he quoted, "'leaves and flowers all darkening and dying.' I read your emails and in one sentence you stop me in my tracks with your use of language; in the next, you have me laughing out loud. That was a nifty reference to Miss Havisham's wedding dress."

"You quoted Keats," she returned.

"True. And that dress, by the way, isn't remotely reminiscent of poor Miss Havisham's. You look very elegant."

"Elegant? I think of French or Italian women of a certain age as being elegant. But not me. I just went with Gin's basic code of The Little Black Dress."

"Elegant," he insisted. "I like the Gibson Girl topknot, too."

"Gibson Girl? Are you dating yourself?"

"Yup. I remember Teddy Roosevelt and his Roughriders as if it was yesterday. Listen, it's still early. How about some coffee? Unless you want to get right home."

"No, coffee would be great. Where?"

"The diner up the Post Road? It's my favorite late-night spot."

"Did Kat or Soupboy tell you?"

"Tell me what?"

"I've been hanging out at that diner since my days at Yale."

"No kidding! It's at least thirty years since I started dropping in for a coffee on nights I worked late. The diner was my transition spot. I'd take fifteen or twenty minutes to clear my head so I didn't take my work home. I'm surprised I've never run into you there."

"We didn't know each other," she reminded him.

"True. Would you prefer somewhere else?"

"No, the diner is fine."

Elena was at the cash register when they came in and offered them one of her brilliant smiles. Coming out from behind the counter, she looked first at Lucinda, then at Eli, asking, "You friends?"

Lucinda and Eli answered together, "Yes."

"I not know this. Come." Elena signaled, leading the way to a booth and slipping into the seat opposite to look again from one to the other. "Is good," she said, smiling away. "How you, Eli?"

"I'm terrific. How are you?"

"Good. And Lucinda, is good see you. I not know you friend to Eli. You nice couple together. Look good." She nodded happily. "Is surprise."

"How's the baby?" Eli asked.

"Baby almost five year old now."

"Five?" Lucinda could remember so clearly stopping in for coffee the day she was to meet her grandmother for the first time, and Elena had glowed, telling how she was soon to be a grandmother herself.

"Five," Elena confirmed. "Goin' to school nex' week. You look ver' beautiful, Lucinda."

Her face hot, Lucinda thanked her.

"Both, you look—" She struggled to find a word. "Is nice, you friends together. I get coffee," Elena said and slid out of the booth.

"It's crazy," Lucinda said with a shake of her head, "her knowing both of us."

"Maybe a little. I have to agree with her. You do look very beautiful."

She was saved from having to respond by Elena's arrival with their coffee. "Is good see you each," she said again before returning to the cash register.

"What was your dream?" Lucinda asked, shifting to lean against the wall so she could look at him.

He drank some of his coffee, then loosened his tie, pulled it off and shoved it into his pocket before undoing the top button of his shirt. Finally, he shifted, too, so they were facing each other. "It was strange," he began. "We were ice skating—"

"I don't know how—"

"It was a *dream*, remember?"

"Sorry." She reached for her coffee and sat holding the cup with both hands, waiting to hear the rest.

"So we were ice skating," he went on. "Just the two of us, in this huge rink. And we were terrific." He smiled at her. "The audience loved us."

"Glad to hear it."

"Then, you skated a solo while I played piano."

"And you don't know how."

"Correct. But it's a dream. In dreams, we are virtuosos."

She smiled at him, then lifted the cup and drank some of her coffee.

"I was terrific," he said. "Played like Artur Rubinstein."

"I'm impressed."

"You should be. Anyway, you were out there, skating a solo in the spotlight, just like the *Ice Capades*."

She laughed explosively, causing the coffee to slosh around in the cup. Carefully putting it back on the table, she leaned back against the wall. "The *Ice Capades*," she repeated. "Hilarious. You're the funniest man on the planet."

"Maybe second or third."

"Is there more?"

"You betcha. All of sudden, I started hitting the wrong notes. No matter how hard I concentrated, I couldn't get it right, and you were out there, off stride because the music was wrong."

"Was I falling down?"

"No. But you were getting very angry. A couple more bars and you were skating down the ice, ready to kill me."

"I'll bet."

"Just as you got to the piano and I was prepared to meet my fate, an entire orchestra started playing behind me."

"An entire orchestra," she repeated.

"I *told* you: It's a dream."

"Right. How could I forget? So then what happened?"

"We skated together and all was forgiven."

She stared at him for several moments, then declared, "You are a complete confabulator!"

"No, I am a *partial* confabulator."

"What was the point of that blatantly fabricated narrative?"

"It wasn't entirely fabricated," he said with amusement.

"What part was real?" she asked, taking another sip of the coffee before putting the cup down.

"The ice skating and the piano playing."

"Talents neither of us possess."

"That's the wonderful thing about dreams. We were out there in front of the crowd, doing spins and jumps, perfectly in synch."

"Eli, I'm beginning to wonder about your mental health."

"I think it was a metaphor."

"We're both going to blossom in the spotlight, performing publicly? What kind of metaphor is that?"

"A pretty good one, really." He stared back at her. "Think about it."

"'Ah'd love ta kiss ya, but Ah just washed mah hay-ah,'" she quoted in a syrupy southern accent. "Bette Davis, *Cabin in the Cotton*, 1932." His eyebrows lifted and she explained quietly, "If I wasn't such a complete coward I would kiss you. It was a lovely metaphor."

"Prefaced with a quote," he said. "Very good. If I wasn't so rusty on the ice, *I'd* kiss *you*."

"The problem is," she admitted, her voice dropping further, "a kiss is merely a prelude. And I can't play the piano."

"The wordsmith wins the round! So much for that confabulation." He drained his cup, then asked, "Refill?"

"No, thank you, Eli."

"Time to go?"

"If you want another cup, go ahead. I don't mind. I'm in no rush."

"No," he said, "let's go. If I have any more I'll be up all night, confabulating."

She laughed, her emotions spinning themselves around him in silkworm strands—invisible to the naked eye.

He pulled up beside his Infiniti in the driveway, turned to her and said, "Are you okay? I didn't cross any lines, did I?"

"Not at all. It was a lovely evening. I'm just a head-case."

"If that's true, what does it make me?"

"Why does it have to make you something?"

"Because I love spending time with you. You're the least boring person I know. And if you're a self-professed head-case, then I must be *something*."

"Maybe you're a head-case, too. Although I truly don't think so."

"What then?" he challenged.

"Generous and very patient. You *love* spending time with me?"

"Let's go sit on the porch and talk," he suggested.

"If we do that, we'll lose the mood. Just stay here and tell me why."

"Do you love spending time with *me*?" he asked. She nodded. "But you can't say it, can you?"

"No."

"I'm starting to get this. I get to articulate for both of us. Right?"

"Yes."

"Out on the high-wire, without a net. Do I scare you that much, Lucinda?"

"I'm more afraid of how I feel than I am of you. I'm not sure I *want* to feel this way."

"Me, too," he confessed.

"Okay. We're on the same page. I'm satisfied. I've had one of the best evenings of my life, Eli. If you have no plans for the weekend, come for lunch and a swim on Saturday. Renee's dropping Jason off in the afternoon."

"Are you going to sit and watch again?"

"Maybe. I don't know."

"One of these times you're going to have to get wet."

She laughed, opened the passenger door and got out of the car. "That might be Sunday or Monday."

"An open invitation?" he asked, walking up the path with her to the porch.

"Yes. I will be here."

Arriving at her door, he waited until she got it unlocked and turned back to say good night.

"Close your eyes," he said.

"Why?"

"Just do it," he coaxed.

She closed her eyes and was jolted when he kissed her briefly on the lips. Shaken, she opened her eyes again to see he was already moving down the steps. At the bottom he smiled and said, "Good night, Lucinda. It was one of my best evenings, too," and continued on to his car. Rooted in place, she remained in the doorway until he'd driven off.

Chapter Thirteen

For a time she continued to stand in the doorway, hearing him say over and over, "Close your eyes. Close your eyes." A kiss. Was it stolen or bestowed? Bestowed, she decided. A gratifying shock to the system, a tiny fragment of time which contained the essence of affection. Yes, a kiss was a prelude; it was a door opened. In that moment she'd have turned herself over like a pocket watch to be carried away and kept close to him, her heart a smooth internal mechanism contained inside the polished protective case, ticking away. The little engine that could. How long did love take to happen? Did it require a moment, or months? And what happened to the internal mechanism if love was denied, the watch going unwound for too long? Could it be repaired? Could it be returned to functionality as Gin insisted? The size of the risk was beyond measure. But resistance was infinitely more dangerous than risk. You could lose a life while you weighed all the factors; you could be on the verge of passing into the unknowable darkness of the end, before you decided you should've risked your heart after all. Why not give yourself over? Why not just let go and fall? Hearts were rarely broken irreparably. They got injured, bore nicks and scars, but they healed in time. Wait too long and everything atrophied, shrinking away until what remained was a desiccated nubbin of something that had once been healthy and strong. Consider Anne, she reminded herself. A lesson there to be remembered.

Slowly, she became aware of several clumsy, heavy-bodied moths colliding repeatedly with the glass globe of the porch light. Idiot kamikaze bombers determined to die, she thought, at last going inside and locking the door.

She found herself on the living room threshold, looking at the pinspot-lit portraits of her parents, thinking about that night at the drive-in restaurant with Lily—the night they'd gone there instead of to the Awards show because Lily had been so convinced she couldn't possibly win. "Wonderful, Wonderful" had been playing on the car radio and Lily had said, "I love this song." When Lucinda asked why, Lily had paused before taking another bite of her burger to say, "I just do. Someday you'll know why."

Lucinda thought she'd known why with Cort, but she'd purposefully moved him out of her life with the use of monumental roadblocks she'd known he could never get past. She had said and done things that had ensured she'd have an isolated existence, although that wasn't what she'd anticipated. Her secret visions had been of variations on a theme of the happy-family reunion. But the predominant variation, the one that eventually replaced the primary theme, had been comprised of chords in a minor key: a somber solo, played by a mournful cello that underscored endless lost or wasted days.

Close your eyes. I will slip past those now-crumbling roadblocks and resuscitate you with insight and laughter; I will touch my mouth to yours and bestow the kiss of life.

Reaching out, she touched the light switch and the living room went dark, the portraits now no more than retinal afterimages. Her eyes hurting, a steel hand closed over the back of her neck and began to squeeze. As if she'd been suddenly submerged in deep water, her ears began to ache. Like nitrogen bubbles in the bloodstream, she had the bends from rising too quickly to the surface.

Hands beginning to tremble, she stepped out of her shoes and went to the kitchen. Leaving the room dark, navigating by the light of the stove, she got a bottle of water, then fumbled with the child-proof top on the prescription bottle. She hated these impossible tops that were on everything from mouthwash to toilet bowl cleaner. They were adult-proof, she thought grimly, as the top finally shot off and pills scattered across the counter, some falling to the floor. They'd have to wait until morning. She didn't dare bend down to retrieve them.

The pill washed down, she held onto the rim of the counter for a minute or two, collecting what remained of her energy while willing the capsule to stay down and not ride back on the surging nausea that had taken over her midriff. Sensory overload, perhaps a fall in the barometric pressure. Or possibly cosmic revenge, although she wasn't given to believing she'd been singled out, like some Greek mythological figure, to suffer unduly. She merely had a limited capacity for outside stimulus.

She made it to the bathroom just as her stomach overturned. Involuntary tears leaking down her cheeks, she knelt on the cold tiles, waiting for the next spasm. *Elegant*, she thought and emitted a brief laugh that culminated in another wrenching series of heaves.

At last, exhausted and emptied, she flushed the toilet a final time, gagged down another pill, then sat on the floor with her back against the tub, trying to find the strength to undress. She reeked, the room reeked. Light flares burst behind her closed eyelids and the grip on her neck had tightened so severely that only another minute or more and her head would separate from its stem and topple to the floor—a grotesque bowling ball suitable for the Queen of Hearts. Something appropriate to Wonderlandish games and adventures; an item from one of Arthur Rackham's exquisitely detailed 1907 illustrations. Snarks and Cheshire cats, and a questionable unacted-upon obsession/love for a little girl named Alice Liddell. When she thought of Alice, she could only think of Julia Cameron's photograph of an angry-mouthed young woman of twenty glaring defiantly at the camera. Perhaps by then Alice was simply fed up with being photographed. That did happen, as Lucinda well knew. There were only so many photo ops a small child could tolerate before any latent rebelliousness set in.

She had planned to write her thesis on Carroll/Dodgson and Alice, with the title *The Other Love that Dare Not Speak Its Name*. But aside from his lifelong close association with young children, there'd been no evidence that Dodgson had ever made so much as a single untoward gesture to any child. He'd told them stories, he'd photographed them. He'd clearly loved them, especially Alice—perhaps for her defiant whimsy and her moody beauty as a little girl. But was pedophilia of the mind (like Jimmy Carter's lust in his heart) something for which one should be condemned and vilified? Dodgson had written wonderful stories, riddled with hugely imaginative events and entities, that had timeless value. So, in the end, she'd set aside her research notes, and her thesis had been *The Cultural Influence of Film on Modern American Society.*

Forcing her fingers into compliance, she managed to get her clothes off, but not without tearing her silk slip. She didn't care. Leaving the garments in a heap on the floor, she staggered to her bed where she lay shivering as residual minor spasms rippled through her abdomen. She tried first her left side, then her right, each time victimized after a minute or two by positional vertigo that at last had her dragging the pillow and bedclothes to the floor. On her back, she blinked at the shifting shadows on the ceiling, swallowing repeatedly, thinking wryly about elegance; thinking with a pang of Eli's mouth touching against hers; thinking that it was real—his caring was genuine, as was her own—and she knew why Lily had loved that song. Her thoughts darted about, touching present, then past, repeatedly reviewing that snippet of time when he'd told her to close her eyes before daring to demonstrate his affection, until at last the medication took her sliding down the rabbit hole after Alice.

When she opened her eyes again, it was almost three o'clock on Friday afternoon. And as soon as she tried to sit up, she knew she wasn't going to make it to dinner with the family that night. Her eyes throbbed in syncopation with the pounding in her head and the thudding against her eardrums. She felt as if she'd been beaten, hurting all over, as she huddled on her knees, summoning the energy to get to the bathroom and the spare container of medication.

More spilled capsules. Her bare foot crushed a few as she clung to the sink and choked one down with a mouthful of bottled water. Unable to tolerate the stink of her body and the greasy feel of her face and hair for even a minute longer, she got the shower going, adjusted the shower head, then sat in the tub under the pounding spray, her breathing labored as, stiffened muscles protesting almost audibly, she shampooed her hair and lathered her body—the gently scented body wash and lemon-verbena shampoo carrying away the fetid smells that had accumulated with the pain. Migraines fouled the body chemistry, pushing noxious odors from every pore and follicle on her body—a truism in her lifelong dealings with these attacks.

It took forever, but she stayed in the tub until the beaten feeling began to subside under the steamy flow of the water and she had enough mental stamina to examine the signally important exchange that had prefaced Eli's kiss.

Eyes closed, she reviewed his so-called dream, viewing it as a collective of metaphors that comprised an apologue. The exercise in analysis brought to mind the advanced English course so many years before, when dismantling language had been equivalent to a thrilling treasure hunt where the clues to be collected en route were such that only the most diligent students could unravel them. Cort, who'd dropped the course in frustration after only three weeks, had, before departing, quoted Churchill's famous statement: "It is a riddle wrapped in a mystery inside an enigma."

... we were ice skating. Just the two of us, in this huge rink. And we were terrific. The audience loved us. Then, you skated a solo while I played piano ... In dreams, we are virtuosos ... All of a sudden, I started hitting the wrong notes. No matter how

hard I concentrated, I couldn't get it right, and you were out there, off stride because the music was wrong ... you were getting very angry. A couple more bars and you were skating down the ice, ready to kill me. Just as you got to the piano and I was prepared to meet my fate, an entire orchestra started playing behind me. We skated together and all was forgiven.

Ignoring the radiating pain inside her skull, she concentrated on the subtext, reducing it further and further until only the distillate remained. Then she studied that, as if through a high-power microscope's lens, until completely satisfied with her interpretation. It was, she was compelled to conclude, the product of a fine mind at one with a fine heart: the ultimate prize at the end of the hunt.

Her hair swathed in a towel, body warmly wrapped in the heavy terrycloth robe Gin had given her the previous Christmas, she sat on the floor by the bed with the telephone in her lap and called Elise.

"I won't be able to come this evening," she said almost inaudibly—the sound of her own voice heightening the horrific thrum in her eardrums.

"Ah, *pauvre petite.* You have the migraine (she pronounced it me-gren). I am so sorry. You will be missed. Rest yourself," she said, "and we will speak tomorrow."

"I love you," Lucinda said tearfully. "I hate losing out on time with the family."

"It is not time lost," Elise said, "but merely deferred. Perhaps I will see you tomorrow."

"I would like that."

"Also me. You had a good evening with Eli?"

"Wonderful."

"As I expected. So now you must go to your bed. *Je t'aime, chérie. Au 'voir.*"

"Au 'voir," Lucinda said, putting down the receiver. Then picking it right up again she dialed Eli's home number. The answering machine came on and she listened closely to his message, absorbing the tone of his voice, its mellow cadence. At the tone, she whispered, "I've been felled like the proverbial oak but I insist on being better by tomorrow. Come early, we'll have lunch. I can't wait to see you." She disconnected, turned off the ringer and set aside the phone. Then, down to the dregs of her energy, she lifted the pillow and blankets from the floor, got into bed, bathrobe and all, and went plummeting at once back into drug-induced sleep.

Saturday morning she was able to go downstairs, her now-weightless head feeling separated by several body lengths from her feet. Performing a top-to-bottom mental survey, she decided that the worst of the migraine had passed. She wasn't hungry but long experience had taught her to eat. While the coffee was brewing she went to boot up the computer, her movements not yet steady, her hands still taken by minor tremors. She studied them with interest as she hit the Browser key on the launcher, loving the speed of the cable connection. Admittedly stupid but the fact that Eli had the same service provider pleased her. Their emails shot back and forth almost with the speed of instant messaging—an invention she loathed but one that everyone she knew under forty seemed to love. Jason and Katanya had IM'd every evening, throughout the winter. He also now IM'd with Emma in Chicago, although he still didn't speak of her.

The chime indicating mail in her inbox brought her attention to the screen.

Dear Lucy:
Since you haven't been emailing, I decided you must have one of your migraines and I didn't want to disturb you by phoning. Then I spoke to Elise and she confirmed it. I'm sorry. I know they're dreadful and I'll keep my fingers crossed that this one is over for you quickly.

I wanted to let you know that Elise and I have come to an agreement and we're both pretty excited about it. I've talked to Mrs. Weinburg who has finally given in and will be moving to Larchmont to live with her son—who's going to take care of getting the apartment listed and moving the things she wants to keep to the "granny apartment" they're already having built for her. As of the fifteenth of September, I'll be doing a reverse commute to Westport every day to learn the ropes from Gwyn for a couple of weeks before she moves out west.

This means that I've got to get a driver's license. So I signed up right away for an accelerated course, which Elise very generously offered to pay for. I've already had three lessons and seem to be taking to this as if, as Mr. Shakespeare said, to the manner born. I'm studying the manual and don't think I'll have any trouble with the tests, either the written one or the driving one. Getting to know the roads, etc. in CT might take a little doing but I love the idea of being so close to you and also getting to help Elise.

I hope this isn't one of the really bad spells that puts you down for days on end. All three of us will be more than ready for our weekend with you on the fourteenth.

Take good care.
Much love, big hugs, Jen.

Lucinda had to smile as next she read an email from Katanya cataloging the new outfits (primarily more overalls in sundry colors) and shoes she'd bought for school, and complaining mildly about how much she disliked being back in the city.

Everything's so dark and sooooo _dirty_ after Connecticut. I really saw it, coming home this time. I miss you and Soupboy like crazy, but I'm pretty psyched about being a senior …

There was a short email from Loranne extolling the virtues of her new job and asking, as her mother had done, if Lucinda was down for the count with another headache.

With the email done, Lucinda played the one message on the answering machine, which was from Gin who'd called from Toronto the previous evening.

"Hey, kiddo. Just checking in. I've got another week's worth of meetings here in Hollywood North before I head to Boston next Sunday night to have one last session schmoozing the money man over dinner Monday at the Ritz. Then Tuesday the eleventh I'm catching the 7:45 a.m. flight to L.A. for an overnighter to finalize a couple of last-minute things. With luck, I'll be home by that Wednesday night, or early Thursday morning on the red-eye. We're set to start principal photography the twenty-fourth, *finally*. I'm just on my way out to dinner with some of my key tech people here, but I'll call again tomorrow so you can fill me in on your big date with Eli. I think I'm gonna break down and buy a cell phone when I get back over the border. It's such a pain in the ass trying to find phones everywhere. Anyway, everything's right on schedule, I'm happy to say. Okay, gotta run or I'll be late. Love you to pieces, Ella. 'Bye."

Lucinda put the previous day's paper in the blue box for recycling and read that morning's copy of the *Times* as she ate a piece of whole wheat toast with honey and drank a cup of coffee. She had one bad moment after the first couple of bites when her stomach protested, suddenly cramping. She sat motionless, alert, prepared to have to fly to the bathroom. But her stomach seemed to yawn, then settle, and she finished the toast, licking the residual honey from her fingertips as she poured another cup of coffee.

She had acknowledged the context of Eli's dream and the declaration it contained; she had also—somewhere in the depths of her migraine-induced maundering—owned up to her feelings for him. She certainly wasn't going to be carrying a banner in an affection parade, but it was a major step for her to have taken—even if it was restricted to the confines of her mental arena. As she put her cup and plate in the sink before going upstairs to tidy the bedroom, she decided that, no matter what, today she was going to get into the pool.

She had a shaky moment when Eli arrived. He came into the foyer and put a small gym bag on the floor, then he stood and looked at her so intently that she suddenly wondered if she'd misinterpreted everything, if she'd said and done absolutely all the wrong things. But then he smiled a little wickedly and, mimicking the accent she'd used, said, "'Ah'd love ta kiss ya, but Ah just washed ma hay-ah.'"

She laughed giddily, wanting to look away, but forcing

herself to maintain eye contact. "Very good," she told him. "You're a quick study. You might have a future in acting."

He leaned against the wall, the intent in his eyes holding. "It was such a treat, Lucinda. I had to take the cassette out of the machine so I could play your message two or three hundred times."

She shrugged. "It was an ordinary message, Eli. No big deal."

"Hey! My first message from you. Please! Of course I had to save the tape."

"So it's not a digital machine, huh?"

"Nope. Lucky me. I'm thinking I'll have some copies made. One for the car, one for the Walkman when I'm on the treadmill. One to play on the stereo while I'm having my sandwich or cereal. One—"

"I get the idea. Would you like something to drink, coffee or a soda?"

"'If we do that, we'll lose the mood,'" he quoted her again. "Let's just stay here for a minute and I'll tell you why I'm keeping the tape."

"Okay."

"We're never going to agree on this, so you'll have to accept my version of this particular reality. Agreed?"

"You're making me nervous."

"Don't be. I told you: I find your shyness very touching. I probably like all the things you hate about yourself. Anyway, these past few months I've come to believe you're one of the bravest people I've ever met."

"Oh, I'm not—"

"I told you: This is *my* version. You don't *have* to agree. Everything, as you know so very well, is subject to interpretation. I dropped by to see Elise on Friday and she told me then that you were down with a migraine. I was sorry to hear it. I take it you're better?"

"Yes, I am."

"Good, good. Initially, I was kind of put out because I wanted to phone you right back. I mean, you left me a message in that nice low voice, saying you couldn't wait to see me. Our sudden moves rule is still in play, even though it only seems to apply to me." She smiled at this. "I don't mind. You played Sherlock Holmes, deciphered that confabulation, found the subtext and returned an encoded message of your own. This could be an intellectual match made, as they say—Who are *they*? Don't you ever wonder?—in heaven. As you pointed out, I had water for almost thirty years. The past three years or so have been long and dry, pretty bleak, really. Then I dropped by to see Elise, and you and I met. You have become oxygen to me. Necessary."

"Thank you," she said, a fluttering in her chest. Her breathing shallow, she said, "Close your eyes, Eli."

It took a second or two to register, then he nodded and closed his eyes.

She touched her mouth to his, then stepped back, saying, "So, would you like some coffee or a soda? I hope you're hungry because I made lunch. Nothing special, though," she warned. "Just sandwiches and some salad."

"To quote Elsie Gottlieb, one of my favorite seniors at the nursing home, 'I could eat.'"

She smiled, said, "Great," and took his hand as they started for the kitchen. With a Yiddish accent that made him whoop with laughter, she said, "I also could eat a liddle somethink."

Chapter Fourteen

Upon waking at six-thirty, she looked out the window to see that it was a glorious morning, the sky a deep cloudless blue. Summer had gone very quickly. And, as she'd observed to Eli in an email, the sad season was approaching when the trees would lose their foliage in an outrageous dying flourish of color. With the first frost, she would open the door one morning to see that the late-blooming flowers had wilted, shriveled overnight on their stalks. But this day had all the splendor befitting a prologue, and she was brimming with energy. Pulling on some baggy pants and a T-shirt, she went directly outside to dead-head some of the perennials. The warmth of the new-morning sun tempered by an intermittent breeze, she worked steadily, satisfyingly, for the better part of an hour. After dumping the cuttings in the trash, she returned inside to shower. Then she had coffee and a slice of toast while she read the paper, all the while marveling at how well she felt. She was filled with optimism, and happy—a state of mind and being so long forgotten that it seemed new, something never previously experienced.

The school-year routine had resumed the week before but she no longer had to go to collect Jason. He'd announced that he didn't want to be picked up anymore, "... like a baby. Only the little kids get picked up." So now the yellow bus dropped him at the foot of her driveway and she only had to be there, waiting, when the vehicle lumbered to a stop. She did miss the daily trip to the school, waiting in the row of cars with the young mothers and nannies. Still, her baby-sitting duties were nowhere near an end. Renee would be graduating this semester and she already had résumés out; she'd even received a "maybe" for an opening in January with the city of Bridgeport. She wasn't especially keen on Bridgeport. "Such a dangerous city," she'd said. "Still, if nothing else materializes, I may have to take it. Even if it's only for a year, it'll be something to put on my résumé. But I'm seriously considering starting up my own consulting firm."

Lucinda wasn't about to go near that idea, but she did wonder just how Renee thought she could start a consulting firm with no experience and no clients. Sometimes, Renee's thinking was sufficiently off kilter to keep Lucinda on her toes. She thought of it privately as the William Tell syndrome, where someone aimed to shoot an apple off the head of a live person. The slightest miscalculation and you had an arrow through that person's forehead. From the beginning, Lucinda had opted to ignore some of Renee's more outlandish remarks and observations. It felt like the safe way to go. Lucinda didn't want to say or do anything that would affect her relationship with Jason. She knew she represented approval and acceptance for him, that he never feared sharing his thoughts with her.

With the better part of each weekday free, Lucinda had begun making notes on the novel, *Awake or Dreaming*, which Gin had optioned as their next project—another finely written interior study of yet one more quietly heroic woman. No question, Gin could pick them. Lucinda had enjoyed the book so much she'd gone online and ordered the four other novels the author, Claudia Mason, had written.

On top of everything else, Gin had launched what was sure to become a full-scale campaign to persuade Lucinda to come to Toronto during the shoot. "It's time you went farther than fifty miles from home," she'd argued over the phone from Boston the previous evening. "If you don't want to fly, you could drive up, spend a few days, maybe a week. Bring Eli!" she'd suggested. "I'll betcha he wouldn't say no."

"We'll see."

"What'm I, your kid? Don't 'we'll see' me, Ella. Just plan to do it. We're going to be shooting there for five weeks. It's a beautiful city, great food, good shopping, lots to see and do. Clean like you wouldn't believe. And it's not as if you'd have to sit around, watching the set-ups, for Pete's sake. We've only got two night shoots scheduled which means we'd have time in the evenings to be together, eat, take in some shows, whatever. I *want* you to come, and no is not an acceptable answer. We'll talk about this when I get home, which'll probably be Thursday now. Those dolts in L.A. keep putting back our appointment times. So ask Eli! Guarantee you he'll be all over it."

"I'll think about it," Lucinda had said. "Now leave me

alone and go eat with Mister Money. If you don't get off the phone, you'll be late."

"Hey! I'm a *movie star*. I'm supposed to be late." She laughed.

"Sure, I forgot. Silly me. As if you're *ever* late."

"It's been known to happen. Okay, I'm going. Love you, Ella. Ask Eli!" she'd said again, then put down the phone.

Ask Eli! Well, maybe she would, Lucinda was thinking as she poured a second cup of coffee and scanned the business section of the paper. More likely, though, she wouldn't. A trip together had serious implications, and she was nowhere near ready to get into bed with Eli. Not that she didn't think about it, because she did. He'd started appearing in her dreams, in charged sexual encounters that took place with effortless ease. As was so typical of dreams, their interactions weren't complicated by extraneous dialogue or of feelings, particularly of the self-conscious, fearful variety that continued to underscore her actual dealings with him. Granted, her doubts were diminishing. But it was going to take some time, possibly forever, to get past her hyper self-awareness. If the relationship was meant to move forward to the next step, she told herself repeatedly, it would happen in its own time, spontaneously. Lily used to say, "You could think anything to death. Sometimes, Luce, you've just got to take things at face value and stop analyzing everything to pieces." It was true. Lucinda was intensely, perhaps even morbidly, analytical, capable of examining a piece of information, a casual remark, even a tone of voice repeatedly, sometimes for days on end, until she was confident she had a grasp of what had been intended. Now, after all those isolated years of endless introspection, it was a tough habit to break. Yes, she'd come a long way. But not far enough to invite Eli to accompany her on a trip.

She finished the newspaper and put it into the blue box, left her cup in the sink and settled on the sofa with the outline she was creating for the screenplay. After reviewing her notes, she reread the next chapter, placing Post-its on the key pages where she would lift either a scene or a segment of dialogue. At a nearby house a lawn mower started up with a roar and a minute or two later the smell of fresh-cut grass with an underlying whiff of gasoline wafted through the open window.

When she heard the computer chime, she got up and went to check her email. It was a news bulletin that seemed to make no sense. A plane had crashed into the World Trade Center. Clicking open her browser, she went to her home page. How was it possible? she wondered, going quickly to several other sites, seeking more information. How could a plane fly into a Manhattan skyscraper on a clear, cloudless day? She remembered Lily telling her about the military plane that had flown into the Empire State Building in 1945. It had been a rainy, overcast morning with heavy fog. Lily had been in New York on a publicity junket and was supposed to fly home that afternoon. But one look out the window of her suite at the Waldorf and she'd phoned Eddie to say she was staying put until the weather cleared up. Just as she didn't much care for driving, Lily wasn't fond of flying, especially in bad weather. Typically, once the decision not to go that day had been made, she quickly become bored. So she'd grabbed an umbrella and gone for a walk down Park Avenue, thinking she'd head to B. Altman's and look around, and after that go someplace nice for lunch. She'd described hearing the ominously loud rumble of an engine in the sky, and looking up had been stunned to see a plane flying that low. "It was so loud," she'd said. "Scared the dickens out of me. I actually ducked." And then she'd heard the crash …

Lucinda turned to look out the window. The sky, as before, was perfectly cloudless and perfectly blue. The gas mower continued its noisy travel, coming near, then retreating as it crossed an expanse of lawn. Nothing had changed.

Looking back at the computer screen, she hit the Reload button, to see if there was any update on the story. She couldn't help thinking this was no accident, that something was very wrong. She searched online for three or four minutes then suddenly stopped, saying aloud, "How stupid are you? What the hell are you *doing*?" and grabbed the TV remote. She tuned to CNN and stared at the screen, immediately gripped by anxiety. The camera showed thick black smoke gushing out of the side of— Which of the towers was that? She tried to pay attention to what was being said, dismissing thoughts of special effects, computer-generated images in films she'd enjoyed in the past or had, more recently, lauded in her online column for their simulated disaster scenes—the train wreck in *The Fugitive* for one and the plane crash in *Cast Away,* both of which had seemed exceptionally authentic. But this was no simulation. It was real, yet from moment to moment she lost the context, thinking again of films. But no. *Real*. She went from ABC to NBC to CBS to MSNBC, back to CNN, then again to NBC, spending a minute or so on each station. The background images were all the same but shot from varying angles, only the talking heads and voiceovers were different.

Back on CNN they were saying it was the side of the

north tower. From a distance it didn't look that bad. The towers were so high and the damage seemed localized. But then the camera zoomed in, revealing tremendous destruction—entire floors consumed by raging fire, with gusting billows of dense smoke, high up, near the top of the building. It had happened, they said, at 8:47. According to the digital readout on the screen, it was now 8:54. The on-air voice said it was an American Airlines flight that had, at top speed, flown directly into the tower. No attempt had been made to avoid the building. From all appearances, the crash was intentional.

All at once weak in the legs, having trouble catching her breath, she made an ungainly rush to her desk, glancing over repeatedly at the TV screen as she pushed through stacks of notes and papers, trying to find the sheet with the details of Gin's flight. Couldn't find it. A grocery list; a list of items to order online; a library list, another for miscellaneous *things*. Her life was a series of goddamned lists! Where *was* it? Papers slipped to the floor, slithering over each other, a scattered mess. She knocked the receiver off the phone. Fumbled it back into its cradle. Abandoning the effort to find the page and, increasingly distraught, she went back to stare at the TV screen. 9:02. Switching over to NBC, the camera was fixed on the towers. Then, in horror, she watched as a plane appeared on the right of the screen, coming about in a loop to fly directly into the south tower. A tremendous crash with an instant explosion of brilliant orange fire, debris showering down. People on the ground were screaming, panic and disbelief—the camera another set of eyes gazing upward at the consuming inferno. She hit the Recall button. On CNN Aaron Brown's voice was oddly contained, his expression quite calm, as he tried to put words to what was impossible to describe. It was so far beyond anyone's experience that only cinematic terms seemed viable. This devastating assault was being broadcast *as it happened*. It was its being live, its happening in real time on TV that lent the event such an artificial aura, making it so hard to absorb.

Lucinda couldn't think. Her synapses were misfiring, her brain seizing. No matter how hard she tried to focus on what she'd been told, she couldn't remember whether Loranne's new office was in the north tower or the south one. And Gin was on one of those planes—which one? Did it matter? Not any more. No one could survive those crashes. She couldn't think about that. Loranne was in one of the towers. But she was quick-witted, resourceful. She'd get out, maybe she was already down there, on the street, running as fast as she could. Lucinda wanted her to be out and away, bolting toward safety. She had to focus on Loranne, not think about Gin and those planes, the countless lost lives.

Maddie and Steven, Michael all worked in midtown. She'd have to call, though, make sure they were okay. She thought about her poor angry, frightened aunt Anne and was glad she hadn't lived to see this. Something this monumental would have sent her over the edge. Anne had had no coping mechanisms, only anger. And anger was as useless as fear. Lucinda looked over at the portrait she loved of little-girl Anne, then returned her attention to the TV set.

Was this how the end of the world began? Sirens wailing, masses of people fleeing from the vicinity of the towers, thick smoke erupting volcanically into the sky. Lucinda was immobilized, unable to stop watching, mad thoughts, fear and grief tumbling about, colliding, ricocheting off the hard inner surface of her skull; mixing, tangling, snarled.

Too much to take in, to process. Untold numbers of dead on the airliners and inside those grievously wounded towers. Hundreds, possibly thousands of lives vaporized in a holocaust fed by jet fuel. Concrete reduced to powder, glass, papers, fragments of steel, pieces of the plane, all flying through the air; debris raining down as everyone on the streets quickly moved away, some looking back over their shoulders (as if they, too, were caught in the cinematic mind-set) as they headed north toward midtown, or west toward the Hudson, frantic to escape, to find somewhere safe to stand and catch their breath while they tried to make sense of this. Blocks away, frozen faces gazed up at the jagged fire-breathing maws of the newly made torn-steel dragons. Hands over their mouths, eyes wide and unblinking at the sight of the ravaged monoliths, strangers clutched each other, sobbing. Eyes fixed on the towers, people used their cell phones to call home, to say I'm okay, I love you, don't worry. Or exclaiming, Oh my god turn on the TV, look what's happening! We're being attacked. We're at war … or *something*.

Was there a name or an explanation for an event of this magnitude? The perfect blue sky was being obscured by roiling gray-black plumes of smoke. Tongues of flame licked at the exposed ribs of the structure, reaching out from the crevices of what had once been windows. And a voice-over stated somberly that two other commercial planes had deviated from their routes, were out of contact. A total now of four missing aircraft; two had flown into the towers, two had unknown destinations.

Digital minutes ticked by. People leapt from the towers, some hand-in-hand, some alone. Jumping from smashed-out windows, to dive into space. Better to fall hundreds of feet and die on impact than suffer prolonged terror that culminated in incineration. Live network feeds were coming in from everywhere, voices cutting in on top of each other, halting voiceovers stating that all takeoffs and landings to or from New York, Boston and Newark had been canceled. Then, minutes later, all New York City airports had been closed. Next, the New York City Port Authority was closing all bridges and tunnels to the city. Then word that American Flight 77 out of Dulles in D.C. en route to Los Angeles had also gone out of contact, believed hijacked. Communication had been lost with United Flight 93 out of Newark bound for San Francisco. Hijacked, hijacked. Four planes. Were there more? How many? What did it all *mean*? Was this the end-product of hate? Taking thousands of lives to make some sort of statement; the kind of message sent by suicide bombers who boarded buses or who strolled into late-night cafes in Israel, becoming human incendiary devices in the mad belief that these acts would deliver them to paradise. What kind of statement was that? It spoke only of fanaticism and carnage, senseless deaths.

9:26. The FAA had grounded all flights. But was it too late? How many commandeered planes were still bound for major destinations? Were there legions of terrorists in appropriated planes aiming for landmarks nationwide? Were the towers merely the beginning? Where would the next strike be? Nuclear power plants, skyscrapers in Los Angeles, San Francisco? Limitless possible targets containing thousands of people. She was sweating and shivering simultaneously, her throat aching. 9:32. The New York stock exchange was closed. 9:43. An airplane had crashed into the Pentagon. A cutaway from Aaron Brown on CNN to a scene shot from a distance of smoke gushing from the low building. Jamie McIntyre in a voiceover telling Aaron about evacuating the Pentagon.

Then confirmation: The plane that hit the north tower had been American Flight 11 out of Boston, en route to Los Angeles, carrying as much as *ten thousand gallons* of fuel. Available information indicated that onboard there had been nine flight attendants, two pilots and eighty-one passengers—including one petite blonde, probably in jeans and a T-shirt, not looking in the least like an international film star. A flight to L.A. was bound to have been carrying people in the business, Lucinda thought. Producers or writers or actors, as well as ordinary people—on holiday, on a honeymoon. Then there were the thousands of workers in the towers, and down on the street. Firefighters, police, paramedics. It was too much to take in, too terrible altogether, an assault on the senses. A calamity that dried the mouth and squeezed the heart; images seared like brands on the brain.

Lucinda stood benumbed, eyes on the screen, whispering prayers for the lives of those she loved and couldn't bear to lose, and for the people in the towers and on the ground, repeating her mantra: *ohpleasenopleasegodno godohgodohgodpleaseplease* and then ... 9:59. The unthinkable. Her brain couldn't assimilate what her eyes were seeing. The top of south tower was buckling dangerously, then imploding, like a reverse atomic bomb, complete with mushrooming cloud. The tower fell into itself, disintegrating in an earth-shuddering roar, floors collapsing down one on top of the other, down, so quickly, downdowndown. And then it was gone. Just—gone. The camera's view showed the north tower, its upper stories smoke-shrouded. Everything behind it was obscured by impenetrable rolling waves of solid matter that seemed like clouds. But no ordinary cloud had ever contained such fearsome components.

Her knees unlocked and Lucinda was sitting on the edge of the sofa, a hand over her mouth, crying, oblivious to anything but the unfolding apocalypse, knowing with absolute conviction that nothing, ever again, would be the same. *Nothing*. From this moment forward, everyone, everything would be permanently altered. Innocence lost. No one was truly safe. Repeating her prayer mindlessly: *godohgodohgod-pleaseplease. Let them be alive.* Like a small child, she promised she would do anything, *anything* if only her friends were still alive. *Please*!

Chaos. Camera-eyes scanning the people, the devastation, the desperate crowd's surprisingly orderly flight toward safety. She thought of that famously painful audio clip of the Hindenburg disaster, with announcer Herb Morrison's gut-shot voice crying, "*This is the worst of the worst catastrophes in the world! ... Oh, the humanity, and all the passengers screaming around here*!" None of the on-air people Lucinda saw allowed their emotions to show—if they had them. Surely they did. But maybe Herb Morrison had been an anomaly, a caring, feeling man who just happened to work in broadcasting and was in New Jersey on a day of tragedy. Aaron Brown's face revealed nothing, although he spoke of what a calamitous event this was, how shocking, how terrible, how frightening. But his face ... Perhaps it was a broadcasting mandate: Show no emotion! Just report the breaking news.

10:02. The Sears Tower in Chicago was being evacuated.

10:06. The fourth missing plane had crashed in a field in Pennsylvania.

Hearing this, Lucinda could only think that the passengers must have fought back and overwhelmed the hijackers, refusing to allow them to reach their goal. Rural Pennsylvania could not have been the target destination. More likely it had been The White House or The Capitol building, but those buildings, too, had been evacuated. The President had been rushed onto a plane and secreted away somewhere.

Minutes ticked by, speculation running rampant, and reports coming in simultaneously. Fiery deaths at the Pentagon where the crash site collapsed at 10:15. Views now alternated between D.C. and Manhattan, with live feeds from Pennsylvania. The media scrambling to deal with the flood of information. 10:24 all flights to the U.S. had been diverted, most to Canada. *Gin gone forever?* She couldn't be … No! *No*!

10:28. The north tower was suddenly coming down in a great, gusting roar and in only four or five seconds it, like its twin, was gone. Vast plumes of smoke. On the streets, people were running for their lives as the pulverized ruins, like an ocean, flooded outward. The tip of Manhattan was obscured by choking gray-black clouds. People emerged from the area, ghostly, coated in ash, walking like zombies. Their clothes torn, some people bleeding; everyone moving away, away. They had survived, after a fashion.

Wiping her face with her sleeve, Lucinda watched and watched. Then, suddenly, she needed to talk to her grandmother and got up, her joints stiff, her body creaking, to go to the telephone.

Gwyn answered, her usual British cool tone gone. Her voice raspy, she said, "Please wait a moment, Lucinda," and put down the receiver. Lucinda listened to her heels click away. Then Elise said, "You are watching, *chérie*?"

Lucinda whispered, "Yes."

"A great tragedy. I am … I have no words."

"I just wanted to hear your voice," Lucinda said, trying to hold herself together. Failing, she cried, "Gin was on Flight Eleven! And Lorrie's new job was in one of the towers, but I can't remember which one."

"Ah, no!" Elise said mournfully. "So terrible. *Je suis désolée.*"

"I … I can't talk."

"Nor can I," her grandmother said. "It is too much."

"I don't know why, but I keep thinking of Anne."

"I, too," Elise said. "Why is that?"

"I'm glad she's not here to see this. I don't think she could've handled it."

"You are right." Her grandmother sounded surprised. "She could not. She would have gone mad with fear and worry."

"I know it sounds strange, but I love her now. When it's too late."

"To love a memory is a good thing, I believe."

"I'll call you again later. *Je t'adore.*" Lucinda put down the handset and looked out the window. The day remained perfectly beautiful, the sky still perfectly blue. It was hard to look at the clear, vivid colors out there. The brightness of the light hurt her eyes as she studied the way the breeze lifted the leaves and set the flower-heads nodding. And at her back, the voiceovers continued, documenting the events taking place less than fifty miles away. How could it be such a seemingly peaceful day beyond her window while untold thousands of lives now lay in ruin?

Chapter Fifteen

Half an hour later, she was back on the sofa, staring at the TV screen with the feeling that she dared not move, for fear of missing some vital piece of information. There was no way of knowing if there was more to come, if the attacks were over.

The doorbell startled her. She jumped, her heart jolted, stood up and, for a moment, couldn't think what to do. Then she ran to open the door. Eli stood there. His tie hung loose, the top button of his shirt undone. His hair was messy, as if he'd been caught in a windstorm. And his eyes were red. He'd been crying. She flew forward to embrace him, grateful for his presence, hanging on for long moments, unable to speak. Then, taking his hand, she brought him into the house. He stood in the hallway for several seconds, his brows drawn together, as if he, too, was having synaptic difficulties and forming a cohesive statement was a problem.

"Manny was supposed to be at a breakfast meeting this morning, at the towers." He stopped and looked at her.

"Is he all right?" she asked tremulously.

Eli nodded slowly, as if the movement was painful. "I just heard from him. He was running late and just coming out of the subway when the first plane hit. He actually saw it and had to run for cover because of the debris coming down. He called home right away but couldn't get through to me—the lines are all messed up. I had my cell off while I was at the nursing home—as a courtesy, you know—and forgot to turn it back on until I tried to phone you and couldn't get through."

"But I just spoke to my grandmother—" She looked over at her desk, remembering that she'd knocked off the receiver. But no. She'd spoken to her grandmother after that.

"The phones lines are completely screwed up. You can make some local calls, some you can't. Forget long distance. Anyway, he's okay. He had to walk all the way back uptown and kept trying to call me and his brother every couple of minutes. He got through to Raf before he was able to get me. But he's *okay*." He got the words out and then choked up. "I was terrified that I'd lost him," he confessed, dragging a well-used handkerchief out of his pocket to mop his face.

"I know," she whispered, stricken by his display of emotion. "Gin was on Flight Eleven, Eli. And I can't remember which tower Lorrie works in." She looked down at her trembling hands. "I don't know what to do. There's nothing I *can* do. That was Gin's *flight*! I'm sure of it. I can't find the paper I wrote the information on, but she told me it was American and that was the only one. I, ah ..." She shook her head, her eyes drawn back to the TV. Then she looked at him, the prayer murmuring inside her head. *Godohgodohgodpleasepleaseplease.* "All our lives she and I have been close, like sisters, Eli ..." She couldn't get any more words out. Just looked inward at a future without Gin and felt eviscerated.

Eli held her. They stood, her wet cheek against his shoulder, his arms around her, for long minutes, while the newscast went on and on, an endless narrative of horror intercut with moments of heroism, first-person accounts of escape, people quaking as they spoke in high, taut voices of seeing jumpers in the final moments before the second tower went down. Lucinda thought about little Ginny Holder in her outrageous dresses, a miniature ten-year-old Mae West, with a tiny body as shapeless as a lozenge, in the studio schoolroom, saying, "If you're lookin' to get anywhere, you're gonna have to drop some of those pounds and do somethin' with your hair."

Six-year-old Lucinda telling her, "That's okay. I only like *watching* movies. I don't want to be *in* them."

"So how come you're here?" Ginny asked.

And Lucinda explained, "My mama works on the lot."

"Oh! Okay. So whaddya think of my dress?" Doing a slow turn to show off the diagonally striped black and white, knee-length, form-fitting garment that had puffed sleeves to the elbow and a big white collar.

"It's ..." Lucinda had to search for the right word. "It's amazing."

"Yeah, isn't it?" Ginny beamed and stood, one hand on her hip, eyes alight with pleasure. And Lucinda had liked her better than any other kid she'd ever met, knowing they were going to be friends.

She couldn't be dead, Lucinda thought. The world would

be a cold, dark cave without Gin's radiance. And Kat would crumble without her mother. Jeneva would be left, as Elise had been, trying to find some logical order to a child predeceasing her mother. It was all too cruel, too crazy, too excruciatingly painful.

At last, Eli said, "Have you got any coffee, Luce?"

She raised her head to study him. They'd broken past some previously unrecognized barrier. It was the first time he'd ever called her anything but her full name.

"Yes, I do."

"I could really use a cup of coffee," he told her. "I can make it."

"No, no. I'll do it." Any action, even the smallest, gave her some sense of purpose, took her mind off what was happening a short train-ride away. Getting lost for a moment, she wondered if the commuter trains had been stopped. How would all those people get home?

"If you have it, you should put on your call forwarding," he said, "and turn on your cell phone. In case."

"Yes," she agreed, glad to follow directions. "Good idea. I'll do that." She went to the desk and activated the call forwarding, then said, "My cell's in the kitchen." Again, she took his hand. He was keeping her anchored, she realized. And perhaps she was anchoring him as well. All sorts of barriers had fallen or been eradicated; because she didn't question her need to hold on to him, to take his hand, to heed his instructions. She wasn't self-conscious or concerned with how he might interpret her actions. Her previous fears seemed selfish, petty, inconsequential. All that fretting about minor issues; fussing over semantics and appearances when the world beyond these walls had been heaved into chaos. Remarkably, Eli seemed to have no qualms about asking for coffee, suggesting what she should do about the phones. Because of the circumstances, they had stopped being entirely separate. There was a blurring of the lines, a dismantling of the self-imposed constraints. The morning's events had wiped away trivial matters, facilitating a different, more important level of communication. They had drawn close in a time of tragedy when their positions were shown to be small, scarcely worthy of notice—except to each other and those they loved.

She busied herself making a pot of coffee, forgetting the cell phone altogether, from moment to moment seeing that second plane go flying at full speed into the south tower. Then, the towers came down, one right after the other—a time-lapse sequence, with otherworldly ash-covered souls emerging from the debris clouds. The scenes played over and over behind her eyes, and she couldn't believe she was doing something as mundane as brewing a pot of coffee when her dearest friends were very likely dead. But she couldn't go there. It was a door she was terrified to open, so fearful was she of what lay on the other side. So she kept viewing the loop, and the buildings came down again, then again, and again. She poured water into the reservoir, put filter paper in the basket, then added coffee. The carafe in place, she pressed the On button. Functioning by rote. She could hear the voices on TV but, mercifully, couldn't make out what was being said. She didn't think she could take in anything more. *Gin, you can't be gone! Please don't be gone.*

Eli unplugged her cell phone from the charger and powered it on. He looked at it, then said, "You've got messages, Luce," and held the phone out to her.

Addled, she took the absurdly small thing—scarcely bigger than Lily's old powder compact—and looked at the screen. Message indicator flashing.

"You do it, please," she said hoarsely, handing the phone back to him. "I can't."

He said, "No problem. What's your PIN and the access number?"

She told him, and watched as he entered the numbers, then listened intently for what seemed a long time. He smiled at one point, then his expression sobered. He pressed a button and said, "There's some good news and some not so good news. You'd better listen."

"I don't think I can handle bad news, Eli."

"It's not optional, Luce," he said gently, giving her the phone. "Just press this button and listen."

Nearly sick with dread, keeping her eyes on his, she did as he'd said, then held the cell phone to her ear. There was a lot of background noise, then she heard Gin's voice. "My limo driver was so busy trying to impress me with his whatever, charm, bullshit, that he plowed right into the back of a cab. By the time everybody told their stories to the cop and swapped insurance numbers, it was after eight and we'd gone maybe three whole blocks from the hotel. When I finally got to the airport both the L. A. flights were gone. So I said to hell with it, and rented a car at Logan to come home. I just now heard on the radio about the crash and knew you'd be going nuts, thinking I was on the plane. It's about nine-thirty and I'm at some godforsaken shopping center just off I-Ninety-five, buying a cell phone with a car charger. I tried to reach you from the airport but couldn't get through. The phone lines are FUBAR everywhere. The sales-child here—I swear he's about eleven—is letting me use the store phone, but it's so goddam noisy with all the TV sets going I can't hear myself think. And I sure as hell can't believe what I'm seeing. Listen, I'm heading back to the rental now to plug in the gizmo and get this sucker charging. I'll check in with you again in a while, if I can figure out how to use the thing. You know me and equipment. But I'm okay, Luce, so don't worry. I'm on my way home. I love you, sweetheart. 'Bye."

Her chest heaved and relieved tears overflowed, as the next message began to play.

It was Renee, her voice tight and thin. "I can't get through to your phone, so I hope you get this. I'm on my way back from New Haven to pick Jase up from school. This is such a nightmare. I'll talk to you later."

God! She'd completely forgotten about Jason. She supposed that all the schools had closed, yet she hadn't even thought of it. Then she heard Katanya's voice, wobbly and out of control.

"Luce, I'm so *scared*. I can't find my *moms*. My gramma said she's comin' home soon as Mrs. Weinburg's son gets there. She doesn't want to leave the old lady all alone. Gramma's scared about my moms, too but she's makin' out like things'll be okay. She was in the north tower, but I don't think she was up that high, where the plane hit. I wanna go downtown and look for her but I'm afraid to go out in case she phones. And I wouldn't know where to look. I don't know what to *do*. Mrs. Garcia said I should go downstairs 'n' stay with her but I don't wanna leave the phone. Please call me, Luce. *Please*."

Next it was Gin again. "Okay, it's ten-fifteen and I'm at a rest area trying to figure out how to use this idiotic thing. I wish you'd turn on your goddamn cell but you probably don't even know about the phone lines being out of whack.

The highway's just about empty. Rows and rows of trucks are parked here with their motors running, but no drivers. They're all inside, dead quiet, watching what's happening on TV or lining up at the pay phones, calling home. A couple of them were actually crying, telling their wives or kids they loved them. I saw them when I ran in to grab a coffee. The girls working the counters were all in tears. And I just now realized Lorrie's new job is at the Trade Center. I hope to God she's okay. This is such scary shit. Everybody looks completely stunned, as if they've just been whacked with a two-by-four. Okay, I'm on my way. I'll be there in a couple of hours."

The last message was from a now-sobbing Katanya. "Turn on your cell phone and *call* me, Luce! I'm so scared for my moms. And Mrs. Weinburg's son isn't there yet so Gramma can't come home. I *need* you, Luce!"

Lucinda disconnected and carefully put the phone down on the table.

"Call Kat," Eli said quietly.

"Gin missed the flight," Lucinda said dumbly.

"I know. I heard. And I'm as relieved as you are. Now call Kat, Luce. She needs you. If you don't mind, while you do that I'll call Elise to let her know Gin's okay."

"I don't mind. Why did you come here, Eli?"

"You know why," he said patiently.

She thought about that for several seconds. At the worst moments in life one needed to be with the people who mattered most. Then, in acknowledgment, she leaned into him, inhaling the now-familiar scent of Joup, reassured by his arm closing around her shoulders. Wordless communication as the aroma of the dripping coffee floated into the air. She stepped away, maintaining eye contact with him as she sat down at the table. She began to speak, couldn't get anything out, stopped, swallowed, then shook her head, looked down, steadied herself as best she could, and pressed the speed-dial for Katanya's number.

The girl was so fear-struck she was barely coherent. Hearing her, Lucinda knew she had to sound normal in order not to feed Katanya's fear.

"Honey, your grandmother will be there soon. I don't want to tie up your line in case your mother is trying to call you. Kat, please listen. Take a nice deep breath for me. Okay?" She listened as Katanya sucked air into her lungs. "Good. Once more, honey."

"Okay, Luce." Again, the girl drew a ragged breath.

Looking over at Eli, she realized he was speaking to Elise in French. It seemed remarkable—gracious, gentle and accommodating. Right then, a hackneyed old phrase became endowed with new meaning. Eli was going to be the love of her life. What she'd had with Cort had been sweet, a youthful passionate affection. Her feeling for Eli was stirring and intense, multi-layered and deeply complex. It had started forming itself in the many weeks since their accidental meeting in the Westport parking lot. Since then, it had been growing, gathering strength daily. The reality made itself fully known to her in that moment. There wasn't a single thing about him that she didn't like. And she couldn't imagine her future without him in it.

Returning her attention to Katanya, she said, "Good girl. Forward the calls from your home phone to your cell, then go down to Mrs. Garcia's. It's not a good idea for you to be alone just now. And please stay away from the TV, Kat. Don't watch any more. It'll only make you more scared than you already are."

"They keep *showing* it over and *over*," Katanya wailed.

"I know, honey. That's why I want you to turn it off."

"But what if more planes are coming? We could *all* be killed."

"I don't believe that's going to happen, Kat. I think you should go downstairs now. Will you call me, please, the minute you hear from your mother?"

Katanya hiccuped, then managed to say, "Okay. I wish you were here with me, Luce."

"I know, honey. I know. But I'm with you in my heart."

"Are you all by yourself, Luce?"

"No. Eli's here."

"Good. You shouldn't be alone, either."

"Go on down to Mrs. Garcia's now. All right?"

"Yeah, all right. You think my moms is okay?

"I'm praying that she is, Kat. I love you and I'll be waiting to hear from you."

"Love you, too." In tears again, Katanya ended the call.

"Maddie and Steven and Michael are all okay," Eli told her. "After hours of trying, Steven finally found Gwyn's cell phone number and got through to her. Everyone in the family is accounted for."

In an unparalleled state of ongoing apprehension, Lucinda sat next to Eli on the sofa, drinking coffee and watching the continuing news reports on TV. At 12:15 they heard that the U.S. had closed some border crossings with Canada and Mexico. Then, a minute or two later, it was announced that U.S. airspace was clear except for military and emergency flights. Only a few transoceanic flights were still landing in Canada.

"They're locking the barn door," Eli said tiredly as the front door opened and Gin came bounding in.

Without a word, Lucinda jumped up, and threw her arms around her friend, lifting her right off the floor. Gin, who weighed scarcely more than Jason, didn't protest, but wound her arms around Lucinda's neck and laid her head on Lucinda's shoulder.

"The thought that you were gone was unbearable," Lucinda whispered to her. "I couldn't stand it."

"You think I didn't know that?" Gin said as Lucinda set her down. "That's why I kept trying to get through to you."

Freeing herself, she went over to hug Eli, saying, "I knew you'd be here. Is your son okay?"

"He's okay," Eli confirmed. "Thank you for asking, Gin."

"Listen, guys, is there any more of that coffee?" She paused and turned to look over at the TV. "Could we turn that off, give it a rest for a while? My head's ready to explode."

"Good idea," Eli said, and picked up the remote. "Why don't you two take it easy and I'll put some food together." Pulling off his tie, he shoved it into his pocket, then removed his jacket. "Go on," he said, rolling up his sleeves. "Sit down and I'll get your coffee, Gin."

Gin hugged him again, then flopped onto the sofa. "Jesus H. Christ!" she said tiredly. "They're saying maybe as many as seven or eight *thousand* people died in the towers. Hundreds of firemen, dozens of cops. It's a horror show."

"I was watching," Lucinda said, resuming her place on the sofa, her eyes going automatically to the now darkened TV screen. "I couldn't stop thinking of special effects. Kat's frantic. There's been no word from Lorrie."

"Ah, shit!" Gin said, shaking her head. "She's *gotta* be okay. I was thinking about her the whole way here. I've got a horrible feeling we're all gonna know somebody in those towers or on those planes." She ran both hands over her face as if trying to rub away her fatigue, then said, "I have to do something for the limo driver. The goofy guy was getting on my nerves like you wouldn't believe, yacking away nonstop first thing in the morning."

"Not your best time," Lucinda said, able to smile at this.

"There's an understatement. But his ceaseless yacking *saved my life*. It's unbelievable. I have to do something for him. I'm trying to decide between money or a gift. Probably money. You think?"

"A gift, Gin. Giving money could be misconstrued."

"Yeah, you're right. Something expensive, maybe a watch."

"From Cartier," Lucinda said.

"Yeah, with an inscription and the date. I wonder if he even realizes what he did."

"Doubtful. He's probably just embarrassed as hell that trying to impress you got him into a rear-ender."

"Probably. I'll call the limo company, make sure they know he's a hero." Letting her head fall back against the sofa, Gin said, "No news at all on Lorrie?"

"Nothing. Kat was falling apart. Mrs. Garcia was asking her to come down but she didn't want to leave the phone, in case Lorrie called. So I encouraged her to take her cell and go downstairs. Kat just told me, but I keep forgetting which tower she was in. I don't think I want to remember."

"Me, neither. Where's Jen?"

"Last I heard, she was still with Mrs. Weinburg. They're waiting for her son to come, then Jen's going home to wait with Kat."

"Poor Jen must be going crazy. I would be."

"I keep telling myself Lorrie's okay, she got out." Lucinda laced her hands together, those scenes of the towers coming down playing over and over in her mind. "I'm not going down possibility road, Gin. I can't. Until I know otherwise, I have to believe she's safe."

"Me, too. So did Eli just show up or did you call him?"

"He showed up."

"He's a very special guy, kiddo."

"He really is. You know what became very clear to me this morning? Watching it all happen, knowing people were dying, suddenly all my concerns and inhibitions seemed pathetically unimportant. Going up one side and down the other, worrying about subtext, about what people are really saying, what they *really* mean, it's such a shameful waste of time. It can all end in seconds, with no warning. I keep thinking of the people in the north tower, sitting at their desks, maybe talking on the phone or having their bagels and coffee—the usual morning routine. And just like that, they're not only dead, they're gone. Completely *gone*. Someone on one of the stations was saying that the heat of those fires was four thousand degrees or more. Instant cremation. Nothing left for their families. No bodies to identify, no way of knowing for sure that their husbands, wives, children, mothers, fathers are actually gone. I can't waste whatever time I've got fretting over things that are inconsequential compared to that. I can't. It would be unforgivably self-indulgent."

Gin stared at her for a long moment. Then she reached over to hold Lucinda's hand, saying, "I have a confession to make. It's something I've been meaning to tell you for ages, but I kept putting it off because I was afraid you'd be very pissed off with me."

"That would never happen."

"Trust me, it could. This is serious."

"No matter what it is, I promise I won't get pissed off."

"You *promise*?"

"I do."

"Okay. The thing is," Gin said, "I was worried about you turning into a head-case."

"I know that."

"So one night, I was having dinner with all my gay buddies at Huck's house. Huck's my makeup maven. Remember?"

"Right."

"Anyway, his friend Simon was there, a couple of others. All really terrific guys, people I *trust*. Okay?"

"Okay."

"So we're shooting the breeze after dinner and Simon was saying they'd been looking forever but couldn't find anybody with the smarts and the background to write their movie reviews."

"Simon? Oh my god! It was *you*! You were the one who told him about me."

"Yup, I'm the one. Are you mad?"

"No. I'm just—stunned. I couldn't figure out how they knew, how they tracked me down … Gin, why would you think that'd make me mad?"

"Kiddo, nobody *ever* knows exactly how anyone else will react to something. You were the perfect person for the gig, with all that talent going to waste. But I was blowing your anonymity, your privacy. It's not as if I didn't know your feelings on the subject, so, to me, it felt like I was putting our friendship on the line. It was just so perfect for you, though, and you were so perfect for them. And I wasn't wrong, was I?"

"You couldn't have been more right."

Gin let out a big huff of air and said, "Man, is that ever

a relief! There was one little part of my brain that was positive you'd murder me. The rest of me felt good about it. But still, it was an iffy thing to do."

"No, I'm so grateful. And look what you did for Soupboy!"

"Sorry, that one's on you. You're the one who's made him famous. Nothing to do with me."

"Okay, fine. It was me. Thank you, Gin." Lucinda leaned over and kissed her cheek. "It was a typically gutsy, Gin kind of thing to do, and I love you for it."

Eli appeared in the doorway and said, "Food in five."

"Yes, sir." Gin saluted.

"In the kitchen," he added.

"What? No room service?" she quipped.

"I don't *do* room service." With a smile, he left them.

"I dare you to tell me you're not mad about that man," Gin said.

"Oh, I *am* mad about that man," Lucinda said in a very low voice. "I am completely, absolutely, utterly besotted with that man."

"Oh, well as long as it's nothing serious."

Their eyes locked for a long moment and then, too drained to laugh, they smiled at each other.

The two women sat at the table in almost somnolent silence, until Eli brought over a platter of sandwiches, saying, "We have to eat."

Leaning on her elbow, chin cupped in her upturned palm, Gin said, "Why?"

"Why?" he repeated. "Because you"—he pointed at Lucinda—"will get a migraine if you don't. And you"—his finger moved to Gin—"drove for, what? Four and a half hours? And you drank, how many coffees, three?"

"Four," Gin said.

"Okay, you'll *both* have headaches. And I'll feel physically sick instead of just heartsick." Holding out the platter, he said, "Please. Humor me and eat."

"Okay. When you're right, you're right," Gin said, and put half a tuna sandwich on her plate.

Lucinda also took half a sandwich, doubting she'd be able to eat even a bite of it. She couldn't stop seeing those towers fall, couldn't stop hoping and praying Loranne hadn't been inside.

"There's fresh coffee," Eli said. "But, Gin, you should probably have Seven-Up or water. More coffee will make you hypertensive. You won't be able to sleep, no matter how tired you are."

"Water, please."

"Luce? What would you like?"

"I—"

Her cell phone rang. She jumped up and hurried to the counter to grab it.

"Lucy, it's Jeneva." Her voice was wearied but not despairing. Lucinda took this as a good sign.

"Did you find Lorrie? Have you heard from her?"

"She called about half an hour ago. Hernan's gone down to St. Vincent's on his motorcycle to get her. She has a few scrapes and her feet got really cut up from going down sixty-seven flights of concrete stairs with no shoes."

"No shoes?"

"She was just taking off her sneakers when the first plane hit. She didn't hesitate, just grabbed her purse and ran to the fire exit. She's alive, Lucy. That's all that matters."

"I'm so glad, *so* glad. What about you, Jen? Are you all right?"

"I am now. But I'm very shaky. Holding in all that fear for hours, every minute lasting forever, trying not to think the worst. I'm ready to lie down on my bed and have a good long cry. I'll save that for later, after I see my girl, see for myself how she is. I'm worried there are going to be more attacks."

"I think everyone is. How's Kat doing? I wish I could've been with her."

"You did the right thing, encouraging her to go down to Gloria's. That child is as close to a breakdown as anyone can get without falling right over the brink. It's been a terrible, terrible day. The whole city's in a state of shock and grief. Coming back from Mrs. Weinburg's, the streets were filled with people walking home from downtown, most of them crying, even a lot of the men. I've never seen anything like it. There's a prayer meeting at the church tonight. I feel a need to go, to give thanks."

"If I was there, I'd go with you. Thank you so much for letting me know. Give my love to Lorrie and Kat, please. And if there's anything you need, anything at all I can do, call me."

"You're not alone there, are you, Lucy?" Jeneva asked, echoing Katanya's concern.

"No. Eli's here and so is Gin."

"Good. Nobody should be alone today. My love to all of you. I'll call you back later, let you know how we're doing."

"Please. I'd appreciate it. Love you, Jen."

Lucinda put down the phone. "Loranne's okay. Hernan's on his way downtown to St. Vincent's to get her." Returning to the table, she repeated what Jeneva had told her, overwhelmed once more by that cinematic sense of unreality she'd felt so strongly since receiving the emailed news bulletin hours earlier. Now that she knew her friends were safe, she was suddenly exhausted yet still very tense. Everything was a tremendous effort, even lifting the sandwich to take a bite. But Gin and Eli seemed to be moving sluggishly, too.

"It's the shock," Eli said, as if able to see into her brain and transcribe her thoughts. "The aftermath is fatigue."

"I feel exhausted," Lucinda admitted. "Gin, you can spend the night here, if you want."

"Thanks, but after I finish this"—she held up her sandwich—"I'm going to swing by the market to pick up some basics, then go get my dogs from the kennel. I just want to be home with my boys." She paused a beat, then said, "You know, I'm wondering if I'll ever be able to get on another plane."

"I think we're all wondering about that," Eli said. "The airlines and the travel business will be crippled by what's happened today. No one's ever going to feel the same way again about flying. The repercussions will be tremendous across the board. The insurance companies are going to get hit hard, too—a gigantic domino effect."

There was silence as each of them considered what he'd said.

Not one of them consumed more than a few bites of their sandwiches. Eli found the plastic wrap and put the platter in the refrigerator. Then the three of them walked outside into the mild afternoon—the sky still cloudless, still so blue—and stood blinking in the sunlight as if emerging from a long tunnel. After an exchange of embraces and a promise to check in later or the next morning, Gin drove off in the rental car.

"Do you want me to go?" Eli asked, glancing at his watch. It was just after three.

"No. I'd like you to stay," Lucinda answered. "Unless you have housecalls to make."

"I'd like to stay, too. If anything urgent comes up, they'll page me."

"It's so jarring," she said, looking up at the sky. "Coming outside, somehow I was expecting it to be dark. Not night, but *dark*. Let's go see my grandmother."

"Great idea. Would you mind if I clean up?"

"Of course not. Help yourself to one of the bathrooms. I'm just going to call to let her know we're coming."

Elise said, "I would love to see you. I sent Gwyn home some hours ago. And Erica has been with me all afternoon, watching the television."

"Why don't we bring some food and feed you and Erica for a change?"

"That would be splendid, *chérie*. You are very kind."

"Not at all. We'll be there soon. Is there anything you need?"

"Only to see you."

Chapter Sixteen

Eli accepted her invitation to drive when they left Elise's house, and she was so comfortable with him at the wheel now that she dozed off, waking only when the car came to a stop.

"Where are we?" she asked, sitting up to look past the windshield.

"Calf Pasture Beach. I see I'm not the only one who had this idea." He turned off the lights, got out and came around to the passenger side.

Hand in hand they walked to the pier and joined the dozen or so other people who were gazing across the Sound. The fires burning in the ruined area that had once been the World Trade Center complex were a molten glow in the smoke-laden cloud covering the bottom of Manhattan.

The only sound was of the waves washing languidly in to shore, then retreating. Lucinda thought of Jeneva at her prayer meeting and couldn't help but feel that this gathering was of a similar nature. Unexpressed fear and sorrow hung over them in the warm night air, almost as palpable as the odor of burning carried by the wind.

All the people she loved were alive. It seemed miraculous in the face of such losses—not only of lives but of trust, and of the general confidence in personal safety. Random accidents could always happen. But the morning's events had been anything but random. The targets and the day itself had been chosen specifically for their impact. The message had been successfully delivered. *You are not safe. What you perceive as your safety is merely an illusion. We will destroy your illusions, even your lives, in great numbers.*

It was so difficult to think rationally in the face of irrational-seeming acts, carried out by terrorists who were prepared to die for their beliefs. The only way to deter fanatics, of any stripe, was by understanding their mind-set. And even then, understanding was no guarantee of dissuasion. Made-up minds were all but impossible to change. Take Aunt Anne, for example. An embrace merely bewildered her, disrupted her plans—which, themselves, were indirect, never fully formed, never realized.

Back in the car, Lucinda said, "What made you think of coming here, Eli?"

"I guess I wanted to get some kind of perspective. Television makes everything so *small*. This is no small thing. Intellectually, emotionally, I know that. But I wanted to set it to scale. It's like that conversation we had a couple of months ago, the first time I came to dinner at your house. Thinking about death and examining it through a microscope, looking at it this way and that, trying to get a sense of it as an entity. But I can't. It's just not possible."

"I remember," Lucinda said.

"As I recall, you said something to the effect of its being too big to see completely, like standing at the base of a mountain and trying to see all of it—top, bottom, its entire circumference. What you said was true then, true now. But the enormity of this—I have to try to get perspective so I can put my feelings into some kind of order."

"How *do* you feel?" she asked.

"Conflicted. Angry and sad, relieved and frightened. I feel selfish, because my son is okay and I'm glad. Guilty, because a lot of other sons are dead tonight. Angry at the madness of it."

"I don't think it's selfish to be glad your son is okay. How many losses is one person supposed to sustain in a lifetime? I don't subscribe to the Book of Job. I don't believe faith has to be tested by stripping someone of all he values. But then, I'm not a religious person."

"Oh, I think you are," he disagreed. "Just because you don't belong to an organized group doesn't mean you lack a belief system. When you get down to it, an awful lot of harm gets done under the mantle of religious rightness. I happen to believe true religion is a behavioral code; it's how you treat other people."

"Do unto others, you mean."

"Not a lot of people behave honorably, Luce. At a time like this, folks pull together. Something at a primal level moves us to reach out to one another in our anguish. But there will be some who'll look for ways to profit from what happened today. It's inevitable. They see an opportunity for personal gain, they'll take advantage of it. The majority of us will see it as reprehensible. But the con artists, the thieves, the ones with stones where their hearts ought to be will see it as entirely justified because they've got this obscene sense of entitlement. So, for all the good, there's always, *always* an element of bad."

"But that's human nature, Eli."

"Unfortunately, it is. All my life I've wondered about that. I'm not satisfied with simplistic notions of good and evil in the Garden of Eden. It's not even about higher or lower intelligence because I've met some highly intelligent people who were absolutely unscrupulous, entirely devoid of any concern for others. And I've met good, honest and kind people working registers in supermarkets, and parking cars, even panhandling on the streets in the city—people who would not be considered all that smart."

"If that's your thinking, why do you go to church?" she asked.

He smiled tiredly. "Primarily, honestly, because I love the music. That choir is the most joyful thing I know. Maybe true religion is a choir."

"Maybe it's simply music."

"No," he said. "It's love."

"You may be right. I think we should go now, Eli."

"Okay." He turned the key in the ignition, fastened his seat belt, then put on the headlights and reversed the car.

When they arrived back at her house, her thoughts and conclusions of that morning clear in her mind, she said, "Stay here with me tonight, Eli."

Surprised, he said, "Really?"

It took her a second or two to answer. "Really. I would like you to."

"So would I. Nothing has to happen."

Her laugh surprised both of them. "Everything has to happen," she said, "eventually."

"Ah!" he said, climbing out of the car. "The escape clause."

"Actually," she said, "that was entirely for my benefit. Just in case."

"Which is why I said nothing has to happen."

She unlocked the door and stepped inside, saying, "I'm going to take a shower. Do me a favor and lock up down here, then come find me. *Eventually.*"

She heard the water running in the guest bathroom. Not even sure why, (Eli wasn't someone who'd just walk in on her) she locked her bathroom door, then stood under the shower, so nervous she could barely function. Her coordination had vanished. She felt premeditated and clumsy. Her mouth was dry; her heartbeat so rapid it made her dizzy. With one hand braced against the wall, she closed her eyes and reminded herself of all the things she'd said to Gin that afternoon. She'd made a declaration of intent and felt obliged to honor it.

What mattered? she asked herself. This wasn't a contest. There was nothing to prove. It was about commitment. But it had been so long since commitment had any relevance to her life that she had to ask herself if she really knew what she was doing.

Then she thought back to the first evening Eli had come to dinner, how they'd stood in the driveway talking, and he'd spoken about his wife. *"It happened in a kind of extreme slow motion. First the tiny lump, followed by a partial mastectomy, chemo, radiation."* God, sometimes she was so slow! He'd told her that evening that he'd had an intimate acquaintanceship with disfigurement; he'd lived with it for years. It hadn't mattered because—Gin was right—it was about the person, not about the parts that comprised them. Anyone with halfway decent eyesight and average intelligence could look at her and know she wasn't merely flat-chested but without breasts altogether. He'd known from the outset and it hadn't mattered to him.

"Oh! So I'm not an object of lust," she'd quipped, then was shocked at herself.

He'd laughed. "Don't be so sure of that. Depends on the interpretation you put on lust. I like your brain."

The worst thing that could happen was that one or both of them (probably both, she thought, trying to be realistic) would be awkward and it would be less than great. But if they survived their first time, things could only go uphill from there. And there was no reason why there wouldn't be a second time. It was just surviving the first time, revealing herself completely, that was so unnerving.

Finally, somewhat calmer, she turned off the water and climbed out of the tub, reaching for a towel. She could hear music. He'd turned on the radio. *What the hell was she supposed to do next?*

"I'm relieved!" he called out. "I was about to phone the sub-aqua rescue team!"

She broke out laughing as she grabbed her terrycloth robe.

"There'd better not be any lights on!" she called back.

"I can't see my own hand in front of my face!"

"Good! Keep it that way!" she said, then took a deep breath and opened the door. He'd misrepresented only slightly. The curtains hadn't been drawn over the window, so the light from outside lent an ambient glow to the figure of Eli sitting in her bed. "Are you nervous?" she asked, taking a faltering step into the room.

"You have *got* to be joking! I have tachycardia. Listen,

I'm going to close my eyes. Let me know when it's safe to open them."

"Oh, brother!" she said to herself, as she dropped the robe and slipped beneath the covers. "Okay," she said with an effort. "It's as safe as it's going to get." Instinctively, she aligned her body with his and examined the influx of sensation. How could she have forgotten the stirring pleasure of flesh meeting flesh?

"Do you feel guilty now every time you laugh or smile?" she asked.

"No. I refuse to feel that way. Now is the perfect time to laugh and smile, to celebrate life."

"Good. I don't want to feel guilty."

"I have to tell you I'm in no way prepared for this," he said. "I'm not one of those jokers who carries a condom in his wallet, hoping he'll get lucky."

"Would those be the same pretentious cigar-smoking jokers who buy the three-hundred-dollar bottles of wine that turn to vinegar?"

"The very same."

"I see. Well, I think we're all right. I, uhm ... God! I am past prime," she said, then groaned and covered her face with her hand.

"Past prime," he said. "Please wait while I process that."

"Past my sell-by date. I can't get pregnant. And I haven't made love in over thirty years."

"And you think of that as past prime. Odd way of thinking. I would say you are peak prime."

"You lust after my brain," she reminded him, venturing to run her hand down the smooth, muscular length of his arm.

He reciprocated by taking his hand from her shoulder,

down her back to the rise of her hip. "That is true. However, I also lust after your long, gorgeous legs and the way your shoulders taper to your waist."

Small shocks followed the passage of his hand, her entire body startled. The embraces of friends, family, small children were singular, food for the heart. But skin to skin, the exchanges of touch were electrifying, a power source that could restore life. "This is very nice," she murmured, filled with anticipation and extraordinary excitement.

"Hmmn, very, *very* nice," he agreed.

And then words were displaced by an alternative communication that made profound statements.

She was jolted awake at coming up against a solid presence in her bed. For a long moment she was terrified. Then, remembering, the fear subsided. Her head returning to the pillow, she smiled, then waited for her heart to calm itself.

At the door, he said, "I should be back by around two, if nothing urgent comes up."

"I'll be here."

"I'm pretty much counting on that," he said, and put his hand on her cheek.

"Me, too."

When she opened the door, she was surprised to discover Jason sitting on the porch, barefoot, in his pajamas, his arms wrapped around his drawn-up knees. He looked pale, unwell.

"Hi, Soupboy. Why're you sitting out here? Why didn't you ring the doorbell?" Lucinda asked.

He shrugged.

Eli went to squat in front of him and put the back of his hand to Jason's forehead. "You feel okay, Jase? You're not looking too great."

Jason shrugged again.

"I'm coming back later for a swim," Eli said. "I hope you'll be here. I hardly ever see you now that school's started, and I've missed you."

"Me, too." He gulped, then said, "I needa talk to Luce."

"All right." Eli smoothed the boy's hair, then, on impulse, kissed his forehead.

To both Lucinda's and Eli's surprise, the boy erupted into tears, grabbed hold of the man's shirt and fell against him.

"Ah, hey!" Eli said, scooping up the boy and standing with him. "What's the matter, dear heart?"

"I needa talk to *Luce*!" he cried, his fists clutching the sleeves of Eli's shirt.

"Okay, son. Okay," Eli said soothingly. "You can talk to Luce."

"I'll take him," Lucinda said. "You'll be late, if you don't get going."

"I can be late, if this is important."

"It *is* important!" Jason cried and reached out to Lucinda.

"Whatever is wrong," Eli said, transferring the boy into Lucinda's arms, "I'm sorry, Jase. If you want to, we can talk later."

Jason nodded, then let his head fall onto Lucinda's shoulder, his hands now fastened to her robe.

"Want me to stay?" Eli asked her.

"No, you go on. Jason and I will be fine."

"Don't forget to unplug the charger and turn on your cell," Eli reminded her. "I'll call you in a while."

"Or I'll call you. We'll be fine," she repeated.

Looking concerned, Eli went to his car and waved before he drove off.

"How about a cup of coffee?" Lucinda asked as she carried Jason inside. Once a week or so, because he loved the grown-up aspect of it, she and Jason had coffee together.

"Yeah," he croaked.

In the kitchen, she lowered him into a chair at the table where he wearily laid his head down on his folded arms. She fixed him a drink that was half coffee and half non-dairy creamer with a little sugar, then brought it and a fresh cup of coffee for herself back to the table.

"There you go, honey," she said, sitting next to him.

He sat up, lifted the mug with both hands and drank some.

"Are you hungry?" she asked. "Have you had breakfast?"

He shook his head, drank some more, then put the mug down on the table.

"How long were you sitting out there, Jase?"

"I don't know. A while."

"Where's your mother? Does she know you're here?"

"*Who cares*?" he near-shouted. "She's so *stupid*! I *hate* her!"

"Whoa, slow down, honey." She placed a hand on his arm. "What's going on?"

"She's just sitting there watching the TV and crying all the time, not even talking. I'm *sick* of the TV. I said she should turn it off cuz I don't want to see that stuff anymore, but it's like she can't even *hear* me! The whole entire day yesterday and all night, and I come down this morning and she's *still* sitting there like a total gorpo. I had to get my own food last night. She didn't even say good night or anything, wouldn't even *answer the phone*!"

"Your phone is working?"

"*Yes, it's working*!" he barked.

"Jason, do not speak to me that way, please."

"Sorry. But she wouldn't answer the phone and it kept ringing and ringing. Usually she won't even *let* me answer. It was driving me nutso-demento, so I answered." His face twisted, his throat working.

"Have some more coffee," Lucinda said.

Obediently, he took a swallow, then set the mug down and stared fixedly at it.

"You answered the phone," she prompted.

Still staring at the mug, he said, "I go hello and this lady goes, Is that you, Jason? And I go, yeah. And she goes, darling, this is Granny Crane. It's so wonderful to speak to you after all this time. And I'm like, what's this about, how come all of a sudden you wanna talk to me? And she goes, we called so many times but your mother always said you didn't want to talk to any of us, not me or your granddad or your daddy. I go, *huh*? And she says they gave up and stopped calling cuz my stupid, stupid, *stupid fuckhead* mother wouldn't let me *talk* to them! SHE LIED TO ME!" he screamed. "All this time she was lying, *lying*!" He erupted into sobs, his face bright red. "SHE'S A GODDAMNED FUCKING LIAR AND I HATE HER!"

Deeply shocked, Lucinda pulled him into her arms. "I'm so sorry, honey," she said, kissing his hot face, stroking him. "I am *so* sorry."

"Lemme *go*!" He broke out of her embrace and began storming around the kitchen, sobbing and shouting. "She made me think they didn't care and the whole time they were trying to *talk* to me, wanting to come *see* me, my *dad*, too. They did *so* care about me but she lied all the time, calling them names, saying they were horrible. But none of it was *true*. Not one single word. Everything she said was a *lie*!" He threw himself face-down and pounded his fists on the floor, howling incoherently and writhing in outrage.

He was in such a state that all she could think of was finding a way to calm him down, but nothing she thought of seemed sensible. At last, unable to come up with anything else, she bent down and picked him up. Opening the back door, she carried him outside, through the gate and jumped into the pool with him.

The shock of the cool water had the desired effect. Surprised, spluttering, he leaned away, searching her face. "*Why'd you do that*?" he gasped.

"You were scaring me and I couldn't think of anything else," she admitted.

He continued to study her for quite some time as the water soothed him, drawing away the heat of his outrage. Finally, he said, "Eli stayed over last night?"

"Yes, he did."

"How come?"

"I asked him to."

"Why?"

"Because I love him a lot and I wanted him to stay."

"You love me a lot, too?"

"Yes, I do, very very much."

"So can I stay over, like forever?"

"Honey, I know you're very angry with her, but your mother loves you. You can't leave home because you don't like something she did."

"But what she did was wrong and bad, Luce."

"Yes, it was. It was very wrong and very bad."

"*Why* did she *do* it?" he asked plaintively.

"I guess because she was mad at your father for leaving."

"But he left *her*, not *me*. What she did wasn't *fair*!"

"No, it definitely was not."

"It wasn't *right*!"

"No, it was not that, either," she confirmed.

"All this time, I could've been seeing my dad and my granny and grandpa. But she wouldn't let it happen and I don't understand *why*."

"Jason, sometimes when people's feelings get hurt they do things that don't make sense, that aren't reasonable or even rational. I don't think she did what she did to hurt *you*. She wanted to hurt your *father*."

"But she *did* hurt me, though."

"I know. I know."

"I won't ever forgive her."

"Yes, you will, honey. Even though you're furious with her right now, she's your mother and you love her."

His features firming so that she had all at once a clear view of how he'd look as an adult, he said, "It'll never ever be the same. *Never*. *Ever*. I don't care what you or anybody says. It was a bad, bad thing to do. People shouldn't do things like that, not to anybody, especially to kids and their dads. They shouldn't." He shook his head hard.

"You know what, Jason? When Eli comes back, I would like you to talk to him."

"Why?"

"Because when he was a boy, some bad things happened to him, too. And he understands very well how you feel right now."

"So do you."

"Yes, but not the same way as Eli will."

"I don't know." He looked away.

"You think about it. Okay? Right now, we should go inside and get dry, before we both catch colds. Then I'll make you some breakfast."

"Yeah, okay. Luce? 'Member when you said people would think you were a loser-creep? I never would think that ever, cuz you're the truliest one of everybody I know in the whole world."

"Thank you, Soupboy. I love you very much."

"As much as you love Eli?"

"That's different, Jase."

"Why? How?"

"Because I love you the way I love Kat and her mother and grandmother, the way I love Gin and my grandmother and all my relatives. That's a kind of love that's called familial. But the way I love Eli is the guy-girl stuff that makes you say you're going to hurl every time you see the huggie-kissie smoochie stuff in a movie."

"*Gark*! You two do *that*?"

"It's just different. Okay? Now, let's get you out of these wet pajamas and into a hot shower. You left some clothes here last week that you can wear."

She wrapped him in a towel and said, "Go on up to the guest bathroom now. I'll leave your clothes outside the door."

He went running off down the hall and she shoved her sopping robe and his pajamas into the dryer, then wound a beach towel around herself sarong fashion. She was so incensed she wanted to march down the road and take her fists to Renee. But she'd have to be satisfied with raking the younger woman over the coals. Like Jason, Lucinda was never going to feel the same way about Renee—even with the reservations she'd long-since harbored. What Renee had done was truly unforgivable. He might be not quite nine years old, but Jason wasn't given to casual declarations. He meant every last word he'd said. And, privately, Lucinda agreed with him. How could he ever again trust her? Renee had done irreparable damage to their relationship.

Chapter Seventeen

"Poor Lorrie is a wreck," Jeneva was saying. "She can't stop shaking and crying; she jumps at the slightest noise and keeps flashing back to when the plane hit, then she cries and shakes even harder. St. Vincent's sent her home with some pain meds, tranquilizers and sleeping pills. I finally made her take a sleeping pill, and wound up with the two of them in my bed last night. It was like lying between two windmills. Once they were finally asleep, I had to take myself to the sofa so I could get some rest. The worst of it is that because Lorrie's so upset, Kat doesn't know what to do with herself."

"How so?" Lucinda asked.

"It's hard to describe. Now that she knows her mother's all right, she's suddenly very angry, even rude. She stormed around here for an hour this morning, then went marching out without saying where she was going, didn't even take her cell phone. I've never *seen* her like this."

"It's the shock of yesterday, don't you think?"

"That's the root of it, I'm sure," Jeneva said. "There's all kinds of emotion bubbling away under the surface. I'm keeping my fingers crossed that in another few days it'll pass. As for Lorrie, I just don't know. When Hernan brought her home she had that same look I remember on the faces of the boys coming back from Vietnam—as if they'd gone to a place that was so ungodly their minds couldn't contain it. The two who came to tell me about my Jimmy were so young, so sober. I've never forgotten them, wondering what it must've been like for them to be assigned to that unit, having to visit the families of the ones who died. Now, here's my girl with that thousand-yard stare and the shakes as if she's coming off a week-long bender. Her injuries aren't serious, but she's terror-stricken."

"Poor Lorrie. I can only imagine what it must have been like. Bad enough watching it on television, but to have been inside ..."

"Exactly," Jeneva agreed. "Mrs. Weinburg talked about Pearl Harbor. And I kept thinking about the day Kennedy was assassinated. Yesterday was one of the days that, whenever we think of it in years to come, we'll remember exactly what we were doing and how we felt."

"I know." Lucinda hesitated, then said, "Jen, there's something I want to discuss with you. It's about Jason and Renee and I'd really like your input on this."

"Okay. Tell me," Jeneva invited. "What's going on?"

Lucinda repeated what Jason had told her that morning and about his reaction. Jeneva drew in her breath sharply, then exclaimed, "How could she be so damned senseless? It's downright wicked to do that to a child, especially one like Jason who's so attuned to everything that goes on around him."

"She's still not answering the phone," Lucinda told her. "I tried several times this morning. Now that Eli's here, I'm going to go over there. I just wanted your feedback, in case I was overreacting."

"Frankly, I don't see how you *could* overreact to something like that!" Jeneva said. "I was there, I'd slap that woman silly. Such a cruel, cruel thing to do!"

"Eli's in the pool with Jason now, having a talk with him. He adores Eli."

"Oh, we all do," Jeneva said. "He's a lovely man."

"He went through some very rough times as a boy. So I'm hoping he'll know what to say to Jason, because I'm not sure I do."

"As I said, I'd have to hit her," Jeneva said. "I want to hit her right now. Jason's right: She *is* stupid!"

"Jen, I'm thinking maybe you should bring Lorrie and Kat and stay here for a while."

"I'll give that some serious thought, Lucy. I have a feeling we might just take you up on that offer. For now, I want to give it a few days and see if things settle down some around here. Be sure to let me know how it goes with Renee. I'm not going to tell Lorrie about this. The minute I do, that friendship's over. All these years, I've never heard Lorrie say one bad word to Kat about her daddy. Whatever opinions Kat has about the man, she's formed them without any help from Lorrie."

"I'll get back to you. Please give Kat and Lorrie my love. And know that the invitation is wide open. If you decide just to get on the next train, it'll be fine with me. Phone from the station and I'll come get you."

"Thank you so much, Lucy. As I said, we may well turn up. But I'm hoping things will settle down."

"We'll talk later. I love you, Jen."

Lucinda went outside and stood by the gate, looking in. Eli was sitting on the side of the pool, with Jason on his lap. Their words were so quiet they didn't carry. Easing the gate shut, Lucinda returned to the kitchen and stood trying to decide how to deal with Renee. She'd left messages—first to say that Jason was with her, then asking her to call, and finally saying that until she heard from Renee she was keeping Jason with her, overnight if necessary. So far, Renee had either not listened to her messages or she was ignoring them.

After stewing over the matter for another fifteen minutes, she went back to the pool where Eli was floating on his back, with Jason floating beside him, his head resting on Eli's outstretched arm.

"You two look very comfortable," she said from the side of the pool.

"We are," Eli confirmed.

"I'm going to do a little errand," she said meaningfully. "I shouldn't be too long."

"We'll be here, won't we, son?" Eli said to Jason.

"Yeah. We'll be here," Jason confirmed.

~

She rang the doorbell. No response. She knocked on the door, hard. Nothing. She could hear the TV set and knew, from what Jason had told her, that Renee was inside, watching. Lucinda tried the door. It was unlocked. She walked inside and stood looking into the living room. There sat Renee in clothes she'd obviously been wearing since the day before, her hair a tangled mess, picking at her lower lip and staring fixedly at the TV set.

"What are you doing?" Lucinda asked.

If Renee was aware of her, she gave no sign of it.

Lucinda walked over, pulled the remote out of her hand and turned off the set.

"*What are you doing*?" Renee shrilled, trying to grab back the remote.

"More to the point, what are *you* doing?"

"You can't turn it off! Any minute, something else could happen! Give me that!"

"Where is Jason?" Lucinda asked.

Renee waved a hand at the ceiling. "Upstairs. Or in the kitchen."

"You have no idea where he is, do you?"

"He's fine. Give that back!"

"The first time I met you I thought you were rude and presumptuous," Lucinda said, sliding the back off the remote, removing the batteries and dropping them into her pocket. "Now I know you're considerably worse than that."

"What're you *doing*? You can't do *that*! Are you *crazy*?"

"No, but I think you might be. Jason has been at my house since five o'clock this morning. Eli's with him now, trying to come up with some kind of explanation for why you've been lying to him about his father and his grandparents for the last five years."

"What're you talking about?" Renee asked flatly, her eyes on the blank TV screen.

"I'm over here! Look at me!"

It seemed she couldn't. She kept staring at the TV screen, like an addict eyeing a fix. As a kid, at catered "theme" (African safari, or the circus, or even once, the Teddy Bears' picnic) birthday parties, Lucinda had seen that very same expression when one of the mothers would disappear into a bathroom and come back a while later, all smiling and wobbly, her eyes like a cartoon character's—almost swiveling on their stalks, unable to focus. She'd been too young to know what it meant at the time but when Lucinda was twelve, Lily had put it in simple terms for her. "There are people, not just in this town," she'd said, "who are drunks, or drug addicts. Same difference. It's a disease, Luce. They get hooked on booze or dope, and that's the end of them. Unless they can wise up enough to go into a program and get themselves straight. Keep away from people like that, even if they're charming and fun—and I have to tell you, they can be charming as hell and all kinds of fun—because if they don't get what they need they can turn very ugly. It's fine to have a drink now and then. But anybody who *has* to drink, or snort, or shoot something into their arm every day is hooked and has the disease. And stay away from people who *want*, who *need*, Luce. They *gotta* have this or they *need* to have that. They've got a disease, too. Only difference is in what you call it."

What kind of disease did Renee have? Lucinda wondered now. Self-pity, narcissism? Whatever its name, it was a pernicious thing that blocked out everything but Renee's needs and wants.

"You have to pull yourself together, for heaven's sake," Lucinda said. "You need to shower and wash your hair; you need to put on clean clothes and keep the damned TV set off. You're neglecting your son."

"What I *need* is to keep it *on*! Don't you *get* it? Thousands of people are *dead*. Grand Central station could be next, or the New York reservoirs, the Chrysler building. They could poison our drinking water or put bombs in the subways!"

"Watching that box night and day isn't going to change anything, or help anyone, or prevent another terrorist attack. You've got a child who needs attention *right now*. Not tomorrow. Now! You have to explain to him why you lied."

"Todd was a bastard. He left us."

"Maybe. But he's Jason's father, and he wanted to see his son. Jason's believed all this time that he'd been abandoned. He was hurt, and your lying to him only compounded the damage. You have a chance to set things straight. If you don't, you're risking alienating Jason for life. He may never forgive you."

"You don't know everything, even though you always act as if you do."

Here it comes! Lucinda thought, knowing she'd been right to exercise caution with Renee all along.

"You think you're a paragon of virtue but you're just a boring, know-it-all old spinster." She would have said more, Lucinda was certain, but she plainly lost her train of thought. Eyes gone vague, she picked at her lip for a moment, then said, "I have more batteries. I know I do," and walked away to the kitchen where she began rummaging through the drawers, mumbling to herself. Maybe she was having a breakdown and needed medical attention. Certainly, trying to engage her in conversation was futile. Perhaps Eli would know how to deal with her, Lucinda thought, watching Renee searching the drawers, throwing whatever got in her way on the floor. She was so obviously out of control that it was alarming to watch.

Spotting Renee's address book on the counter, Lucinda picked it up and slipped it into her pocket. "Here's your remote," she said, setting it and the batteries on the counter. "I'm going up to get some of Jason's things. He'll be staying with me until your spaceship comes back from Planet Zebulon."

After stowing Jason's backpack (containing all the school-related materials she'd been able to find in his room) and a duffle bag full of his clothes in the bigger of the two guest rooms, she went downstairs to the kitchen. After a quick look through Renee's address book, satisfied that the numbers she wanted were there, she went outside to see how things were going. Jason was laughing, playing some game with Eli that involved a lot of splashing.

Eli, the miracle man, she thought, awed by the depth of his kindness. She watched from the gate for a few minutes as Eli tossed the boy into the air and caught him. Jason squealed with pleasure, crying, "Do it again, Eli! *Do it again!*"

At last, she went back inside.

Her first call was to the Palmers in Greenwich.

It was Mr. Palmer who answered and Lucinda was glad of that. On the several occasions when she'd met the pair, he'd seemed the more grounded, slightly more accessible of the two.

"It's Lucinda Hunter, Mr. Palmer. How are you, sir?"

"Well, considering the circumstances. How are you, Miss Hunter?"

"The same. Look, I'll get right to the point. I think you and Mrs. Palmer should come up and see Renee. She seems to be having some problems right now."

"Problems?"

"You'll see for yourself. For now, I've got Jason here and I'll keep him with me until things are settled with Renee."

"Is she ill?"

"Frankly, I think she's having some sort of breakdown."

"I see. Well, I'll get my wife and we'll drive right up."

"That would be good."

"May I have your number, Miss Hunter? In case?"

After giving it to him, she drank some water and took a cimetadine tablet to calm her stomach. Then she called the Cranes. This time she reached the grandmother.

"Mrs. Crane? This is Lucinda Hunter, I'm a neighbor—"

"Oh, yes, Jason spoke of you last evening. It's obvious he's devoted to you." The warmth of the woman came through in her tone.

"And I to him. Mrs. Crane—"

"Pamela, please."

"Pamela, as you can imagine, Jason's terribly upset about what he's learned."

"Poor boy. He was so shocked. And I did feel awful, upsetting him. But I felt he had a right to know."

"I agree. The thing is, Jason has been here since very early this morning. Right now, a doctor friend of mine is talking to him, helping him deal with the situation. I just came back from trying to talk to Renee, but it was impossible. She's in a very bad way, completely out of it. I've spoken to her father and he and her mother are on their way up to see what can be done."

"A bad way how?" the woman asked.

"Oh, emotionally. I'm by no means qualified to judge, but she seems to be having some kind of breakdown."

"Ah! Well, let me fill you in a bit, if I may."

"Please. I'd appreciate it."

"I did manage in the end to talk to Renee last night." Pamela faltered, cleared her throat, then went on. "I was determined, so I just let the phone keep ringing—it was a good half-hour at least—until she answered." Again, she faltered. "Our … Todd died yesterday at the Trade Center."

"Oh, no! I'm so sorry."

"I suppose in one way we're fortunate, unlike so many of those other poor families. We have a body to bury. Todd was outside, on the street. He got hit by falling debris."

"Mrs. Crane, Pamela, I am truly sorry."

"Thank you. That's very kind." She paused to clear her throat again. "I just couldn't bring myself to tell Jason. It felt too cruel, under the circumstances. But I did tell Renee. I wanted her to be the one to tell Jason. Perhaps that's why she's so distraught."

"Perhaps it is."

"I have to tell you— May I call you Lucinda?"

"Of course."

"Lucinda, whatever she may have told you about Todd, I doubt very much of it was true. My son was a decent man with great integrity. He did *not* take all their money, and he did *not* simply walk out on them. He'd tried for months to tell her he wasn't happy, that commuting into the city every day was wearing him out. He was a conscientious man and put in very long hours, so he was getting almost no sleep. He was also bothered by Renee's inability to deal with Jason. The boy was just out of control, wild, throwing tantrums, screaming—"

"I remember vividly how he was."

"All right. So you know about that, at least. She just wouldn't listen when Todd tried to talk to her. She didn't want to hear. Things were the way she wanted them and she had no interest in changing anything. She refused to move closer to the city. It was her house and she wasn't selling it. And if Todd spent more time with Jason, Jason wouldn't be so badly behaved. But every time Todd made any gains with the boy, Renee undermined whatever he'd accomplished.

"In the end, he was so worn out, in every way, that he packed up and left. But I assure you, he took only his own money. During the divorce, her lawyer tried to make a case that he'd wiped out all the accounts. But Todd insisted on an audit and she *had* no case. He'd never touched her trust fund and he'd left half of everything. He took only what he felt was fair. And he's paid support for Jason faithfully every month, all this time. According to the terms of the divorce, he was supposed to have weekend and holiday visits, yet she wouldn't let him, or us, anywhere near Jason. Todd was deeply, deeply hurt by that. He considered taking her to court but decided it wouldn't be fair to Jason to get dragged into the middle of a mess. So he sent Jason cards and gifts and phoned every couple of weeks. I doubt that Jason received any of what he sent and he certainly didn't know how hard Todd tried to see him, to talk to him. Now, they'll never have a chance to know each other." Pamela sounded as if she was strangling.

"That's so sad for all of you," Lucinda said, wondering if Renee had told the truth about anything, ever.

"Grandparents have no rights, no standing. Nothing we said or did would persuade her to let us see our grandson. Last night, when he answered the phone, it was like a miracle." At this, Pamela's control slipped and she managed to say, "Excuse me," and put the receiver down.

Lucinda waited, pained for this woman's sake, and for Jason's, while Mrs. Crane pulled herself together and then blew her nose. The portrait of Renee that was emerging was not pretty.

Pamela came back on the line. "I'm sorry. It's a terrible time, for everyone. It's as if in one day we lost our son but regained our grandson."

"Pamela, finding out about Todd's death is going to be a terrible blow to Jason. I am going to talk to him, ask if he'd like to see you. I think he will. And I think you should be the ones to tell him about his father. If Jason agrees, would you be able to come here?"

"Oh, yes! It would mean so much to us—especially now."

"I'm assuming from the area code that you live in the city?"

"Yes. Todd's been living with us since he left Renee. This is so hard—" She broke off, in tears.

"I'll phone you back shortly. If you have to come on the train, I'll be glad to pick you up at the station."

"No, no, we'll drive. If Jason wants to see us, I know George will want to leave right away. This is so generous of you."

"That boy is very, very dear to me, Pamela. I want what's best for him, and I think what would be best right now is to see you and your husband."

"What about the Palmers?"

"I've spoken to them and suggested they need to do something right away about Renee. I think she needs to be admitted to a psychiatric unit somewhere. But that's only my opinion. I hope they'll agree."

"Renee is not a well person," Pamela said with mild bitterness. "She never has been."

"No. I have to agree with you. I am so very sorry about Todd, Pamela. Please give my condolences to Mr. Crane. Oh, and let me give you my number."

Afterwards, rattled, Lucinda made a pot of coffee—something to do while she tried to assemble the facts into a cohesive whole. After turning on the coffeemaker, she went out to the pool.

"Soupboy, your lips are turning blue," she said. "I think it's time to come out."

Lifting him well out of the water, Eli put his face close to Jason's, then said, "They are definitely blue! Time for the showers, son." He set Jason on his feet at the side of the pool and Lucinda wrapped him in a beach towel.

"I'll put Jason in the guest bathroom, so you can use mine, Eli."

"Thank you, ma'am."

"I just put on a fresh pot of coffee, by the way."

"Thank you again."

She held open the gate as Jason went through, saying, "Go ahead, honey. I brought a lot of your things over. Everything's in the guest room."

"You did? I can stay here with you?"

"For now, yes."

"*Yes*!" He made a classic clenched-fist power gesture and went hurrying inside.

Drying himself briskly, Eli stopped and said, "What?"

"Renee's gone tilt-a-whirl. I've spoken to her parents and they're coming up. I've also spoken to the Cranes. Jason's father was one of the people killed yesterday."

"Ah, damn it all to hell!"

"Mrs. Crane sounds like an intelligent caring person. I think they should see Jason, be the ones to tell him. She told me some pretty shocking things about Renee. I'll fill you in when you come back down."

"All right. Are you okay, Luce?" he asked.

"I'm angry and worried for Jason, but I'm okay."

"No, I mean about last night."

"Eli, I *loved* last night," she said, smiling as heat rushed into her face.

"Good. Me, too."

"You're invited to stay tonight, if you like."

Mimicking Jason, he said, "*Yes!*" and made the power gesture, then gave her a quick kiss. "Would I be right in assuming all hell is about to break loose around here?"

"You would be right. But perhaps we'll be surprised and everyone will behave well."

"Just in case, I'll make my shower a fast one." He stood for a moment, then said, "You are an amazing woman, Lucinda Hunter."

"Oh, I'm not. I just do what needs to be done."

"That's what I mean. Most people would run for cover, but not you. Okay, I'll see you in five," he said, and headed inside.

She could hear her cell phone ringing and hurried inside.

It was Gin, asking, "I had to turn off the TV. It's too damned hard to watch. How are things at your house?"

"I have a lot to tell you. I think the lines are straightened out, so let me call you right back."

She powered off the cell phone, picked up the handset and dialed. Gin answered on the first ring.

"Okay, what's going on?"

Lucinda gave her a short-form version of the events of that day so far, winding down with, "So I'm sure the Cranes *and* the Palmers will turn up here this afternoon."

"That bitch!" Gin fumed. "That's taking payback way too far. I always had a feeling about her."

"I know. And you were right, as you usually are."

"How's Soupboy?"

"For the moment, he's all right. Eli's been wonderful

with him, spent hours in the pool, talking to him, playing with him. But I'm very worried about how he'll react to the news about his father. It's like a double whammy."

"That poor kid," Gin said. "You want me to come over for moral support?"

"Why don't you plan to come for dinner later? I'll call you after all the grandparents have been and gone."

"Okay. God, but I'd love to strangle that nutty bitch."

"You'll have to get in line."

Chapter Eighteen

George and Pamela Crane were only a little older than Lucinda, which was a surprise. For some reason, Lucinda had imagined they'd be older—perhaps because the Palmers were well into their sixties and she'd assumed the Cranes would be, too. Pamela was a dainty, handsome brunette with shoulder-length auburn hair and the same large, deep-set brown eyes as Jason. In tan slacks and a beige shirt, with loafers and a brown Shetland cardigan draped over her shoulders, she carried herself like a dancer, with innate grace and perfect posture. Her handshake was firm and warm, as was her husband's. Her eyes were red-rimmed, bloodshot. George Crane was tall and lean, ruggedly good-looking, obviously athletic and clearly as anguished as his wife. He managed nevertheless to be every bit as warm as she was. They were immediately likable people and Lucinda couldn't imagine why Renee had painted them in such ugly colors.

As Lucinda showed them into the living room, Pamela paused to look at the portraits on the far wall. Then she looked back at Lucinda, adding it up. To her credit, she made no comment and merely offered a smile.

"Jason's still getting ready. He's very nervous," Lucinda explained. "Do sit down. Would you like tea or coffee, a soda? Something stronger?"

"We're nervous, too," George said. "Perhaps later?"

"Of course. My friend Eli is helping Jason dress. He wants to look just right."

Pamela's eyes filled and she opened her bag for a tissue.

"I'll let him know you're here," Lucinda said. "Be back in a minute. Make yourselves comfortable, please."

Jason had chosen to wear jeans, a long-sleeved yellow and gray striped rugby shirt with a white collar, and his huge-looking sneakers. He'd gelled his hair so that the sides were flat and the top stood up in spikes. Lucinda thought he looked adorable.

"Honey, your Crane grandparents are here."

"C'n Eli come with me? Are you gonna stay?"

"Yes to both. Take your time and come down when you're ready. Okay?"

He came over and leaned against her, grabbing a handful of her skirt. "Luce, what if they don't like me?"

"Son, anybody who didn't like you would have to be crazy," Eli said.

"He's right, Jason. You're a wonderful boy. They will absolutely, definitely like you." She put her hand over the back of his neck, still sun-warm and tanned. "They seem like very nice people."

Pulling away from her, he reached for Eli's hand and said, "Okay. I'm ready, I guess."

Jason clung tightly to Eli's hand as the Cranes got to their feet.

"Hello," Eli said, advancing into the room and bringing Jason with him. "I'm Elijah Carter. Please call me Eli. And this, as you know, is Jason."

Lucinda had to admire the Cranes' restraint. They didn't rush at him or try to embrace him but instead introduced themselves as George and Pamela, Todd's mother and father, and shook his hand before inviting him to sit between them on the sofa.

"Would you like some juice, Jason?" Lucinda asked.

He murmured, "No, thank you," and sat stiffly, looking first at Pamela, then at George. "I remember you, kind of."

"Do you?" George looked inordinately pleased.

"I think so. Do you look like my dad?"

Both the Cranes were stricken by the question but covered well. "I think your dad and I look a lot alike," George said, grappling to control his emotions.

"And you look like both of them," Pamela said, drawing Jason's attention and giving her husband a chance to pull a handkerchief from his pocket and blot his eyes.

"I do? Cool."

"I like your hair," Pamela complimented him.

"Yeah? Thanks." He touched the palm of his hand to the stiff spikes.

"We thought you might like to see some photographs," Pamela said, opening her handbag.

"Sure. Are they of my dad?"

"Some are," George said.

Taking advantage of the timing, Lucinda said, "Jason, Eli and I are going to get some refreshments for everyone. We'll be back in a few minutes. Okay?"

"Yeah, okay." Turning again to George, Jason said, "My mom says you've got lots of other grandchildren."

Taken aback, George Crane said, "No. We have only one other grandchild, your cousin Emma. She's our son Allan's daughter."

"I have a cousin *Emma*?" Jason said. "My *best friend* is *Emma*! She lives in Chicago. We email and IM all the time! She's got black hair and purple eyes and she can do t'ai chi!"

"What a coincidence," Pamela was saying as Eli and Lucinda slipped away. "Your cousin Emma is almost eleven and lives in New Jersey."

"This is awful," Lucinda said quietly, filling the kettle with water. "Renee even lied to him about how many other grandchildren there are."

"It's beyond awful. Any idea what's happening with the Palmers?"

"I'm sure they'll let me know." She looked over at the telephone as she plugged in the kettle. "It's been a few hours and when I spoke to them they said they were leaving right away."

"Are you sure it's a good idea for me to be here tonight if Jason's staying?"

"I've already explained to him," Lucinda said. "He doesn't miss a thing, you know. He asked me if you'd stayed over last night."

"And you said?"

"I said you had. And he wanted to know why, so I told him it was the guy-girl stuff that makes him gag."

"Okay." He smiled and leaned against the counter, saying, "Shouldn't I be doing something to help?"

"You can get Jason a juice box from the fridge."

He did that and poked the small straw through the hole in the box, asking, "What else?"

"Cookies." She pointed to the cupboard. "Eli, I'm so afraid for him."

"Me, too. But he's a strong kid. He'll get through this. And he's got lots of support here. They seem like good, caring people."

"They do, don't they?" She crossed the room and leaned against him. "What if Renee never comes back from Planet Zebulon?"

"*What*?"

She straightened and said, "I went into 'fabulously articulate' mode with Renee. I was just so angry with her, I couldn't help myself."

"What did you say?"

She repeated what she'd said and he covered his mouth with his hand to stifle his laughter. "You actually said 'until your spaceship comes back from Planet Zebulon'?"

"She's a sick woman. It wasn't nice of me." She thought of remarks she'd made to her aunt and was ashamed all over again.

"Hey! Sick or not, she deserves far worse. Man oh man!" he said, shaking his head. "I'm going to have to start writing down some of your better lines."

"Should I make both coffee and tea?" she wondered aloud.

"Might as well. I'll do the coffee." He picked up the carafe and moved to the sink to fill it.

"Eli?"

"Unh-hunh?" He looked over his shoulder at her.

"You've been wonderful with Jason."

"I love kids."

"So do I."

"I had noticed that," he said, pouring the water into the coffeemaker's reservoir.

"I was thinking. I know it's a bit premature ... *God*! Look, if you'd like to leave a few things here, I wouldn't mind. That way you wouldn't have to keep going home to change."

Looking pleased, he said, "I don't know what constitutes premature. I think time is a limited commodity and I dislike wasting it. Finding two exceptional women to love in one lifetime makes me a very fortunate man. I want to spend all my time with you. Do you have any reservations?"

"No, none."

"Me, neither. So I'll stop by the condo at some point and bring a few things to leave here."

"Good," she said.

"I've told my sons about you."

"You did? Why? I mean when?"

"After the first time I came to dinner with you and Kat and we started emailing. I told them I'd met someone I knew they'd like because *I* liked you so much. They think it's great. Dad's finally stopped mooching around the house, using up his energy swimming at the Y and playing racquetball. We can quit worrying about him."

"Is that what you were doing, Eli?"

"Pretty much. I was reading a lot, renting movies, eating sandwiches and cereal, ordering in the occasional pizza. And working out until I was too tired to think."

"I was certain you were being overrun by women; I pictured them lining up to get to you."

"For a while it was exactly like that. The jerks with the cigars might enjoy being pursued but to me it felt like an endless audition. It was depressing. Initially, I was missing Maria and angry as hell with her for dying and leaving me alone to deal with all those brittle, predatory females—like

'Pig.' Then I got past being angry and was just plain lonely, dying for some rational conversation with someone who had no agenda."

"I always thought men liked having women after them."

"As I said, the *jerks* like that sort of thing. Even if I wanted to, I couldn't join that club. I hate cigars."

She wrinkled her nose. "Me, too. Rational conversation," she repeated. "I do enjoy that, especially with someone who can quote Keats. We'd better get back in there or Jason will think we've abandoned him."

Jason reacted to the news of his father's death as if he'd been struck a forcible blow. He went very still and sat looking at his sneakers as the Cranes instinctively reached to touch him—Pamela stroking his arm and George placing a hand on his shoulder.

"It's not fair," Jason said at last, eyes still on his shoes. "*It's not fair*!"

"No, it isn't," Pamela agreed. "We're so very sorry, Jason."

The doorbell rang and Lucinda went to open the door to the Palmers.

"Thought we'd stop by, see the boy, fill you in on what's happening with Renee," said Mr. Palmer in his typically clipped manner of speaking. About five-ten, with thinning gray hair, portly with a paunch, in gray flannel slacks, a white shirt and navy blazer, he had the telltale broken veins across his cheeks and nose of a hard drinker. "Hope you don't mind."

Mrs. Palmer simply stood on the porch expectantly, an Aunt Anne clone (although not as thin) in navy designer slacks with matching sweater set and flat-heeled shoes, her short hair permed and precise, a Louis Vuitton signature bag over her shoulder.

Lucinda stepped outside and drew them away from the door, saying, "Let's sit for a moment, so I can fill *you* in."

The Palmers sat side by side on the wicker settee. Lucinda took one of the chairs and said, "The Cranes have just told Jason that his father was killed yesterday."

Mrs. Palmer's hand fluttered to her breast and she said, "How dreadful! The poor people. Poor Jason."

"Bad business," Mr. Palmer said tersely. "Madmen flying planes into buildings."

"How is Renee?" Lucinda asked.

"We've admitted her to Silver Hill for evaluation. Once we've got a diagnosis," he said, "we'll go from there, find someplace long-term."

"She was so distraught," Mrs. Palmer said. "The whole world seems to be falling apart."

"It does, doesn't it," Lucinda agreed. "I'm sorry. What are your names again?"

"Lydia and Jim," Mrs. Palmer answered. "I thought you knew. Sorry."

"Lydia and Jim, I think all of us need to sit down together and talk to Jason about what's happening. He needs to know. What I think *you* both need to know is the extent to which Renee has misrepresented everything, not just to Jason but to all of us." Quickly, she filled them in on the key details of Renee's claims about Todd and on her denying access to Todd and his parents.

"Her trust fund was never touched!" Jim said, scandalized. "I'm an attorney and the executor of the trust. I'd have known."

"She told me they didn't *want* to see Jason," Lydia said,

frowning in dismay. "What is *wrong* with that girl?" She directed her question at her husband. "She's always been high-strung," she told Lucinda. "But we were under the impression that she'd settled down and was doing well. School and all that."

"I was under the same impression. But what's important right now is Jason," Lucinda said. "Now that you've got some idea of the background, I think we should go inside and see if we can't settle a few things."

As the Cranes and the Palmers exchanged greetings and Eli was introduced, Jason sat unmoving, still looking at his sneakers, repeating quietly over and over, "It's not fair, it's not fair, it's not fair."

"Good heavens, his hair!" Lydia Palmer whispered to her husband.

"Be quiet, Lyd," Jim Palmer snapped.

"It's not fair, not fair, not fair."

Lucinda could see that Eli wanted to pick the boy up—just as she did—and take him off somewhere quiet to comfort him, but that was out of the question. After tea and coffee was offered and accepted, and Eli persuaded Jason to take the juice box, Lucinda said, "I think what's most important right now is to agree on where Jason is going to stay."

"Much as we'd love to, we can't have him," Lydia said at once, and reached for her husband's hand. "We're simply not equipped for a child."

Jason at last looked up. "I don't even *want* to stay with you!" he told the Palmers. "You hate my clothes and my hair. Probably hate me, too!"

"Oh, no!" Lydia Palmer said. "That's not true at all. We care about you, Jason."

"Bullshit!" Jason muttered under his breath, glowering.

Pamela Crane said, "Jason scarcely knows us. More upheaval in his life right now is the last thing he needs." Directing herself to Jason, she said, "Just know that we love you and you're always welcome in our home. I hope you'll want to see us again."

"I wanna stay with Luce!" Jason declared fearfully, his eyes on Lucinda.

Unable to stand another moment of this, Lucinda held out her arms to him. Jason pushed the juice box into Pamela's hand and flew across the room to climb into Lucinda's lap, at once clutching a fistful of her skirt and hiding his face against her chest.

"Look," Jim Palmer said calmly. "I have Renee's power-of-attorney. I suggest we leave Jason with Lucinda for the time being, provided Lucinda is willing."

"Yes, I am willing," she said, feeling Jason shivering in her arms as if in the grip of a fever.

"We'd like to come visit, if Jason has no objections," Pamela said.

"Can't see why not," Jim Palmer said. "I'll draft papers appointing Miss Hunter Jason's guardian, something to protect all parties—"

The front door opened and Gin walked in. "Hi all. Sorry to barge in. I won't stay but a minute. I just came to ask Jase a favor."

He lifted his head and whispered, "Hi, Gin."

"I know it's a lot to ask, but this guy needs someone to look after him," she said, revealing the puppy she was holding. "His name is Bartholomew and he's six weeks old. He's paper-trained but still has accidents. Do you think you could take care of him for me, Jase? You'd be doing me a huge favor."

"Yeah." Jason accepted the puppy and at once began petting him. "What is he? How long for?"

"He's a golden Lab and he's the smallest guy in the litter, so he won't ever be too big. Phone me tomorrow, okay, and we'll talk about how long. His food and stuff is on the porch and he'll need to be walked in about an hour. He had a little run a while ago, but because he's still in training he needs to go out pretty often. Think you can handle it?"

"Unh-hunh."

"Good. So here's his lead. Okay?"

"Yeah."

"You promise you'll take good care of him for me?"

"Promise."

"Okay, good. Love you, Soupboy." Gin kissed him on both cheeks, made a phone gesture with thumb and little finger to Lucinda, waggled her fingers at Eli and left.

"C'n I take him upstairs?" Jason asked Lucinda.

"Sure. Eli will bring Bartholomew's things inside for you."

"'Kay." Climbing down off Lucinda's lap with the puppy cradled to his chest, Jason started to go, then turned back. "C'n I have that picture of my dad?" he asked Pamela. "The one from his school?"

"Of course you can." Pamela opened her bag and quickly went through the photographs, to find Todd's college graduation picture.

"Thank you," Jason said politely. "I have to go now. You gonna come see me again?"

"Soon," George told him.

"Very soon," Pamela said.

"Okay." Jason nodded, turned to the Palmers and

said—all stiff formality—"I'm sorry you don't like my hair. Thank you very much for coming," and went off up the stairs with the dog.

Within fifteen minutes both the Palmers and the Cranes were gone. The Palmers were cool and business-like, uncomfortable with emotional displays and painfully polite. The Cranes were barely holding themselves together and each of them hugged both Lucinda and Eli, thanking them profusely. They sat in their car for a good ten minutes with their arms around each other before finally separating and driving away.

"Those poor people," Eli said. "I feel for them."

"Me, too. They're going home to plan a funeral."

"It's brutal." Eli sighed, then said, "I think it's time to walk the dog. Gin's a genius."

"Like you, she knows how it feels to be a kid who got hurt."

They found Jason sitting on the bed stroking the puppy who lay asleep on his lap.

Lucinda sat down beside him, asking, "How're you doing, honey?"

Jason shrugged. "Bartie's a good dog. I've never had a pet, not even a hamster. I wasn't allowed. *She* said I wasn't responsible enough to have pets."

"Well, obviously Gin thinks you are," Eli said, dropping to his haunches in front of him. "How about we take him for his walk now?"

"But he's sleeping."

"Honey, puppies are like babies," Lucinda explained. "They sleep all the time. He'll have a walk and check out the neighborhood. Then we'll have an early dinner and get you to bed."

"Can Bartie sleep with me?"

"Sure."

"Did you ever have a pet, Luce?"

"No."

"How come?"

"I don't know. I do like animals. I guess I just never thought of it. Maybe you'll share Bartholomew with me."

"Yeah, but we gotta take really good care of him. Gin said."

"Okay," Lucinda agreed.

"Come on now." Eli held out his hand. "Let's walk the pup. And maybe we'll get some Chinese for dinner. You like Chinese food, Jase?"

"I never had it."

"This might not be the right night to introduce you. What would you like to eat?" Eli asked, fastening the lead to the collar as the puppy awakened and tried to stand on Jason's knees. "Down we go." Eli lifted the dog to the floor and handed Jason the lead.

"I'm not really hungry."

"But if you were," Lucinda said as they went down the stairs, "what would you want?"

"Bacon and eggs with home fries and another cup of coffee."

"Sounds good to me," Eli said.

"Me, too. The diner?"

"Yeah," Jason said. "I like that lady Elena. Can I bring Bartie?"

"Afraid not, son. Dogs aren't allowed in restaurants."

"You mean we have to leave him home all by himself?"

"Sweetheart, he'll be fine," Lucinda assured him. "He'll sleep the whole time we're gone."

"For sure?"

"Guaranteed," Eli said, opening the door while Lucinda pocketed the keys.

"I wouldn't want him to wake up and be scared cuz nobody's home."

"He'll be fine," Lucinda repeated. "That's a promise."

"Where's my mother?" Jason asked as they got to the foot of the driveway.

"She's in the hospital."

"Why?"

"They're going to check her out, try to get her fixed up."

"I hope she dies," Jason said flatly.

Chapter Nineteen

Dear Lucy:

Your grandmother's been so understanding. Instead of the 15th as we'd planned, I'll be starting work for her in two weeks. For the moment I don't want to go too far from Loranne. She's a bit better, but she's still having nightmares and can't eat without getting sick. And Kat seems to have gone right off her head. She actually stayed out all night last night. I was worried sick and Loranne was just scared to death. The girl waltzed in at six this morning, reeking of pot and booze, and ignored us when we tried to talk to her—just went slamming into her room and turned on her boombox at top volume. I had to go in and unplug it because she wouldn't answer me through the door. Lucky for her she didn't give me any sass because I was powerfully tempted to hit her. Instead, I told her to take a shower because she smelled like a saloon.

Again, lucky for her, she didn't argue (didn't say a word, in fact), but went into the bathroom and did as she'd been told.

I know all of this is fallout from 9/11, but knowing doesn't help me deal with her. Loranne is devastated because Kat won't talk to her, either. It's as if she blames her mother for everything that's happened, as if she'd have preferred it if Loranne hadn't made it out of the building. She's shutting Loranne out, won't look at her, ignores her when she tries to speak to her. I'm going to try to talk to her about how cruel she's being to her mother (as if Loranne hasn't been through enough, without this)—when she wakes up. It's now almost three and that girl is still sleeping.

Loranne and I have agreed to wait out this week, to see if Kat calms down and returns to her senses. If not, we would like to take you up on your offer to come stay for a time with you. Your grandmother has said that I'll be able to use the Ford station wagon that's meant for Erica but which she almost never drives. That'll make it possible for me to get up to Westport every day.

Sorry to go on and on about our problems that way. Every time I think about the things Renee said and did I become even more appalled. I feel heartsick for darling Jason. But I am glad he's with you. You've always had a calming influence on him, and he's always relied on you. I think you've been the only constant in his life, the one person he could count on to be attentive and loving.

It's wonderful that Eli has been such a support. I'm not surprised. It's been obvious all along that he cares deeply for you, and you for him. I just wish I could get through to Kat. But I have to confess that if she doesn't snap out of it, I'm hoping you'll be able to work your particular magic with her. In the meantime, I'll keep you posted.

Love always, Jeneva.

PS: Passed the driving tests and now have a license!

Dearest Jen:

That doesn't sound like Kat at all. I'm sure you're right, that this is fallout from the WTC attacks. The three of you are welcome here any time. I'll pick you up from the station, or, if it's easier, I'll drive in to get you.

Eli spends most nights here and, at my invitation, he's brought a lot of his clothes so that he doesn't have to go back to the condo to change every morning. I still can't quite get my mind around his being here. But the timing couldn't be better, because he's endlessly patient with Jason. Every evening after dinner, Jason climbs into Eli's lap with the puppy and just stays there until it's time to walk Bartie before bed. Jason has been far too quiet, spending most of his time with the puppy, or in his room. I had hoped (foolishly, I think now) that once school started up again last week he'd begin to come around. But he's simmering away like a small cauldron and I'm waiting for him to boil over and go off the deep end, the way Kat has. He's not reading, which is an ominous sign because this is a boy who always has a book in his hand, and it's all I can do to get him to do his homework or to watch any of the review videos with me. He seems unable to concentrate on anything for more than a few minutes.

Congratulations on getting your license. I never doubted for a moment that you'd ace the tests. My grandmother is so looking forward to having you with her. She's excited at the prospect of having someone around who loves movies and music as much as she does. And you must take it as a given that I feel the same way. I have to confess that I renovated the barn in the hope (which seemed faintly far-fetched at the time) that the three of you might one day come to live in it. Nothing would make me happier. I've become addicted to family, to being able to phone my aunt and uncle, my cousins and, of course, my grandmother. I live for the Friday night dinners when I'm free to glut myself on the sight and sound of all the people I love. I keep thinking it's slightly disgusting of me to have such a huge appetite for family (and I include the three of you in that group) but I know that you understand, which makes me feel less peculiar and more normal.

Please give my love to Lorrie, and to Kat, too—if she'll stand still long enough to listen. I don't know about any "particular magic" I might possess, but I'm willing to try to get through to her. You three are welcome here whenever you decide to come.
Much love, Lucinda.

She shut down the computer and looked over at Eli who was sitting on the sofa watching an interview on CNN—yet another segment of the ongoing coverage of 9/11. Part of her wanted regular programming to begin again, and part of her was drawn to watch as they reran the clips of the planes flying into the towers over and over. It was a terrible ambivalence she dealt with by keeping as busy as possible.

An open book sat across Eli's knee and he was following the interview intently, holding his reading glasses as if he intended to put them on again at any moment and return to the book. She slipped away and went upstairs to look in on Jason. He was asleep in his Harry Potter pajamas, with Bartie snug inside the circle of his arm. She adjusted the blankets over the pair, then collected the tangle of Jason's clothes from the floor and carried them to the hamper in the guest bathroom. After one more look at Jason, she left quietly and returned downstairs.

Eli had turned off the set. She sat at the opposite end of the sofa with her knees drawn up under her skirt, saying, "From minute to minute, I'm still startled to find you here."

"Is that a good or bad thing?"

"It's definitely not bad."

"How are things with Jen?"

"Shaky." She gave him the gist of Jeneva's email, then said, "I think they'll be coming soon."

"And that will make you happy." It was a statement, not a question.

"That will make me happy," she confirmed. "I can't help thinking I've evolved into a Frederick Clegg replicant."

With a smile, he said, "Double whammy. A book and a movie. I must, however, with all due respect, disagree. For one thing, the butterfly motif is absent. For another, you're not an obsessive. As well, I have first-hand intimate knowledge that you are genuinely human, with no implanted memory-stick."

"Good grief! One offhand reference and you not only know the book, you also pick up on the movie. You amaze me."

"I liked *The Collector* and *The Magus*. Fowles got kind of wobbly after that, seemed to lose his edge. And *Blade Runner* happens to be one of my all-time favorite sci-fi movies, along with *Soylent Green*."

"I agree about Fowles, and about both movies. We are," she said, "alarmingly compatible."

"Surely not alarming."

"Yes, a little. I've never lived with a man. It's a brand new experience."

"You consider me to be living here?"

"Of course you are. And I like it. It feels"—she cast about for the right word—"appropriate. I do very much envy you your self-containment. You seem so comfortable, wherever you are. I'd like to be that way. But I feel as if I'm still gathering up bits and pieces of myself, assembling it all into something like a patchwork quilt."

"You're all of a piece, Luce. It's more a case of your getting re-socialized. It's one thing to spend years traveling to the outside world via a computer; it's another thing altogether actually to go outside and rub up against reality. It's that minimalist view you had for so long from seeing everything framed by a screen. Life is just a hell of a lot bigger than that, as you know perfectly well. And going from something small and manageable to something immense and unwieldy is a big jolt to the system."

"Yes, it is," she said thoughtfully. "But I do love your being here. If you want to, you can stay forever."

"Forever," he repeated, tasting the word in the same way he'd taught Katanya to taste the good wine. "I would like that. I love being here with you."

"Good. Because otherwise I've been considering a Cleggish maneuver where I lock you up and throw away the key."

He smiled and said, "Won't be necessary. I'll go for voluntary confinement."

"I'm going to take a shower. Will you check the doors before you come up?"

"I will check the doors *and* the windows."

She smiled at him, then went upstairs, her smile dissolving as she wondered what could be done for Katanya and Jason. She was terribly worried about them. And yet, with Eli there, her worries were contained, controllable. Whatever happened, he had yet to display any qualms about stepping in to help and offering practical suggestions.

The next afternoon Jason didn't even acknowledge her when he climbed off the school bus. He marched into the house, tossed his backpack down at the foot of the stairs and ran upstairs. Lucinda followed him but stopped when she realized that Jason had gone directly to the telephone in his room. Pausing on the landing, she listened for a moment as he finished dialing. There was silence as he obviously waited through the ringing at the other end. Then he said, "Hi. This is Jason. Is that you, Gramma? … I'm fine, thank you. I wanted to ask you if my dad got put in the cemetery …"

Lucinda tiptoed away and went downstairs to her desk in the living room. Her chest heaved painfully and her eyes filled. Aware that he might come back down at any moment, she wiped her face and clicked open her browser, performing on auto-pilot as her home page sign-in came up and she typed her log-in and password.

A minute or two later, Jason walked right past the living room and into the kitchen.

"Have you got homework, Jase?" she called.

"I'll do it!" he snapped back. "I've got all night. I've been home like fifteen minutes and I've gotta walk Bartie."

"Bartie can wait a few minutes. Would you come here, please?"

"What for?"

"I have something for you."

He clomped down the hall and slouched into the room. "What?"

She gave him the unwrapped box and suspiciously he asked, "What's this?"

"It's a picture frame. I thought you might like to put your dad's photo in it."

Instantly enraged, he threw the package on the floor, the glass inside the box shattering. *"I don't want that!"* he yelled and stormed off up the stairs.

"Damn!" she whispered as his door slammed. His reaction caught her off guard. She had thought he'd be pleased. But each day he was a little angrier than the day before and she just couldn't reach him. Even Eli was unable to get him to talk. After picking at his dinner, each evening he'd sit in Eli's lap breathing heavily like an asthmatic, and stroking the puppy. She had no more idea of what to do for him than Jeneva did for Katanya. They hadn't come to visit since the week before the Labor Day weekend. It was now September twentieth. She picked up the phone and dialed the Manhattan number. As if she'd been waiting, Jeneva answered on the first ring.

"It must be telepathy," Jeneva said. "I was just going to call you."

"How is everything?"

"Getting worse by the day. How is Jason?"

"The same. I simply do not know what to do."

"Me, neither. Kat's turned unruly and mean as a snake.

She cut school three times this week. I got a call. Once more and she'll be suspended. I'm at my wits' end."

"Come for the weekend! Just get on the train and come. Maybe a change of scene for Lorrie and Kat will do them some good. And maybe seeing Kat will improve Jason's mood."

"Know what? I'm all for it. If those two kids want to act out, we'll ignore them and have ourselves a visit. I'm losing patience with Kat. Lorrie's a whole other matter. She's starting to come around and I know getting her out of the city will do her a world of good. So come hell or high water we'll be there the usual time tomorrow. I've been missing you something fierce."

"Me, too. And don't think about bringing food. Just come. I'll be at the station, waiting."

After the call, Lucinda went upstairs to knock at Jason's door.

"What?" he asked.

"I'd like to come in, Jason."

"Whatever."

She opened the door to see that he was sitting on the floor by the window, playing with Bartie.

"It's time for his walk. I'd like to come with you, if you don't mind."

"Whatever."

"Kat and her mother and grandmother are coming tomorrow evening for the weekend."

He shrugged.

"And we'll all be going to my grandmother's house for dinner."

Another shrug.

"Let's take Bartie for his walk," she said, trying to ignore the gradual tightening at the base of her skull.

He stood up, found the lead and fastened it to the puppy's collar. Then he walked right past Lucinda, down the stairs and out the door to the porch where he stood waiting, huffing impatiently, one big sneaker tap-tapping.

Reminding herself that he had good reasons for his anger and upset, Lucinda came down the stairs, got her hat, sunglasses and keys, and locked the door. The moment she was done, he hurried off.

"Jason," she said firmly, "stop and wait for me!"

With another exaggerated sigh, he stopped and waited until she was beside him, then set off again. Frustrated, she said, "I can't help you if you won't even talk to me."

"I don't *want* help."

"Okay. What *do* you want?"

Another shrug.

"You know you're behaving badly," she said without inflection. "I don't need to tell you that."

"No, you don't!"

"But I'm going to tell you anyway because what you don't perhaps know is that I feel hurt when you behave this way. Just because I'm an adult, doesn't mean I don't have feelings. You should also know that even when you act like a little shit, I still love you."

He snickered at her swearing. Then, as if determined not to be persuaded away from his dark mood, his face shut down again. He started to speak, but she cut him off.

"If you say 'whatever' again, I swear I'll clobber you. It's so beneath you to hide behind a cheesy catch-all word like that. You're one of the most intelligent people I know. If you're going to act all pissy, at least use that intelligence to come up with something a little more meaningful than 'whatever.'"

Jason had to stop because Bartie was sniffing at a hedge, and then, as if he'd decided this was the perfect spot, he squatted. Waiting, Jason began to whistle tunelessly, studiously avoiding making eye contact with Lucinda.

"I would think," she persevered, "you could come up with a new word to express your anger or disgust. Given your talent for coining words, I'm certain you'll think of something. I'm not going to say anything more now, so please don't feel that you have to smart off at me or act as if you're stuck with taking a puppy *and* an elephant for a walk." She couldn't ignore the band of pain clamping down on the nape of her neck but didn't want to give up on the small progress she felt she was making in getting through to the boy.

Again he snickered, then again he shut down.

After Bartie had stopped half a dozen times, Lucinda said, "Let's head home now, Jason. I think I have to lie down."

At last, Jason looked at her. "Are you getting a headache?"

"Afraid so." Her stomach was riding up and down like an out-of-control elevator and brackish fluid kept filling her mouth.

"I'm sorry, Luce."

"Honey, you didn't give me the headache." She reached for his hand and he allowed her to take it.

"You're just being nice."

"Did I sound nice back there?" she asked.

"No. But you were funny, and you swore."

"You've been marching around, swearing like a little sailor for days on end. Only fair that I should have an equal opportunity." She was going to be sick and wanted to get home.

"I guess."

"You pick up those fancy four-letter words at school?"

"Yeah."

"I thought so."

By the time they got back to the house, Lucinda had the shakes. She went to the kitchen for a bottle of water and her medication, with Jason following anxiously.

"I have to go lie down, Jason. Eli will be here soon. Would you please do your homework in the meantime?"

"Okay."

"Thank you."

"I know it's my fault," he said unhappily, following her up the stairs carrying the puppy.

"I promise you it isn't. If I've caught it in time, I'll be all right again in a couple of hours." She patted the top of his head, then closed herself into the master bedroom and went directly to the bathroom.

When she awakened on the bedroom floor the daylight was ebbing. She could hear faint music from the stereo downstairs and the sound of Eli's voice and Jason answering. Sitting up slowly, she found she was slightly dizzy but the grip on her neck had loosened and the pain had receded; it hovered in the background like a threat. She undressed and got the shower going, leaving the door open to let in enough light so she could see what she was doing.

In the kitchen, Eli was making dinner while Jason did his homework at the table. In passing, she smoothed Jason's hair and went to lean against Eli's back.

"Did you nip it in the bud?" he asked, rinsing his hands and then drying them on a dish towel.

"Hope so."

"I looked in on you when I got home a couple of hours

ago, thought it best to let you sleep. You usually take to the floor with one of these?"

"Positional vertigo. I'm hungry and something smells good."

"Good sign. Dinner's almost ready."

Jason was watching them with a guilty expression and she mouthed, I love you.

Relieved, he pushed off the chair and came to lean against her.

"Hey!" Eli complained. "There's a lot of weight stacking up on me."

"Tough!" Lucinda said.

"Yeah. Tough!" Jason echoed.

"You two keep me pinned here, the food'll burn."

"Can't have that," Lucinda said, standing away.

"Can't have that," Jason said, clutching a handful of her skirt and mournfully looking up at her.

"Come here, you," she said, hefting him into her arms. At once he wound his arms and legs around her. "Let's go watch TV while Eli finishes whatever it is that smells so good."

The package with the broken picture frame was gone, Lucinda noticed, but didn't comment. She and Jason sat on the sofa and she handed him the remote, saying, "Find something we can watch. Just keep the volume down. Okay?"

"Yeah."

He tried, but he couldn't sustain either his contrition or his peaceable mood. By the time they'd finished eating, he'd retreated into silence and while Lucinda loaded the dishwasher, he climbed into Eli's lap with Bartie and remained there, gazing inward, until it was time to walk the dog one last time before bed. Eli went with him, then oversaw Jason's bath.

"I have a colleague who's a much-respected child psychiatrist," Eli said a while later, folding his clothes and leaving them on Lily's old slipper chair. "It might be a good idea for Jason to see her."

"Maybe. It might also traumatize him even more. Let's give him a bit more time and see if he comes around."

"How's the head?" he asked, climbing into the bed and leaning on his elbow beside her.

"Iffy."

"What can we do for you?"

"We?" She smiled and looked around. "Are there others here? Did I fail to notice the crowd?"

"It was the empirical we, the royal we, the collective we."

"Oh! The I'm-Sybil-for-American-Express-don't-leave-home-without-us we."

He emitted one of his booming laughs.

She put both hands over his mouth. "Ssshhhh. You'll wake the baby," she said, which made him laugh even harder.

Finally, blotting his face with the sheet, he said, "How much more time do you want to give him?"

"I don't know. Let's see how the weekend goes. Kat's been great with him since day one. Maybe seeing her will be a help—for both of them."

"You have something against shrinks?"

"No. But under the circumstances, with Renee off at the funny farm for a long-term stay, I don't think Jason would be too receptive to the idea of seeing one. That's all."

"What's going to happen with the house?"

"Jim Palmer phoned this morning to ask if we'd move all of Jason's things over here. He's trying to decide whether or not to put the house up for sale. I gathered, from what he didn't say, that Renee isn't going to be coming home any time soon. And while he didn't come right out and say it, he made it clear that Jason will be here permanently—if I'm willing. And of course I am."

"Works for me," he said.

"Me, too."

"Look, my class is finished by two tomorrow. We could go get his stuff before Jase comes home from school. He needs his computer and some warmer clothes anyway. The weather's starting to turn."

We are a unit, she thought; we are a *we*. "Have I told you," she said, "that I find you unendurably attractive?"

"It drives me into a frenzy when you use polysyllables." He laid his hand over her hip and moved closer. "Un-en-dur-ably," he said slowly. "Well, right back atcha, sister."

It was her turn to laugh.

Then he asked, "Is the door locked? I'd hate to have Jason walk in on us while we're otherwise engaged."

"Locked and loaded, captain," she said, and turned off the light.

Chapter Twenty

At 10:40 the next morning the telephone rang. Lucinda stopped the VCR, pressed the TV's Mute button, set aside her notebook and picked up the phone.

"Ms. Hunter?"

"Yes."

"This is Julia Derwent, the vice-principal. There's been an, uhm, incident. Could you come to the school please?"

"Is Jason all right?" she asked, at once worried.

"Jason is fine. But there's a—*situation*. Could you come?"

"I'll be there in ten minutes."

When she arrived, she was shown by one of the secretaries directly into the vice-principal's office where Jason sat slouched in a chair, arms tightly crossed over his chest, his backpack on the floor beside him. His hands, face and clothes were soiled; he had the beginning of a black eye as well as a split lip but glared defiantly at her as Lucinda approached him.

"Are you okay, Jase?" she asked quietly.

"Yeah," he said in a gruff whisper. "I'm fuckin' great." Tightening his arms even further across his chest, he looked away.

"Not smart to be swearing in here," she whispered back, then straightened.

"Please sit down, Ms. Hunter."

Lucinda looked at the woman behind the desk. Somewhere between thirty-five and forty, with short dark hair in a boyish cut, no makeup except for some lurid red lipstick, a long-sleeved white shirt with French cuffs. A little overweight, a little smug. Lucinda had always disliked the very sight of the woman.

"I'll stand, thanks. What happened?"

"Jason attacked another boy during recess. He broke his nose and knocked out one of his teeth, kicked him in the genitals. The boy had to be taken to the hospital."

"I see." Lucinda glanced over at Jason. "And what were the circumstances of this so-called attack?"

"It was a very real attack, not a so-called one," the vice-principal said indignantly.

"So you say. What was the name of the other boy?"

"I don't see the relevance—"

"The name?"

"Tristan Rafferty."

"Ah!" Lucinda looked over at Jason who made an I-told-you-so face at her, then she looked back at the woman behind the desk.

"Let me make sure I've got this right. Jason attacked the school bully, broke his nose, knocked out one of his teeth and, for good measure, kicked him in the balls. And you've called me here for what purpose?"

"This is very serious," the woman said. "We're going to have to suspend Jason—"

"Excuse me. How long have you been at this school?"

"I—"

"How *long*?"

"Six years."

"Right. And in the almost five years Jason has attended this school, not a thing has been done about that trio of bullies, led by the infamous Tristan. They have mercilessly terrorized the smaller kids while you and the teachers and the principal stood by. Now, one of the smaller kids has finally had enough. He fought back and beat the crap out of this considerably bigger boy. The payoff, if I understand correctly, is that you intend to punish Jason for defending himself."

"We can't allow—"

"Tristan, Aidan and"—she turned to Jason—"who's the other one?"

"Rory!"

"That's right. How could I forget? Tristan, Aidan and Rory have made life miserable not only for Jason but for most of the children in this school. You've known it and you've done sweet bugger-all about it." Lucinda braced her hands on the edge of the desk and leaned toward the younger woman who, instinctively, shrank back.

"Now, just a minute," Ms. Derwent began. "You can't come in here and tell me how to do my job."

Lucinda laughed—a short, unpretty burst of sound. "Don't be naive, Ms. Derwent! Of course I can. It's about time *somebody* did. So here it is. I'm taking Jason home now, and he will be back on Monday morning. Don't even *think* about penalizing him for doing what most of the other kids have dreamed of doing for years. *Deal* with the *bullies*, Ms. Derwent! Do your goddamned job for once, instead of punishing the good kids, or leaving it to the parents to try to get their kids to understand why they have to come back here five days a week when they'd rather hide under their beds. Jason has tried most stoically to live with the situation, so I've been unable to say or do anything before now. But *you* summoned me here, no doubt thinking *I* could be bullied, too. Well, sorry, Ms. Derwent. That's not going to happen. You have two choices. One: Either you suspend those three bullies and make sure their parents and the entire school knows why. Or two: Don't do it but proceed with great caution because I will bring this whole thing down on your head like a truckload of bricks. Those are your options. Think carefully, because if you make the wrong choice, your next job could be asking customers if they want fries with their burgers." Pushing back from the desk, she said, "Come on, Jason." Taking his hot, dirty hand, she walked him right out of the building and over to the car.

As she put the key in the ignition, breathing hard, she said, "Don't say a word! You do not take your fists to people, Jason. You ask for *help*! If you had asked me, I'd have dealt with this long ago. Tristan made the mistake of coming at you when you were fired up with anger that needed an outlet. You kicked his ass and the kids watching probably cheered. But all you proved this morning is that you're capable of lowering yourself to a bully's level. If there's a problem that you can't handle, ask for help! Got that?"

He hadn't expected this and didn't reply, but let his chin sink down to his chest and sat that way throughout the drive home. When she opened the passenger door, he jumped out with his backpack and stomped up the walk to the door where he stood sullenly, waiting for her to let him into the house.

Grabbing him by the arm before he could bolt up the stairs, she said, "Jason, stand still and listen to me." Dropping down so that she was level with him, she said, "Tristan had it coming. No question. Those boys've made your life a misery from your first day at that school. But no matter how angry you are, it's wrong to lash out and hit people—even someone as nasty as Tristan. Once you go down that road and start using your fists on people, it gets to be a habit, because you get a rush from winning."

His expression was softening, although his eyes were still on fire.

"I don't want *you* to turn into a bully now because you did something today that made you feel strong and powerful. You're too nice for that, too intelligent. I'm sorry if I was harsh in the car but I didn't enjoy telling that woman off. It makes my stomach hurt because I'm not a bully, either. Sometimes, though, words are stronger, more powerful weapons than fists. And those are my weapons, the ones I use when someone I love is being treated badly. Do you understand?"

He lifted one shoulder, a half-shrug.

"I want you to take a shower, put on clean clothes and come down. I'll give you an ice pack for your eye and, with luck, it won't get too bruised. Okay?"

He nodded stiffly.

"I love you dearly, Jason. You're a very special boy. You're smart and funny and clever. I want you to grow up to be a good person, not someone so angry that he lashes out because he can't handle his feelings. I know you think I'm being horrible and unfair and you hate me right now, but

I'm trying to do what's best for you. You go get cleaned up. I'll fix you a snack and we'll have some coffee. All right?"

He nodded again.

She kissed him on the forehead, then stood and watched him trudge up the stairs. He was locked up like a bank vault and she couldn't figure out the combination. Maybe Eli was right and a psychiatrist was the answer.

When he came down to the kitchen, he was calmer but subdued and silent. While he held the ice pack to his eye with one hand, he ate only a few soy crackers but drank the entire mug of coffee.

"It'll be good to see Kat," Lucinda said, trying to draw him into conversation. "It seems like such a long time since they were here."

"Yeah," he said listlessly.

"And we'll have dinner with my grandmother tonight. Gin will be there. And maybe Annette will bring Amelia and you'll be able to play with her."

"Whatev—" He caught himself and said, "Yeah."

"How does your lip feel?"

"It's okay."

"Maybe after Bartie's walk you should have a nap."

"Okay."

Feeling hamstrung, she said, "Jason, if I knew what to do for you, I would do it. I know you don't like feeling the way you do."

He put the ice pack down on the table and slid off the chair saying, "I'm gonna go get Bartie for his walk."

God! This was brutal.

~

The moment Lucinda saw Jeneva, Loranne and Katanya come off the train, she knew Jeneva had played down how bad things were. Loranne had lost a lot of weight and looked frail as she limped along the platform beside her mother. Jeneva looked bone weary. And Katanya bore no resemblance to the girl Lucinda had known so well. Gone were the Gap overalls, the sneakers and pastel T-shirts. Gone too was her long corn-rowed hair. What remained was a frizz of dyed blonde curls. She had on a pair of skin-tight hip-hugging jeans and a cut-off sleeveless T that ended at her midriff. Her eyes were heavily made up, circled in black; her lips looked greasy with dark red lipstick. She had a stud in one nostril and a ring in her navel. She could scarcely walk in absurdly high, open-toed canvas wedgies. Defiantly, she trailed behind her mother and grandmother, intentionally distancing herself from them, with a black leather jacket over her shoulders and a big backpack carried in the crook of her arm. Passengers leaving the train were staring at her as she stopped on the platform, fished a cigarette out of her jacket pocket and made a show of lighting it as Jeneva and Loranne came down the steps.

All three of them stood in the parking lot and watched Katanya's performance for several long moments. The girl glanced over at Lucinda, her expression indecipherable—part upset little girl begging for something unknowable, part angry near-woman ready to spit on anyone who so much as attempted to offer whatever the little girl needed. She pointedly turned away and took a hard drag on her cigarette.

Lucinda embraced Jeneva, murmuring, "My god!"

"I'll say," Jeneva agreed, as she stepped away and Lucinda took Loranne into her arms.

"You need some of Erica's cooking, sweetheart," Lucinda told her. "My turn to fatten you up some."

"I've missed you so much," Loranne said tearfully.

"Me, too."

The three women again turned to watch Katanya who was now leaning against the platform railing, the backpack at her feet, blowing smoke at the passengers going by.

"Show's over, little girl," Jeneva said sharply. "Get yourself down here and pretend you remember your manners."

Katanya flicked the cigarette onto the tracks, then, with exaggerated slowness, picked up her pack, minced over to the stairs and descended, almost tripping and throwing out a hand to grab the rail.

"If she knew how ridiculous she looks, she'd give it up in no time flat," Jeneva muttered, as she and Loranne walked with Lucinda toward the car. "I'm an inch away from taking her over my knee."

Katanya caught up with them, finally, and to Lucinda said, "Yo, what up?"

Lucinda laughed. "Are you kidding?" she said, provoking a scowl on Katanya's made-up face.

"*You* be kiddin', bitch?" The girl struck an attitude, one hand placed on her bony hip.

Moving close to the girl, Lucinda said in a fierce undertone, "You have no idea how much I am *not* in the mood for any crap. I'm *not* your mother or your grandmother and you *can* hurt me, but not in the way you're hurting *them*. So stow the attitude and get in the goddamned car!" With that, she went to unlock the car and held the door as Loranne, wincing, got herself into the back seat.

"In with your mother," Lucinda told Katanya who, thrown by this unexpected reaction, got into the car. Lucinda slammed the door and climbed into the driver's seat. Jeneva patted her on the knee as Lucinda fastened her seat belt, then put the key into the ignition.

When they got to the house, Eli and Jason were outside waiting. At seeing Katanya, Jason exclaimed, "What's up with the costume? You look like a total gorpo!"

"Fuck you, little boy!" Katanya growled, and started walking with difficulty toward the barn.

Open-mouthed, Jason turned to Eli, who said, "Don't look at me. I didn't direct this show." While he and Jason greeted Jeneva and Loranne, Lucinda went after Katanya saying, "Just stop right there!"

In a contempt-laden manner, Katanya stopped and turned to look at Lucinda. "*What*?"

"You are not going to my grandmother's house looking like that."

"Then I won't go."

"Yes, you will! She loves you and she wants to see you. So wash off the wannabe Goth paint, put on some sensible clothes and eighty-six the attitude. I can see you, Kat." Lucinda pointed at the girl's eyes. "The girl I've always loved is hiding back there. Bring her out for the night and ditch the We-bonics. It was cute when you were almost ten. It's ludicrous at almost sixteen. Have I made myself clear?"

"Fine! Anything else?"

"Not right now."

"Fine!" Katanya repeated and continued on her way to the barn.

Jeneva didn't ask Lucinda about the exchange. She smiled tiredly, saying, "We'll have a quick wash and be ready when you are."

Lucinda put her arms around the woman, saying, "They're a pair of walking nightmares."

"Isn't that the truth?" Jeneva laughed as they separated.

Looking lost, even bewildered, Loranne stood blinking

up at the sky until her mother took her arm and they followed Katanya to the barn.

"Did you *hear* what she said to me?" Jason demanded, aquiver with indignation.

"I heard," Lucinda said. "I also heard what you said. Try to keep your comments to yourself."

"But she does look like a gorpo!"

"Son, try not to blurt out whatever comes into your head. Let's walk Bartie before we go."

"But that's not fair!"

"You were both wrong," Lucinda told him. "Let's drop it now, please." She put a hand over the back of her neck.

At once, Jason asked worriedly, "Headache?"

"I hope not," she said with a smile for him. "Jason, could I have a hug?"

"I guess."

She leaned down and put her arms around him, breathing in the combined scents of hair gel, puppy, and little boy. "I love you, sweetheart," she said softly.

The best he could do was, "I know."

"Okay, you guys walk the dog while I get ready to go."

As Eli and Jason started down the driveway, Lucinda heard him ask, "How come she keeps saying that?"

"Because it's true, dear heart. Luce never says things she doesn't mean."

She turned back in time to see Eli take the boy's hand as they got to the foot of the driveway. *Was this how it worked*? she wondered on her way to the kitchen. *You gained some love here, you lost some there*? That wasn't reasonable. She loved both these children and they loved her. She knew they did. None of this was personal, she reminded herself as she took some Excedrin Migraine, hoping to fend off the looming headache. This was about events over which none of them had had any control. And the aftermath was ruins, not just the physical site—that vast, smoking jumble of concrete and twisted beams—but the emotional sites, too. Be patient! she told herself. She had to stop lecturing everyone, like the boring old know-it-all spinster Renee accused her of being. She might be a know-it-all, she conceded, and old. But given her current sexual appetite and the energetic lovemaking she and Eli engaged in, she definitely no longer fit anyone's definition of a spinster.

She drank some more water, closed her eyes briefly and offered up a silent prayer for the children.

To everyone's relief, both Jason and Katanya behaved tolerably well—being polite but saying little—throughout the evening. After dinner, Gin steered Lucinda outside to the terrace, saying, "I need a smoke and you need to tell me what's up with everybody. I want to force-feed Lorrie and just cuddle her nonstop for a week. Poor thing looks like crap and trembles like a drenched kitten. Kat's hair is grotesque and so's her attitude. Jen looks like she needs to sleep for forty-eight hours straight. Jason seems like somebody lit his fuse and any second now he's gonna blow sky-high. And you, kiddo. You look like your head's gonna blow up and there'll be bits of your clever old brain all over hell 'n' gone. About the only one who seems okay is Eli."

"Eli's a champ," Lucinda said, sitting beside Gin on the terrace wall as Gin lit a cigarette with her gold Cartier lighter. "Jason is definitely a time bomb, and I think the only reason he hasn't blown yet is because Eli has all kinds of time and patience with him."

"What about you?"

"What *about* me?"

"Are you moving into headache central?"

"I'm trying to fight it off. What's going to happen with the shoot?"

"Postponed, obviously. I'm thinking we'll try to reschedule for April or May. The distribution deal is solid. We'll just have to get the post-production work done faster than usual. My original plan was for an October release next year, but that's toast. With luck, we might squeak through and make December. Anyway, once it's in the can, we can start cranking up the pre-production stuff for *Awake Or Dreaming*."

"I haven't even started the script yet," Lucinda protested. "I'm still taking notes."

"Take it easy. You've got *months* yet. I'm just projecting dates here. So," she said, pausing to take a drag on her cigarette, "how's domestic life with the champ?"

"It's wonderful. I'm ready to suggest he get rid of the condo and move in for real."

"Wow! Not wasting any time, are you? Is this the same Ella who didn't used to answer her phone? My, my, my."

"Well, as it happens, you were right. I am functional. I am so functional, in fact, that I'm all over the man like a cheap suit. Fortunately, he seems not to mind."

"Oh, get over yourself! You're a magnificent-looking woman. Why would he mind?"

"Magnificient!" Lucinda scoffed. "Please."

"You know what? If I had one wish, it would be that for just ten seconds you could see yourself the way the rest of us see you. You'd stop all that self-deprecating nonsense and never go down that road again. You're beautiful, Luce. Thick long hair, big smoky eyes, killer smile. Plus you're tall. Second thought, I'll kill you right now."

Lucinda laughed. "Go ahead. Kill me."

"As if." Gin took another drag on her cigarette, then put it out. "Listen," she said. "Seriously? I'd tread very carefully with those two kids. One or both of them is going to combust spontaneously any moment now."

"I know. So does Jen. We're both trying not to get angry, but it's hard with the two of them working like crazy to provoke us."

"You need help," Gin said, "call me. I know a couple of big bruisers I can send your way."

They laughed, then got up to go back inside. There wasn't going to be any musical performance that evening.

What Lucinda could only think of as a close equivalent to simultaneous acts of spontaneous combustion occurred early the next afternoon just before lunch.

She, Jeneva, Loranne and Eli were sitting on the porch chatting. Jason was on the lawn playing with the puppy when Katanya emerged from the barn. She came sashaying across the driveway, puffing on a cigarette, and Jeneva whispered, "She looks like she's on her way to a damned Halloween party."

"Leave it, Moms," Loranne said. "She wants to get a rise out of us. That's the whole point."

With her eyes ringed in black and the gooey red lipstick, Katanya was dressed in a tiny mini skirt that sat on her hips, leaving her belly exposed, and barely came to the tops of her thighs. She had on a torn T-shirt with a hem that came to mid-chest, with the black leather jacket riding her shoulders. Today she sported striped stockings that ended above her knees and high-heeled sneakers in bright red. At least a dozen bracelets of varying sizes and shapes rode on her right arm, almost to the elbow, and huge silver hoop earrings hung halfway to her shoulders. Squinting, she took a drag on the cigarette, blew out a cloud of smoke then dropped the cigarette and made a great show of crushing it out under her shoe.

At that moment, as if catching her scent, Bartie went scampering across the lawn to nudge at her leg, then eagerly sniffed her shoes. Katanya muttered, "Get away from me, dog!"

The puppy kept sniffing then jumped at her leg and she kicked him away.

Jason screamed and went racing across the lawn, shouting, "YOU KICKED HIM! WHY'D YOU DO THAT? HE'S JUST A PUPPY, YOU ASSHOLE!"

"Keep your idiot dog away from me, runt!"

Jason stood glaring at her, his fists clenched. "I am *not* a runt, you freakazoid!"

"Say *what*, bro?"

"You *heard* me, *freakazoid*!"

"Get the *fuck* outta my way or I'll *kick* your *ass*!"

The four on the porch watched in breath-held silence.

"I *hate* you, *bitch*!"

"Like I *give* a shit!" Katanya said scathingly as Bartie returned and again began sniffing her improbable shoes. For a second time, she kicked the puppy away. The puppy squealed, and Jason went berserk.

"I TOLD YOU NOT TO KICK MY DOG!" he screamed, then hauled off and kicked her in the shin as hard as he could.

Without hesitating, Katanya whacked him so hard across the face that he wound up on his backside on the lawn.

All three women made to move, but Eli whispered, "Let them play it out," and they remained where they were.

The two children were motionless, their anger hanging in the air like a cloud of swarming hornets. Then Jason's hand went to his reddened cheek as Katanya abruptly sat down on the lawn, rubbing her leg, saying, "That *hurt*, Jason!" and started to cry.

"You *hit* me!" Jason accused.

"Cuz you *kicked* me!" she defended herself.

"You kicked my *puppy*!" he shot back, tearfully. "He's just little." He began to cry too as he touched his face. "How could you *kick* a *puppy*? How *could* you? He's only a *baby*."

The baby in question was now circling the pair, watching with as much interest as the four adults on the porch.

"I didn't mean to." Katanya sobbed, rivulets of the black eye makeup starting to travel down her cheeks as she ran her hand back and forth over her shin.

"But you *did*!" Jason persisted.

"I'm sorry. Okay?"

"People shouldn't *do* things like that to little kids!" Jason cried. "It's not fair!"

"They shouldn't fly planes into office buildings either. Is that *fair*?" Katanya shot back.

"And they shouldn't *hit* kids and say never to tell. They shouldn't *lie* and say stuff that's not true and then it's too late cuz people are dead and you can't ever *see* them anymore. *It's not fair*!"

"And scare us cuz maybe they're dead and maybe they're not," Katanya contributed.

"My dad's dead for sure." Jason looked up at the sky and howled in anguish.

Katanya kneewalked over to him and dragged him against her. "I know, I know. I'm sorry. I'm really sorry, Jase. Sorry, really. I am, I am."

The two sat on the lawn and sobbed out their sorrows.

"The worst is over," Lucinda said softly, holding Jeneva's hand tightly on one side; Loranne's head resting on her shoulder on the other side. Her eyes meeting Eli's, she said, "They're going to be okay."

He smiled, then went down the steps to sit on the lawn, gathering the children into his comforting arms.

Epilogue
March 2004

Epilogue

The winner was announced and the camera closed in on the startled woman who first kissed the elderly woman to her right, and then turned to accept a kiss from the attractive man on her left. The camera moved to focus on Gin Holder who was beaming and clapping madly. The applause was polite, even somewhat subdued as the film's theme music began to play. The camera returned to track the progress of a small very good-looking boy in a tuxedo, leading a tall slim woman with loosely upswept hair, in a simple but beautifully cut ankle-length long-sleeved black dress, down the aisle to the stage. There was much murmuring in the audience as the announcer said, "This is the second nomination and the second Academy Award for Ella Van Dyne."

Onstage, the woman accepted the statuette with an uncertain smile and stood holding it, visibly trembling, as the grinning boy went to the microphone and reached to lower it to his level.

"Hi. My name is Jason Crane, but some people call me Soupboy."

In the audience a number of girls screamed, and he laughed.

"My best friend here is very, *very* shy so she asked me to read this for her." He pulled an index card from his pocket and began. "I was born into the movie business, went to school on the studio lot, and grew up in a celluloid world. It is therefore a special honor to receive this award for a second time, and I thank the members of the Academy for deeming my work worthy. I am indebted to my oldest and dearest friend, Gin Holder, who made me write the screenplay for *Exposure* at gunpoint." Jason paused for the laughter. "I congratulate the author, Melinda Morgenthal, for crafting such a fine book. I thank my extaordinary grandmother and my family, including Kat and Jen and Lorrie, for being their generous, loving selves. I am grateful to my darling Eli for his enduring kindness. And most of all, for being remarkable in every way, I thank my lovely, lovely mother, Lily Hunter."

There was a moment of stunned silence as Jason tucked the card back into his pocket and reached for Lucinda's hand. Then the audience went wild. People jumped to their feet, cheering and shouting as, once again, the film's theme music began. Jason and Lucinda both waved, as, hand-in-hand, they left the stage.

About the Author

New York Times bestselling author Charlotte Vale Allen worked (among other things) as a sales person, a waitress, a secretary, an insurance broker, and as an actress and singer before turning to writing full-time with the publication of her first novel *Love Life* in 1976. Born in Toronto, Canada, Vale Allen moved to the US in 1966 and has lived in Connecticut since 1970. Her award-winning autobiography (and only nonfiction work) *Daddy's Girl* is in its 3rd edition after over 30 printings. *Sudden Moves* is her 38th novel.

Please visit the author's website at:
www.charlottevaleallen.com

TELL THE AUTHOR

Dear Charlotte Vale Allen,
I just finished reading Sudden Moves *and wanted to tell you what I thought of the book.*

Sincerely,

*name*____

*address*______________________________________

*city, state, zip code*____

(please print)

If you are reading a library book, please copy this page and leave it for the next reader.

Charlotte Vale Allen
c/o INP
144 Rowayton Woods Drive
Norwalk, CT 06854
U.S.A.

TELL A FRIEND

Dear__________________________,

I just finished reading Sudden Moves *by* Charlotte Vale Allen *and wanted to tell you about it because I think it's a book you'll enjoy.*

Sincerely,